NOBLE VENGEANCE

WILLIAM MILLER

NOBLE VENGEANCE

Copyright © 2017 by William Miller.

All rights reserved. Printed in the United States of America. No part of this book may be used or reproduced in any manner whatsoever without written permission except in the case of brief quotations embodied in critical articles or reviews.

This book is a work of fiction. Names, characters, businesses, organizations, places, events and incidents either are the product of the author's imagination or are used fictitiously. Any resemblance to actual persons, living or dead, events, or locales is entirely coincidental.

Book and Cover design by www.LiteraryRebel.com

First Edition: May 2017

Every novel is a labor of love. This one is no exception. I could not have done it without all the love and support of my family and friends. Special thanks to Gary Clairy for valuable insight and feedback, and to Robin for doing her best to catch my many, many typos.

"From Hell's heart, I stab at thee."

~ Herman Melville

CHAPTER ONE

Jesús Torres had roughly an hour to live. He entered the recently remodeled Buenavista railway station a few minutes after one o'clock. A summer heatwave was turning the streets of Mexico City into rivers of shimmering asphalt. Inside the station, the air conditioners worked overtime. A voice announced arrivals and departures over a grainy loud speaker. Sound echoed in the cavernous hall. Torres passed the ticket booths and terminals packed with sweaty travelers, to a row of long-term storage lockers. He dug a USB drive from the pocket of his faded denims, opened locker 314, glanced around the bustling terminal, then hid the thumb drive inside, using the narrow ledge above the door hinge. He closed the locker, removed the key and gave it a tug to be sure it was locked.

Next he located a row of payphones near the restrooms. He took one look at the bulky, orange card readers and his lips peeled back from clenched teeth. For someone in his line of work, a credit card is like a homing beacon.

He stood there in silent debate. The only other person

using the payphones was a middle-aged woman. She kept waving a hand in the air, sighing, rolling her eyes.

"Screw it," Torres said and reached into his back pocket for his wallet. He picked up the receiver, pushed his card into the slot and then waited for a dial tone.

"*Hola.*" Machado said with the raspy baritone that comes from a lifetime of heavy drinking.

"It's me," Torres said in Spanish. "You have something I want."

"*Sí, amigo.* She has a lot of spirit."

Torres heard a scream in the background. His heart squeezed inside his chest. His knuckles turned white. "*Cabrón!*"

The woman on the next phone over shot him a dirty look.

"My men have been entertaining her for days," Machado said. "I was starting to wonder if you would ever call."

Torres squeezed his eyes shut. If she could scream, she was still alive. That's all that mattered. Machado was trying to push his buttons, force him to make a mistake. He told himself to breathe. She was still alive and he had a chance to save her.

"Let's trade," Torres said. "Me for the girl."

"I'm more interested in the files you stole from me."

"That's part of the bargain," Torres assured him. "Turn her loose and you get the files. Don't, and they go public."

"We pay a terrible price for the women we love," Machado chuckled. "When and where?"

Fighting to keep his voice steady, Torres said, "The airfield. One hour. Bring the girl."

"We have a deal," Machado said.

Torres slammed the receiver and walked out of the train station into the blazing midday sun. His eyes narrowed against the light. He clutched the locker key in his fist. First thing he needed was a post office.

CHAPTER TWO

Gone were the days when cartels used small, single-engine airplanes to fly drugs into America under the cover of darkness. During the eighties, when the cocaine business was run out of Colombia, plane or boat was the most efficient means of moving product. Now that cartels had relocated to Mexico, it was cheaper to load a few hundred kilos onto the backs of immigrants and march them across the border, making airplanes obsolete.

However, planes still provide the best means of travel for paranoid drug tsars. Armored convoys, no matter how well protected, can be blown up by roadside bomb—a tactic employed frequently by rival gangs. Once airborne, the only thing that can bring a plane down is a surface-to-air missile. For that reason, Cessnas and helicopters are the transportation of choice for fashionable drug smugglers.

Torres pulled off the road well in advance of the airfield. He was in a dust-covered Range Rover with balding tires. The air conditioning was on full blast. Heat made the horizon shimmer. The Range Rover rumbled over hardscrabble earth dotted with stunted trees. Torres drove around the east side of the runway where a corrugated steel hangar abutted a security fence topped with razor wire. He cut the engine and raised a pair of binoculars.

In the passenger seat was an SVD Dragunov rifle with a scope and a 9mm Berretta. He had built a silencer from a glass Coca-Cola bottle packed with cotton and had fixed it to the Berretta with duct tape. The handgun looked comical with a Coke bottle duct taped to the barrel, but Torres knew from experience the homemade sound suppressor would work. The glass and cotton trapped the expanding gasses and dampened the report. It wasn't perfect, though. He would get one, maybe two, shots. In order to fit the bottle over the barrel, he had been forced to file down the front sight, which made aiming tricky business. If he had to use the Berretta, he would need to be up close and personal.

Through the binoculars, he counted six cartel soldiers armed with AK-47s, milling around the front gate. They knew he was coming and they'd be keyed up for a fight, but they were teenagers with automatic weapons. Machado hired school kids, gave them guns, and put them to work as enforcers on the streets of Mexico. Most of the boys lived short, brutal lives. The ones that survived to adulthood grew into stone-cold killers. Those were the ones that worried Torres.

He tossed the binoculars into the floorboard. They landed with a thump. He climbed out, slung the Dragunov sniper rifle over his shoulder and took the silenced Berretta. A hot wind seared across the barren landscape like the breath from an open oven. Torres mopped sweat from his brow. His boots kicked up small clouds of dust. He draped the floor mat over his forearm, shouldered the rifle, gripped the Berretta in both hands, and made his way between stunted trees to the perimeter fence.

He took a knee behind a thorn bush and waited. He was watching for foot patrols. If the teenage *pistoleros* caught him in the open, they would cut him down with their AK-47s. The hangar, its powder blue paint gleaming under the sun, lay directly ahead. Fifteen meters of open ground separated him from the fence.

He watched the second hand on a knock-off Rolex with the gold plating flaking off. Thirty seconds. Sixty seconds. No foot patrols. His training told him to wait ten minutes at the very least, but he didn't have the luxury of time. He needed to be inside the hangar before Machado's men showed up with Alejandra.

Torres broke cover, running in a crouch with the silenced Berretta leading the way. The fence was eight feet tall. Torres, only five foot seven, had to jump to drape the floor mat over the razor wire. It sounded like the brass section of an orchestra falling down on stage. He wedged the toe of his boot into one of the diamond-shaped openings and hauled himself up. The Range Rover's floor mat protected him from the razor wire. Torres dropped down on the other side and pulled the carpet down. The brass section took another tumble.

He dropped the floor mat in the dirt and moved around the building to a side door. Apart from the main hangar doors, this was the only other way in. A collection of cigarette butts and crumpled beer cans littered the ground.

Torres tried the knob, found it locked and banged on the metal door with an open palm. He heard the lock turn and the door swung open. The hangar attendant, a short man with a sagging gut and a gun tucked in his waistband, stuck his head out. "*Qué?*"

Torres leaned around the door and fired two rounds. Empty shell casings leapt through the air, trailing smoke, to land among the cigarette butts. The hangar attendant rocked back on his heels with a pair of dime sized holes in his forehead and broken glass in his face. His body teetered for a moment and then fell. He hit the concrete floor with a flat *whomp*. The first round had exploded the bottom of the bottle. The second made a loud clap.

A sixty-five million dollar Gulfstream and a smaller jet helicopter took up most of the hangar space. Skylights reflected off their gleaming white fuselages. There was a large fuel tank on one side of the hangar and a small office on the other. The smell of jet fuel hung in the air.

Torres closed the door, locked it, and then went to a small window in the main hangar doors which looked out toward the front gate. Machado's hirelings loitered in front of the chain link fence, smoking cigarettes and telling jokes. He could knock down all six from this distance, but he would need a stable shooting platform.

He scanned the hangar bay, spotted a large red tool chest and wheeled it across the floor. It was constructed of heavy gauge aluminum and filled with tools; it should stop a few bullets. Next he located a stepstool that the mechanics used to work on the engines and placed that in front of the big tool chest.

Torres laid the Berretta atop the chest, climbed the step-stool and shrugged the Dragunov off his shoulder. The weapon was chambered in 7.62mm with a ten-round magazine. He flipped down the bipod legs, settled the stock into his shoulder and adjusted his vision through the scope.

His front teeth felt like they were electrified and his heart was trying to beat its way out of his chest. He exhaled, and focused on his breathing.

A dirt-splattered BMW rolled up to the front gate, pulling a train of dust. The cloud blotted out the car momentarily before the wind pulled it apart. Through dark window tint, Torres counted five heads. Two in front. Three in back.

CHAPTER THREE

Torres watched as the driver's side window buzzed down and Santiago ordered the guards to open the gate. Machado had not come himself. Santiago was his second-in-command: a tattooed ex-cop who wore gold-tinted aviators and slicked back hair. One of the cartel soldiers shouldered his rifle, brought out a set of keys, and moved to the padlock.

Torres centered the crosshairs, exhaled, brushed the trigger. The Dragunov kicked. The window exploded out of its frame. The *pistolero* pitched over onto the tarmac, dead.

The others turned and unleashed a hail storm of lead. The sound split the air like a swarm of angry hornets looking for something to sting. Bullets chewed through the corrugated steel doors and impacted the rolling tool chest with heavy metallic *thwaps*. Torres ducked his head and waited.

Santiago leapt out of the BMW waving his arms in the air. "Hold your fire! Hold your fire! You'll ignite the tanks!"

He finally yelled loud enough to be heard over the rattle of AK-47s. "I said hold your fire!"

The guns tapered off. The sound rolled away over the flat landscape like retreating thunder. Smoke drifted from rifle barrels. The hired guns kept their weapons trained on the hangar. A few were smart enough to spread out. One took a knee, making himself a smaller target, not that it mattered.

Santiago hunkered down behind the car and yelled, "Diaz! I knew you were *federales* from the start. Who do you work for? The *Americanos*?"

Torres took a burner cell from his pocket and dialed Santiago's number. He put the phone on speaker, placed it on top the tool chest next to the Berretta and centered his crosshairs on the top of Santiago's head, just visible over the hood of the car. It rang a dozen times before Santiago realized his phone was vibrating in his pocket. "*What*?"

"I want to see the girl," Torres told him.

Santiago took the phone away from his ear and barked a command.

The back door opened. Ramone, a bulldog of a man with a barrel chest, hauled Alejandra out and dumped her, naked, by the side of the road. Her black hair hung in tangles. Dried blood caked one side of her face.

Ramone hurried back around the car and out of sight.

Santiago said, "Like what I did to her face?"

Torres trained his scope on her for a closer look.

The bastard had cut her. A deep slash ran down the right side of her face from her eyebrow to her chin. Bruises covered the other half. Her lips were busted and her nose was broken.

Torres turned his face away. A vein pulsed in his forehead. Tears blurred his vision. He had screwed up. He should have cut her loose when he realized he was falling for her, but she was under his skin, like a melody that you can't get out of your head. He dashed away the tears and trained the scope on the *pistoleros* at the gate. It was an effort to keep his voice under control. He said, "Order your men out of the car."

"Everybody out of the car," Santiago said.

They piled out, left the doors standing open and took cover in a shallow ditch on the opposite side of the road.

"Give the phone to Alejandra," Torres said.

Santiago tossed the cell over the hood. It landed in the dirt. She crawled to it on hands and knees. "Diaz?"

"Alejandra," Torres said. "Get in the car and get out of here, baby."

She shook her head. "N-no. Not without you."

"Listen to me," Torres said. "I'm not coming with you, baby. Now get in the car and drive."

"No," Alejandra moaned.

"Santiago!" Torres yelled through the window. "You want me? Put the girl in the car!"

Santiago jogged around the car, grabbed Alejandra by the hair and hauled her to her feet. She shrieked. He dragged her around the front bumper and shoved her into the driver's seat.

Torres' throat cramped. He swallowed the lump and yelled. "Alejandra go!"

Crying, she shifted the car into reverse and stamped the gas pedal. The BMW shot backwards, kicking up a cloud of dust.

Santiago and his crew flattened themselves out along the shoulder of the road.

Torres watched the BMW hurtle backwards. Alejandra reversed a hundred meters, then cramped the wheel. The car slewed around, then stopped while she changed gears. The back tires threw up gravel. The engine revved, but the BMW stood still. Torres' heart caught in his throat.

"No," he said. "No-no-no. Not now."

The brake lights flashed. Alejandra shifted into low gear and the BMW lurched forward.

Torres watched her disappear into the distance. As soon as she was gone, the fear was gone, replaced by a murderous rage. He said, "Santiago? Can you hear me?"

"I hear you," Santiago yelled from behind the berm.

"You want me?" Torres said. "Come get me."

"Kill him," Santiago ordered.

The cartel soldiers ran at the hangar, firing full auto from the hip. Bullets punched through the door and zipped around inside the corrugated steel building. A round starred the windscreen of the jet helicopter. Torres sighted on the closest threat and stroked the trigger. The man threw his hands in the air and went down face first. Torres fired twice more. The second shot missed. The third forced a gunman to double over, screaming.

Torres felt a sharp sting and knew he'd been hit. It felt like someone had snapped him with a wet towel. A bullet had drilled through the tool chest and into his left side. He looked down and saw a deep red stain spreading above his left hipbone. Seeing somehow made the pain worse. The sting became a pulsing stab.

He cursed, grabbed the Berretta and stumbled down

from the step stool. He limped across the floor, trailing blood to the back wall.

The heavies reached the hangar doors. One of them thrust the barrel of his AK-47 through the window and fired blind. Bullets hissed and snapped. One ricocheted off the fuel tank without rupturing the skin.

Torres sat down with his back to the wall.

The hangar door rolled open enough to admit a man. Torres sighted on the opening and pulled the trigger. The bullet ripped open the man's neck and he sank to his knees, bottlenecking the entryway. It bought Torres a few precious seconds.

He pressed a hand against his side and winced. The hole in his gut would kill him, but not right away. It would take hours to bleed out. Santiago would spend that time questioning him. Torres would resist at first, but when the pain got bad enough, he would talk. Falling for an asset was bad enough. Giving up information was an unpardonable sin.

He rested the back of his head against the wall. "Hail Mary, full of grace, blessed art thou among women and blessed is the fruit of thy womb, Jesus. Pray for us sinners, now and at the hour of our death."

Torres put the Berretta to his temple and pulled the trigger.

CHAPTER FOUR

Jake Noble was on his belly in the dirt, at the base of a towering pine tree. The drooping evergreen branches provided good cover. He was dressed in black with a dark watch cap on his head. The luminous hands on his TAG Heuer pointed to 4:47 a.m. The stars were dimming as the first hint of dawn tinged the eastern horizon. The whole world feels still and quiet in the hours just before dawn. Nature seems to hold its breath in anticipation of a new day. Man's circadian rhythm is at its lowest. That's when Special Forces Operators like to launch surprise attacks. The enemy is tired and thinking longingly of their beds.

The mansion was two stories of river stone and blonde timber with floor-to-ceiling windows that looked out over rolling green foothills. It had several chimneys and a back deck with more square footage than Noble's first apartment. Decorative lamps illuminated the porch and a propane grill. A little girl's tricycle was parked next to the leg of a swing set. Several miles to the south, the lights of Colorado Springs winked in the dark landscape.

A heavyset man leaned against the deck railing. The bulge of a handgun was visible under his gray windbreaker. He shook a cigarette from a pack of Lucky's, flicked his lighter, and filled his lungs. It was his third cigarette tonight. He craned his head back and exhaled. It was almost daybreak and he was fighting to stay awake.

Noble sympathized. He had caught himself dozing several times through the night. He couldn't get too comfortable though; a root was digging into his ribcage and an insect had spent the last two hours chomping on his right butt cheek. Every couple of minutes he felt a sharp pinprick that sent a jolt to his sleepy brain. He was far enough from the house that he could have killed the insect without attracting any attention but his training stopped him. He let the little bugger feast and used the pain to keep himself awake.

On the porch, the guard's radio emitted a brief hiss of static and then a voice filled the silence. "Element Two, this is Control. Status?"

Noble took a deep breath, filling his lungs with thin mountain air and holding it for a count of ten, forcing oxygen back into his brain. He rolled his shoulders and made fists with his toes, preparing his body for action.

The heavyset guard plucked the radio off his belt. "Nothing to report. Over."

"Roger that."

Element Two finished his cigarette and stubbed out the butt on the sole of his shoe, and flicked the filter into the woods where his employer wouldn't see it. He ambled to the south side of the house. Like every building along the Rocky Mountain Range, the house was built on an incline with the south side of the basement exposed. A gravel drive led up to a pair of garage doors, inside of which was the owner's Jaguar XF.

Element Two paused long enough to be sure the door was closed, threw a cursory glance along the gravel drive toward the main road and, seeing nothing out of the ordinary, started back to his perch.

Noble chose that moment to trigger a garage door opener tuned to the same frequency as the one clipped to the sun visor inside the Jaguar. The electric motor came to life with a soft whirring. The garage doors swung open. A shaft of yellow light spilled across the gravel drive.

The guard wheeled around and tugged the radio off his belt. He mashed the transmit button. "Control, this is Element Two. The garage door just opened. Do you copy?"

"I copy. Check it out. I'm coming around to back you up. Over."

Element Two reached under his coat and produced a Glock pistol. Moving slowly, careful not to lose his footing in the dark, he crept down the incline to the driveway and approached the open doors with his gun leading the way.

Element One came around from the front at a slow jog, breathing heavy from the effort. He outweighed his partner by a good fifty pounds. His large hands made his pistol look tiny. Sweat glistened on his forehead. "What's up?" he asked in a hoarse whisper.

"Don't know." Element Two shrugged. "Opened up all on its own."

Noble scrambled out from under the low-hanging

branches, mounted the steps to the deck and moved in a crouch to the back door of the house. Around the corner, he could hear the guards discussing the possibility of a malfunction. He took a set of lock picking tools from the pocket of his cargo pants. Working quickly, he slipped the tension tool into the lock, selected a pick and manipulated the tumblers into place. The whole operation took less than thirty seconds. The lock disengaged with soft click. The door popped open. Noble stepped into a dark kitchen.

Outside, the security team was still puzzling over the garage doors. Their voices were just a murmur from inside the house. The kitchen had a slate floor and stainless steel appliances. A collection of expensive cookware hung from a rack. Noble helped himself to an apple from a bowl of fruit on the counter.

An alarm pad mounted on the wall was flashing the word *BREECH*. The numeric keypad glowed green, awaiting the code that would prevent a silent alarm from going out. Home security systems are based on fairly simple technology; when a door or window is opened, the system starts a sixty second countdown. If the countdown reaches zero, an alert is sent to the monitoring company who will then call the homeowner and the local police.

There are two ways to stop the alert from going out. The first is to enter the code into the keypad. The other is to disable the main box, preventing the system from communicating with the monitoring company.

Counting in his head—he had fifty-seven seconds left—Noble moved through the darkened first floor to a coat closet near the front entryway. Forty-eight seconds. Pushing aside the winter coats, he found a small metal box affixed to the back wall. A simple lock, like the kind found on executive desks, secured the box. Noble clutched the apple in his teeth and went to work with his lock picks. Thirty-two seconds. He felt the tumblers click into place and turned the latch. The box swung open. Twenty-six seconds. Noble spent a few precious seconds studying the wiring, selected the one that sent signals back and forth to the monitoring company, and yanked it.

Eighteen seconds to spare.

Noble grinned.

With the alarm disabled, he climbed the stairs to the second floor. The landing was completely unguarded. All the security was outside. A balcony looked out over the downstairs living room where leather sofas flanked a massive stone fireplace. Noble stopped at a door decorated in crayon drawings of colorful ponies with stick legs, balloon bodies, and smiley faces.

He peeked inside. A little girl, six or seven, was sprawled on the bed in cartoon pajamas. Her mouth was open and her limbs were flung out in the kind of deep slumber achieved only by the innocent.

Noble closed the door gently and proceeded down the hall to the master bedroom. He had to be more careful here. Even the smallest noise can pull an adult from sleep and the man inside had more cause than most to be worried, hence the security.

Noble laid his hand on the knob and slowly twisted until he felt the latch disengage. Then he waited and listened. Nothing. The door swung in on silent hinges.

He stepped into a spacious bedroom with deep white carpet. On his right was a private bath with a nightlight in case someone needed the toilet in the middle of the night. There was a makeup table and a mirror along with a chest of drawers, probably an antique.

The owner and his wife slept in a California king with silk sheets. A floral print comforter lay crumpled on the floor. The man had one arm draped over his wife's shoulders, snoring softly. The wife slept a little more fitfully. Her blonde hair was a tangled haystack. Her legs twitched under the sheets. Spaghetti straps hinted at a silk nightgown.

Noble lifted the chair from the vanity table, placed it beside the bed and straddled it with his arms propped on the back. He took a noisy bite from the apple. The wife came awake with a small shriek like chalk on a blackboard. The man sat up with fear and surprise etched on his face.

Noble reached over and flicked on the bedside lamp. "*Bang*," he said around a mouthful of apple. "You're dead."

Shawn Hennessey reached for his glasses. He had a pudgy face, large expressive eyes, and hair that had gone gray early. He was the type of guy that wore sweater vests and corduroy pants.

His wife was ten years younger and took better care of herself. It showed. She recovered from the shock of waking up with a stranger in her bedroom, uttered an angry oath and pulled the sheets up around her shoulders.

"Mr. Noble," Shawn said. One pudgy hand went to his chest. "You scared me. How did you get in here?"

Noble swallowed. "You paid me to assess your security."

"And?" Shawn asked.

"It sucks."

CHAPTER FIVE

Fifteen minutes later, Noble was perched on a stool at one end of the battleship-sized kitchen island. A pot of coffee was percolating, filling the room with the rich aroma. Shawn Hennessey and his wife were dressed in bathrobes. The security team had been briefed on their failure and sent back to their posts. Element Two had given Noble the look of death on his way out.

Mrs. Hennessey handed Noble a mug emblazoned with *The Hennessey Bulletin—the Spin Stops Here!*

He accepted it with thanks.

She had taken the time to comb her hair and put on makeup. "Cream or sugar?"

He shook his head. "Black is fine."

Shawn Hennessey cleaned his glasses on his bathrobe. His gray hair was mashed flat in places. "What's your assessment, Mr. Noble?"

"These Black Diamond security guys are one step above mall cop." Noble pulled off the watch cap, folded it, and stuffed it in a pocket of his cargo pants before raking a hand through his hair. "And disabling your alarm system was child's play."

Mrs. Hennessey reached over and gripped her husband's forearm while Noble spoke. He explained how he had distracted the guards, picked the lock, and disabled the alarm pad.

"What about the garage door?" she asked. "How did you manage that?"

Noble took the garage door opener out of his pocket. He slid it across the kitchen island. She picked it up, turned it over in her hands, and then pressed the button. They heard the garage door motor whir to life. She pressed it again and the doors started back the other way.

"Those openers use fairly simple technology," Noble explained. "A twenty-dollar scanner from Radio Shack gave me the right signal. After that, it was just a matter of buying a garage door opener and tuning it to the same frequency."

Shawn Hennessey exchanged an anxious glance with his wife. Rich people think money can buy safety. They had installed an alarm system and hired a security team. They had done everything they were supposed to do and they still weren't safe in their own home. It wasn't what they wanted to hear, but they had hired Noble to assess their security and he wasn't going to sugarcoat it.

He said, "Yesterday when you were on the back porch grilling..." Hennessey nodded. "I was twenty yards away," Noble told them. "Watching you the whole time."

Mrs. Hennessey sucked air through her teeth. One hand closed the top of her bathrobe in a subconscious gesture. Shawn's lips pressed together. They were smart people. They could read between the lines. If Noble had a gun and had wanted to kill them, they'd be dead.

He cradled his coffee cup in both hands. "If someone wants to kill you bad enough, Mr. Hennessey, they'll find a way."

Mrs. Hennessey looked at her husband and then at Noble. "We've been getting letters and phone calls. They sound serious."

Noble nodded. "You can't go on cable television every night, say the things you say, and not expect to make enemies."

Hennessey put his mug down. "Our government is hopelessly corrupt and our nation is headed for disaster. I have a duty to warn people."

"I'm not saying I disagree. I'm saying people are going to resent you for it." Noble sipped.

Shawn asked, "What do you suggest?"

"Buy a gun. Learn to use it," Noble told him. "You might also think about hiring a bodyguard. A real bodyguard. Someone with combat experience."

"Someone like you," Hennessey pointed out.

Noble grinned but shook his head. "With all due respect, I'm not interested in babysitting a T.V. personality, Mr. Hennessey."

Hennessey thrust his chin at the window where they could see Element Two on the deck smoking a cigarette. "I'm paying them good money. They are supposed to be the best in the business. You breezed past them like a ghost walking through walls. You're just the sort of man I want protecting my family."

"I know some guys," Noble told him. "Guys that are

every bit as good as me. I'll get you their contact information. No promises."

Shawn nodded in understanding but his expression said otherwise. "I wish you would reconsider. You obviously know your stuff and you don't cater to me because I'm on television. I like that."

Noble scratched an eyebrow. "My situation is complicated."

Mrs. Hennessey whispered something in her husband's ear. It sounded like *pay the man*. Shawn excused himself. His wife picked up her mug and examined Noble over the rim. She said, "What do you think the chances are someone will make an attempt on my husband's life?"

Noble thought about how to answer that. He decided on the truth. "I'm surprised it hasn't happened already."

From her expression, he could tell she was thinking the same. She drew her shoulders up like she was fighting off a chill. "Thank you for being honest."

He nodded. "Must be hard."

"Most days are alright," she said. "Some days are unbearable. Sometimes I wish we could run away. Go someplace where no one could find us."

"I know the feeling."

She laughed and shook her head. "Shawn would never stop. It's not in his nature."

"Part of what makes him so successful," said Noble.

"He definitely doesn't back down," she said. "What about you?"

"I've been doing this so long I don't know any other way."

"Are you married?"

"No ma'am."

"Call me Paige," she said.

"Jake," he said.

"I find it hard to believe a guy like you hasn't found a girl to settle down with."

"I thought I had."

She raised an eyebrow. "And?"

"And I guess it didn't work out." Noble worked a smile onto his face to disguise the hurt.

"Sorry to hear that," Paige said.

Shawn reappeared with a check. "I hope it doesn't bounce," he said with a smile.

"Me too." Noble narrowed his eyes. "I know where you live."

Shawn laughed and stuck his hand out.

Noble shook it.

CHAPTER SIX

Noble caught a United flight from Denver to Tampa International. He landed at two-thirty in the afternoon, exited the terminal with his carry-on slung over one shoulder and rode the elevator to the long-term parking garage. A 1970 Buick GSX was slotted between a pair of modern sedans. Noble checked the garage to be sure he was alone, then placed his carry-on on the ground, dropped to his hands and knees, and checked the undercarriage.

He had spent the past four days in Colorado Springs—plenty of time to rig an explosive or tracking device. The likelihood someone would attach a bomb to his starter was slim—he had been out of the game five years now—but he had made enemies, most recently in the Philippines and Hong Kong where he had busted up a pair of human trafficking rings. Since a healthy dose of paranoia is vital in the espionage business, Noble scanned the bottom of the car. "Suspect everyone" had been one of Matthew Burke's favorite sayings.

While Noble checked the undercarriage, the elevator

arrived with a ding. A young couple, walking arm in arm, strolled through the doors. They stopped when they spotted Noble on his hands and knees.

He stood up and gave them an awkward smile. "Dropped my keys."

They climbed into an electric car and drove off without comment.

Noble dug the keys out of his pocket, unlocked the door and tossed his carry-on into the passenger seat. He settled behind the steering wheel. It took three tries to start the old Buick. Finally, a throaty rumble filled the parking garage. Noble shifted into reverse. Tires squawked on the smooth surface and he left the airport, headed west on I-275 to Saint Petersburg. The mercury hovered close to one hundred degrees. Even with the air conditioner on full blast, sweat beaded on his forehead.

He drove south on 4th Street to Central and then circled the block. Finding parking downtown in the middle of the day is like finding hen's teeth. A Ford pulled out of a spot directly in front of him. Noble challenged a Chevy pickup for the slot and won. The driver of the pickup gave Noble the finger. He returned the sentiment, got out, and dodged traffic across 1st Avenue.

Sweat formed a greasy patch between his shoulder blades. July in Florida is sticky hot. Regular afternoon thunder showers only make the heat muggy and unbearable. Residents hurry from one source of air-conditioning to the next. Noble stepped under the shaded loggia at the central post office, grateful to be out of the blazing afternoon sun.

Saint Pete is home to the country's first open-air post office. Built in 1916, the Mediterranean architecture and

Spanish tiles keep the covered walk cool in the summer. Gargoyles crouch atop Italian arches and a terra cotta frieze gives the impression that you are stepping back in time. Noble liked it because the open-air design gave him twenty-four-hour access to his P.O. box.

Inside he found overdue bills, junk mail, and a beige envelope with no return address. The check from Shawn Hennessey would help with the bills. It wasn't nearly enough—was it ever?—but it would keep the lights on. Noble frowned at the strange envelope. He shook it, then explored it with his fingertips. It felt like a key.

He tucked the unpaid bills under one arm, ripped open the envelope and turned it over. A small, brass key fell into his open palm. 314 had been etched onto it. There was no note. Noble bounced the key on his open palm. The handwriting on the envelope was block letters in black sharpie.

On a hunch, he pulled out his cellphone and dialed Samantha Gunn. It was mostly wishful thinking. He hadn't heard from Sam in six months. Last September, he had helped Sam rescue her best friend from a Triad gang. When it was over, she went home to Boston to recuperate from a gunshot wound and Noble returned to Florida. They had talked and texted fairly regularly at first. They even kicked around the idea of her coming to Florida for a visit. Then, six months ago, she stopped answering his calls.

The holidays had been fast approaching. Sam was young, good looking and razor sharp. Noble figured she found a guy. There would be no shortage of available men in her life. And Noble... Well, he was a thousand miles away and a decade older.

As he stood under the shaded porch, listening to the

phone ring, he told himself to be happy for her. She was a great girl. She deserved a normal relationship. The kind of relationship he couldn't offer. He told himself that she was better off without him. It was the type of lame platitude friends offer each other after a break up.

The phone rang a dozen times and then went to voice mail. He stuffed the key in his pocket. Who had sent it and why? Someone at the CIA? An enemy sending him a message? A warning? Without more information, all he could do was guess.

He waited for a break in traffic and then legged it across the searing asphalt to the Buick. He tossed the unpaid bills in the passenger seat with his carry-on and slotted the key in the ignition. The engine grunted like an old man clearing his throat, but refused to start.

"Come on," Noble whispered.

He tried a half dozen times. The motor struggled heroically but failed. Noble cursed, collected his baggage, then got out and walked.

CHAPTER SEVEN

SAMANTHA GUNN SAT IN THE BACK OF A TOUR BUS crowded with aides, policy advisors, strategists, and various campaign staff. They were somewhere in New Hampshire. Sam was pretty sure the city was Manchester, but it might be Concord. She had lost track. Every night was a new rally in a new city. After a while, they all started to blend together.

Sam was dressed in a tailored suit with sensible flats and her hair pulled up in a ponytail. The temperature inside the tour bus was turning her toes into little blocks of ice. She should have worn long johns and UGGs. Secretary of State Helen Rhodes, nicknamed the Ice Queen by her staff, was uncomfortable in anything over 68 degrees.

Rhodes was on her cellphone, a vein pulsing in her neck. "Tell the editor if he runs that piece, I'll bury him."

She reminded Sam of a particularly sadistic grade school teacher named Ms. Wormer. The kids had called her Wormer the Witch. When they really got mad they used the B-word, one of the worst curses a third grader can utter, second only to the hallowed F-bomb, which could only be whispered when absolutely certain no adults were in earshot.

Rhodes had just gotten word that the editor of the Wall Street Journal was going to publish a less-than-glowing op-ed. It was an election year and the presidential primaries were only three months away. Rhodes was running against a bombastic Republican insurgent and tensions inside the Rhodes campaign were high. There were television ads to organize, speeches to write, town halls, news interviews, and debates to prepare for. Rhodes' stump speech was met with wild enthusiasm in all the DNC strongholds, but it was tanking hard in flyover country. Her poll numbers were dropping. Worse, the Director of the FBI was hinting at filing official charges against her for discussing top-secret information over an unsecured private email server.

Her cadre of aids and advisors had been working round-the-clock putting out fires. Rhodes clutched her cellphone in a skeletal grip as she said, "Don't give me any of that right to know, freedom of the press bull crap, Harvey. Tell him to kill the story or he'll have a hundred IRS auditors going through his personal finances with a fine-tooth comb."

There was a pause while she listened. Then she said, "I knew you would see things my way." She put the phone down and turned to her top aid. "What are the latest numbers?"

Mateen Malih, a pretty Arab girl with ties to the Muslim Brotherhood, pulled a face. "Not good. Every national poll has you trailing by at least four."

Guy Taggart, a handsome Harvard grad with a used car salesman smile, said, "Other news outlets are running with the FBI Director's remark. And you know Shawn Hennessey will be all over it. We need to be proactive. I think you should make a statement."

One of the other analysts, a dishwater blonde, shook her head. "The only statement you should make is a denial. Deny, deny, deny."

Guy Taggart disagreed. "We need to turn this around and make it about a sexist FBI Director and his war on women."

Several advisors voiced agreement for the idea. It was a popular card in their deck of talking points. They played it often. Taggart said, "Claim the FBI Director is inflating the issue in order to sabotage your bid for the White House. He's a misogynist dinosaur that doesn't want to see a woman president."

The interior of the bus became an echo chamber of progressive sound bites. Sam felt like she was back at Yale listening to her classmates rehash highlights from the latest lecture by openly Marxist professors. Her phone vibrated in her pocket. She dug it out.

The number belonged to Jake Noble.

She chewed her bottom lip. Thoughts of Jake stirred up a confusing maelstrom of emotion. Butterflies zipped around inside her stomach but a painful knot of grief and loss formed in her chest. It was more than her job was worth to answer the call. She had worked too hard to get here. She was good at what she did and she was making a real difference. The only catch was she had to leave everything behind. She had even taken on a new identity. She was now Vanessa Klein.

Helen Rhodes said, "Is there a problem, agent Klein?"

Sam slipped the cell into her blazer and hitched a smile onto her face. "No, ma'am."

Rhodes tapped one long finger against her chin. "Let's see what kind of dirt the FBI Director is hiding."

Guy Taggart said, "I hear he's a real boy scout."

"Everyone has secrets," Rhodes said. "I want you on the first plane back to D.C. Dig into the FBI Director's life and come up with something we can use. Does he gamble? Does he drink? Go deep. If he pissed his pants in the second grade I want to know about it."

"That might require certain extra-curricular activities for which I'm not trained," Taggart said.

Rhodes flicked a hand at Sam. "Take Agent Klein with you."

Sam cleared her throat. "With due respect ma'am, my job is to protect you."

Rhodes fixed Sam with a hard stare. "And right now I need you to protect me from FBI Director Standish. Criminal charges in the middle of the election would destroy my shot at the White House. I don't expect you to understand the intricacies of the situation—you're a blunt instrument after all—but I'm trying to make America something we can all be proud of. Sometimes we have to bend a few rules and cut corners to make that happen. You understand that, don't you?"

Sam nodded. She understood all too well the double standard of beltway politicians. If Sam had been caught passing classified information on a private email server, she would be in jail. Simple as that.

Rhodes leaned back in her seat and worked a smile on her weathered face. "Tell me, agent Klein, how do you like your job?"

"It suits me."

"You have the makings of a top-rate agent and you come highly recommended. I can see you in a position of authority one day. Making it to the top in Washington is about who you know. As President, I'll need people on my security team that I can trust," Rhodes said. "But I have to know you are a team player. Are you a team player, Klein?"

"Yes, ma'am."

"Excellent," Rhodes said. "Think of this as a natural outgrowth of your protective duties. I believe you and Taggart will make a fine team."

Sam glanced at Taggart.

He bared his teeth in a smile, but his eyes were lifeless blue orbs. It reminded Sam of a reptile. She wanted to crawl right out of her skin. Taggart was the kind of guy that would take a chainsaw to a basket full of kittens if it furthered his career. Lies came to him as easy as breathing.

She met his smile with a tight grin.

Rhodes changed topics, laying out her plans for the upcoming debate. CNN had forwarded an advance copy of the questions the moderator would ask and the team worked through them one by one, deciding what their talking points would be, trying to predict what her opponent would say and then coming up with a series of rejoinders. Most of it boiled down to the same tired, clichéd sound bites. The aide reading the list of questions came to one Rhodes didn't like. It had to do with an assault on a diplomatic compound in Libya by Islamic radicals. Rhodes had abandoned the ambassador and his staff to be killed, and the compound was burnt to the ground.

"Call Reed at CNN," said Rhodes. "Tell him to take that question out or I'll have his balls for breakfast.

CHAPTER EIGHT

Two days later, Noble was in the hold of his sailboat, the *Yeoman,* replacing the alternator. The Buick had been towed to a mechanic on 4th Street South. Estimated repairs had totaled over two thousand dollars. Forced to choose between the boat and the car, Noble elected to fix the boat. Mostly because repairs to the boat were cheaper and because it currently doubled as his living space.

He was dressed in khaki shorts, topsiders and a grease-stained T-shirt. His hair hung in limp tangles. The humidity in the hold made the bulkhead sweat. Perspiration beaded on his forehead and formed a sticky bib on his chest.

He removed the burned-out alternator and dropped in the new one, bought with cash he couldn't spare. Now he just needed to adjust the belt. This all seemed a lot easier when he was ten. Back then, he had mostly held the flashlight while dad turned the bolts. Some of his best memories were here in the hold, helping his father work on the boat. He was so focused on the belt he almost missed footsteps creaking overhead.

Noble wiped his hands on a dirty shop rag and took a .45 caliber 1911 pistol from the toolbox at his feet. He pressed the slide back. A hollow-point round winked at him from the chamber.

Overhead, someone padded across the deck to the cabin door, knocked and called out, "Anyone home? We'd like to interest you in Scientology."

Noble recognized Matt Burke's rich baritone. He shoved the pistol in his waistband and climbed the ladder.

Burke filled the door frame. A smile showcased the gap between his front teeth. He was a barrel-chested black man in a wrinkled linen suit that strained against his shoulders. Matt had played college football before joining the military. He made a name for himself in the Army's top-secret 1st Special Forces Operational Detachment-Delta before making the leap to counter intelligence. But his days doing field work were behind him. Now he rode a desk at Langley and it had taken a toll on his physical fitness. He held up a copy of *Dianetics* by L. Ron Hubbard. "You interested?"

The cult had taken over neighboring Clearwater and was making inroads into Saint Petersburg with large sums of cash provided by gullible Hollywood celebrities.

Noble snorted. "Where did you get that?"

"A group is handing them out for free in Straub Park," Burke said. "How 'bout it? Want to join up?"

"I'll pass. What do you want?"

"Can't a fella drop in on an old friend?" Burke asked.

Noble crossed his arms over his chest and leaned against the bulkhead.

Burke tossed the book on the galley table, opened the fridge and helped himself to a bottle of water. He twisted the cap off, took a swig, and leaned against the countertop. "How you been, Jake?"

"I haven't changed my mind if that's what you're asking."

After Noble had rescued the daughter of a Filipino diplomat last year, the Company offered to reinstate him. Noble declined. No way was he going back to work for the people that burned him.

"Who says I'm here to recruit you?"

"Why are you here?"

"Thought we might catch up. Talk about old times." Burke tugged on his earlobe as he spoke. It wasn't an absent gesture. Someone was listening.

Noble got the message. "You wasted a trip. I'm not interested in reliving the glory days. You and the other bureaucrats back at Langley tossed me out to cover your own butts, and now you have the stones to come down here and ask how I'm doing?"

"Water under the bridge, Jake." Burke said. "All is forgiven. You can come back to work with a clean slate."

Noble gave a humorless laugh and raked a hand through his hair. They were acting for the microphones. "Sure, until the next time they need a fall guy. Maybe next time I go to prison. That's where Foster wanted to put me, remember?"

Burke said, "I had nothing to do with that."

"You didn't do anything to stop it either," Noble said.

Burke pulled a face. "Politics, Jake. That's all it was. I regret that I couldn't do more."

Burke had been like a father. He was the one guy Noble expected to be in his corner when the CIA started looking for someone to pin the blame on. Instead, Burke had turned his back. Wounds like that run deep. Noble doubted he would ever get over it.

"We were friends once, Jake." Burke laid a hand on *Dianetics* and tapped the cover. "I hope one day we can be friends again."

"Not likely," Noble said. "Now if you'll excuse me, I've got an alternator needs fixing."

"So long, Jake."

Noble inclined his head.

Burke left.

Noble watched him through the cabin windows as he crossed the deck and walked along the dock to South Yacht Basin. Burke had wanted him to know the Company was listening. They probably had a microdot hidden on the boat. It was the latest in audio surveillance technology. A tiny microphone was imbedded inside an adhesive plastic dot that could transmit a signal up to one hundred meters. Because of their small size, the battery only lasted forty-eight hours, but they were easy to conceal. It would be impossible to find without knowing where to look.

Noble picked up the Scientology book and turned it over in his hands. One of the plastic dots could be hidden in the spine, but that would be too easy. He could simply drop it overboard. No, the listening device would be hidden on a door frame, in a cabinet, or under a cushion. But Burke had *wanted* him to look at the book.

He flipped it open. It was *Dianetics* all right, complete with diagrams depicting something called body thetans and how they attached themselves to human beings, causing negative energies. Noble shook his head. He could solve all his money problems if he took the time to write up a bunch of pseudoscience hocus pocus and market it as religion. Sitting down at the galley table, he leafed through the book. On page 110, he found a hand-written note in the margin.

The Hangar. 2:30

Noble checked his watch. 1:10. That didn't give him much time. If Burke wanted a clandestine meeting it meant there was some kind of dust-up between the spymasters running the Clandestine Service. It wasn't unheard of for intelligence officers to run conflicting operations. In an organization the size of the CIA, it's a rare day when everyone is rowing in the same direction. The unfortunate truth is that all too often, individual personalities take over. The people who go to work for the CIA want to protect America from her enemies—their hearts are in the right place—but they often disagree on how best to go about it.

Noble quickly flipped through the remaining pages to see if there were any other instructions. All he found was information on the life-affirming joy that could be his if he joined Scientology. He tore out page 110, rummaged through the galley drawers, found a pack of matches, and lit the edge. Orange flame crept up the page and blackened the paper, erasing the evidence. He dropped the page into the sink and watched it turn to ash. Then he climbed on deck and dropped the book in the bay. It hit the water with a plunk and bobbed back up to the surface. It would take several minutes for it to waterlog and sink.

Noble stripped out of the grease stained shirt, pulled on an olive drab polo, collected his TAG Heuer wrist watch and his wallet and headed topside. The alternator would have to wait.

CHAPTER NINE

A SURVEILLANCE VAN WAS PARKED UNDER THE SHADE of an oak tree on Bay Shore Boulevard across from Pioneer Park. The engine was running and the air blowing through the vents made a steady hum. Repair vans and delivery trucks are everywhere in downtown Saint Pete. One more white van didn't attract any attention.

Ezra Cook sat behind the wheel, dressed in generic workman blue, pretending to read *Off Grid* magazine. He was a small man with thick black hair and too much nose. He had graduated the Farm—Langley's top-secret training facility—just six weeks ago. This was Ezra's first field mission and right now he felt like Jason Bourne and James Bond rolled into one. Too bad he couldn't tell any friends about this.

Over the top of the magazine, he spotted a large black man cross Demens Landing and climb aboard a wooden sailboat christened the *Yeoman*. The man was wearing a wrinkled linen suit and carried a book in one meaty paw.

"Head's up," said Ezra. "I have an African-American

male, early fifties. He just boarded the target's boat. Are you two seeing this?"

Gregory Hunt thrust his head between the seats. "He's a black guy, Ezra. We aren't the police. You don't have to be politically correct. Call him a black guy. And, yeah, we see him."

Hunt was perched on a rolling stool in the back of the van looking at a wall of surveillance equipment. A high definition monitor hooked up to a tiny camera hidden in the grill of the van was pointed at the ship.

Gwendolyn Witwicky, another recent graduate of the Farm, leaned in to the monitor and wrinkled her nose. She and Ezra had been in the same class together. Both were collecting the requisite field work before they settled down to desk jobs as analysts. It was a new program the CIA had implemented for recent graduates. The idea was for desk jockeys to get a better understanding of what covert operatives went through in the field.

Gwen had mousy brown hair, coke-bottle glasses, and bore a striking resemblance to a young Carrie Fischer, in a nerdy sort of way. None of her CIA coworkers knew it, but she had gone to several comic cons dressed as Princess Leia. It did wonders for an otherwise non-existent love life. Looking at the screen, she said, "Is that...?"

"Matthew Burke," said Hunt. He was the team leader and the only agent in the van with any real experience. This was babysitting as far as Hunt was concerned. He had more to offer the Company than playing nursemaid to junior analysts. And the target was a washed-up operator who dropped the ball on a mission in Qatar and got drummed out of SOG. Why the Company was wasting Hunt's time and talents keeping tabs on a burn-out like Jake Noble was a mystery. Until now, Hunt had spent the morning thinking of ways to get in Gwen's pants.

The arrival of Burke had piqued his interest though. Maybe there was more to this than he had been led to believe.

Ezra, still pretending to read his magazine, said, "Who?"

"Colonel Matthew Burke," Hunt supplied. "He was a Delta Force Commando before making the switch to full-time spook. He's a Cold War dinosaur who thinks intelligence work is best done by ex-Special Forces types. He's also second in line for the Deputy Director of Operations."

"No love lost between the two of you," Ezra remarked.

"None," Hunt said.

"What is he doing here?" Gwen asked.

"We are about to find out." Hunt pointed at the recording controls.

The van was equipped with solid-state hard drives hooked up to the audio and video surveillance monitors. Gwen dutifully pressed the record button. The microdot Hunt had planted in the cabin of Noble's boat picked up the conversation and transmitted the audio to a receiver in the van. Hunt and Gwen listened on noise cancelling headphones while the computers recorded the dialogue to the hard drives. The conversation was brief and, when it was over, Burke disembarked, crossed Demens Landing, and walked south on Bay Shore Boulevard.

"What was that all about?" Gwen wanted to know.

Hunt shook his head. "I have no idea."

"You hear that?" Gwen pressed the headphone against her ear. "Sounds like he ripped a sheet of paper."

Hunt nodded. They had no video feed inside the cabin of the ship. Burke could have written a message down while he and Noble were speaking. They might have a prearranged code. The whole conversation could have been a coded exchanged for all Hunt knew.

Gwen said, "Is he burning something?"

"Sounds like it," Hunt said. "Does he smoke?"

Gwen consulted an operation file. "No record of it."

A moment later Noble appeared on deck.

"He just tossed a book into the water," Ezra said.

Hunt considered telling Ezra that they had seen it on the monitors and thought better of it.

"Should we try to retrieve the book?" Ezra wanted to know.

"He burned whatever information Burke gave him," Hunt said. "The book was a decoy."

"What's going on?" Gwen asked.

"Is this part of the exercise?" Ezra asked.

"This isn't an exercise," Hunt told them.

Noble reappeared on deck a few minutes later, dressed and clearly headed somewhere. It didn't take a rocket scientist to figure out that Burke had somehow arranged a meeting.

Hunt grabbed a navy blue blazer off the back of the passenger seat and shrugged into it. "Let's see where he's going."

Gwen grabbed Hunt's arm. Thick lenses on her glasses magnified her eyes. "This is a surveillance op."

Hunt offered up a devil-may-care grin and patted her

cheek. “Relax,” he told her. “I’m going to perform a little mobile surveillance.”

She turned scarlet.

Hunt waited until Noble was twenty meters down the road before opening the back door. It was eighty-nine degrees in the shade and ten degrees hotter in the sun. He was going to bake inside the blazer but it covered the gun in his waistband. “Keep the home fires burning,” Hunt told them. “I’ll be back in a bit.”

He closed the back door with a *clomp* before either analyst could protest.

Ezra turned around in the driver’s seat. “You think this is a test?”

Gwen threw both hands up. “How should I know?”

CHAPTER TEN

Noble spotted the surveillance van the moment he stepped on deck. It was parked close enough for a microdot. A Jewish guy in his early twenties sat behind the wheel, dressed in work coveralls. He didn't have the complexion of a manual laborer, more like the sallow skin of a habitual video gamer. The survival magazine he was pretending to read only called more attention to the inconsistencies. It was a sloppy cover identity thrown together without much forethought.

Noble, careful not to make eye contact, turned south on Bay Shore, stuffed his hands in his pockets, and strolled along at a leisurely pace. The average city dweller is in a hurry. It makes tailing them easy work. Even a sloppy surveillance team can blend into a crowd of business workers rushing to the next meeting. It's harder to tail someone moving slowly. People who take their time, stop frequently and change directions unexpectedly make covert surveillance difficult.

Noble stopped to watch a gaggle of college girls trying

to windsurf in South Yacht Basin. A gust caught the brightly colored sail, toppling it. The girl hit the water with a splash. Her friends laughed and applauded her failure. Noble grinned, strolled a little further, stopped again. He bent down, picked up a pebble and skipped it across the water. He used the action as an excuse to check his tail.

Twenty meters back, he spotted a man with an athlete's build and the type of sculpted hair normally only seen in the pages of *GQ* magazine. He wore khaki slacks and a navy blazer over a white polo. He looked like a member of the yacht club, but his footwear was all wrong. Instead of the ubiquitous deck shoes worn by country club members the world over, he wore black lace ups with a rubber sole: the kind of shoes you wear when you're expecting a fight, shoes with good non-slip soles and steel toes for extra protection. He was careful not to look directly at Noble and did a better than average job of loafing along nonchalantly. He took a smart phone from his jacket pocket and thumbed a message.

Noble headed for the Dali museum. The city of Saint Petersburg had recently spent several million dollars giving the building a major facelift. It looked like a towering cube with a gigantic soap bubble clinging to one side. In the garden is an enormous fiberglass sculpture of Dali's mustache.

Noble hauled open the heavy door and heard the low hiss of a pneumatic hinge. It felt like stepping into a walk-in freezer. Priceless works of art, oil paintings in particular, are susceptible to heat damage. Curators go to great lengths to keep the temperature inside their galleries steady. Noble purchased a ticket, passed through the first floor gift shop and ascended a spiral staircase to the second floor. As he reached the top, he caught sight of Mr. GQ entering the lobby. Noble ducked through a pair of double doors into the main exhibit.

The lighting was dim with pockets of deep shadow in the corners. Spotlights singled out the art work. Giant canvases depicted melting clocks and alien eyeballs. A large clay sculpture looked like a cockroach on its back, legs wriggling in the air. People stopped and pondered the exhibits with deep expressions on their faces, as if they possessed some special insight into the artist's mind. A sharp, manufactured odor made Noble wrinkle his nose. Someone was wearing too much cologne and the scent lingered. He picked up the pace, looking for a bathroom or a corner where he could hide and wait for Mr. GQ to pass by. He zeroed in on a single mother with a stroller. She was young, blonde, and Noble didn't see a ring. She kept the stroller moving back and forth while admiring a fantastical landscape of trees and more melting clocks.

Noble joined her in front of the landscape. He stood close enough that, to an outside observer, he might be mistaken as part of the family unit. Mr. GQ hadn't rounded the corner yet. Noble paused to admire the painting and then glanced into the stroller. Inside was a baby girl, fast asleep, with a pink bow atop a head of gold curls.

There's something disarming about a napping baby. Noble grinned. "She's beautiful. How old?"

The mother smiled and kept the stroller moving. "Eleven months."

"Precious," Noble said. "My ex and I... We tried for the longest time."

Her smile vanished, replaced by sympathy.

CIA officers are taught to quickly profile a target, figure out what they want most, and dangle it on a string. People will betray their country, even their own family, for the right incentive. Feminist doggerel not withstanding, single mothers are always on the hunt for dad. Noble offered up exactly what she was looking for: an available man who wanted kids.

It was a dirty trick. But it worked.

He hunkered down in front of the stroller, giving himself an excuse to turn his back on the crowd and changing his height in the process. "Do you live in the area?"

"Tyrone," she said. "Over by the mall."

"I'm just down the street at the Saint Pete One," he lied. It was an expensive high-rise condominium building with a view of Tampa Bay. Noble couldn't afford to have dinner in the lounge, much less live there.

Her smile returned. She offered her name. Noble lied again.

Mr. GQ walked past with his head on a swivel. He was looking for a five foot ten man in a hurry, not a doting father. Disappearing into a crowd can be as easy as changing the number of people in a group. Mr. GQ continued to the end of the hall and turned the corner.

Noble stood, offered his hand and said, "It was nice meeting you."

A hint of confusion flitted across her face. Better to disappoint her now than offer a fake number and leave her waiting by a phone that would never ring. Noble knew what that felt like. He said goodbye and went out the way he had come in.

He exited the exhibit, hurried down the spiral staircase and out the main doors into the baking summer heat. Sunlight reflected off the sidewalk in blinding waves. After the dimly lit exhibit, Noble had to squint. He turned south toward Albert Whitted Airport.

Burke's message would have confused anyone unfamiliar with the area. They would wonder which hangar he was referring to. Tampa Bay has two major airports, dozens of smaller airfields, and a number of flight schools. Only a native would know that Burke meant *the* Hangar.

CHAPTER ELEVEN

GREGORY HUNT REACHED THE END OF THE EXHIBIT. The main hall looped around in a circle and deposited him back at the upstairs landing where a knot of Japanese tourists were busy snapping pictures with state-of-art digital cameras. Noble was nowhere in sight. Hunt spotted a sign for the men's room and pushed through the door. In true Dali fashion, the urinals along the wall appeared to be melting. Hunt didn't need to pee but if he did, he wouldn't use one of the oddly-shaped urinals for fear he'd end up with piss all over his shoes.

Hunt bent down and spotted a pair of topsiders in the very last stall. The rest were empty. He entered the next stall over. The toilet, thankfully, was normal. He climbed on the seat and peeked over the dividing wall.

Instead of Jake Noble, he found a middle-aged man with receding hair. The guy grunted, reached for toilet paper and caught sight of Hunt. His face turned purple. "Get the hell outta here, ya' sicko!"

A stream of curses followed Hunt out the door. He

hurried through the lobby and outside into the sunshine. Noble was gone.

Hunt's lips peeled back from clenched teeth. Usually blacklisted agents came with drinking problems and a beer gut. Frayed nerves at the very least. Hunt had been expecting a broken-down old race horse. Noble still had moves.

He closed his eyes, took a breath and then put a hand in his blazer for his cellphone. He wouldn't underestimate Noble again, and he had a feeling their paths would cross. He dialed and put the phone to his ear.

The Deputy Director of Intelligence picked up on the other end. His anal-retentive voice filled the line. "This is Clark S. Foster."

"Burke paid a visit to Noble," Hunt said without preamble. He briefly described the meeting and the strange dialogue. "Noble left his boat right after."

"Where is he now?"

This was the part Hunt was dreading. He cleared his throat. "He gave me the slip, sir."

The statement was greeted by silence.

Hunt rushed to fill the void. "He ran a surveillance detection route through the Dali Museum, sir."

Foster said, "Noble has been out of the game for five years. You graduated top of your class at the Farm. You're telling me he gave you the slip?"

"He's not quite as rusty as I thought, sir," He said. "It won't happen again."

"Get back to the van. Noble has to go home sometime. Pick him up and stick with him. Don't screw up this time, Mr. Hunt."

"Yes, sir," Hunt said, but Foster had already hung up.

He stuffed the phone in his pocket.

Burke and Noble were cut from the same cloth; both were Special Forces hot shots, recruited by the Company for their ability to pull a trigger. Real spy work is about infiltrating the enemy network and collecting usable intel, not riding in, guns blazing. They were the old guard. Noble especially. He had been kicked out of the Company shortly before Hunt joined and the stink lingered, so Hunt had heard the rumors. If Burke was sharing information, he was breaking the law. Hunt would make sure he paid the piper. Burke's demise was long overdue anyway. Out with the old and in with the new.

CHAPTER TWELVE

THE HANGAR IS A BAR AND GRILL IN ALBERT WHITTED Airport, located on the second floor, with a view of the landing strips. Noble smelled grease and onion rings before he reached the top of the steps. Black-and-white photographs of old prop planes covered the walls. *Blue Suede Shoes* was coming from a jukebox in the corner and a wooden propeller was tacked over the bar.

Burke had squeezed his bulk into a booth by the windows. There was a half-eaten bacon cheeseburger in front of him. He tipped a barely perceptible nod to Noble, picked up a strawberry daiquiri, sipped.

Noble scanned the rest of the patrons. No one set off alarm bells, but good surveillance wouldn't. He slid into the booth. Leather creaked. Beyond the windows, a twin-engine Cessna taxied toward the runway. A waitress came over. Noble ordered coffee.

"French fry?" Burke motioned to a pile of thick cut potato wedges on his plate.

Noble shook his head. “I had a tail. Six foot. Blonde hair. Dressed like a member of the yacht club.”

“Gregory Hunt,” Burke said. “Foster’s new fair-haired golden boy, literally.”

“Ex-military?” Noble asked.

“That clown?” Burke snorted. “Yale. Recruited right out of college. Making a bit of a name for himself in the Company. He’s good.”

“Not good enough.”

“You gave him the slip?” Burke asked.

Noble gazed out the window at the Cessna as it geared up for take-off. “I hope you didn’t come all this way to test the new recruits.”

“We lost contact with Torres,” Burke said.

A block of ice dropped into Noble’s gut, pinning him to the seat. He had served side by side with Jesús Torres in the Green Berets. They had fought and bled together on three different continents. Torres had saved Noble’s life more than once. He leaned back in the seat and chewed the inside of one cheek. “What happened?”

“He was in Mexico City, infiltrating the Los Zetas drug cartel. Heard of it?”

Noble shrugged. “Only what I see on Fox News.”

“Then you are better informed than most.” Burke picked up his burger, took a bite and spoke around a mouthful of food. “They make the Medellin cartel of the eighties look like the JV team. They’re one of the most ruthless gangs in Mexico. Nearly half the cocaine coming across our southern border is courtesy of the Los Zetas. The guy running the show is called Machado.”

“The Axe,” Noble translated.

Burke nodded, wiped his mouth with a napkin and said, "He was a foot soldier during the drug wars of the late eighties. Made a name for himself as a cutthroat killer. Likes to chop his victims up. Sort of his calling card."

"Sounds like a real charmer," Noble observed.

"You don't know the half of it," Burke said. "Ten years ago, Mexican authorities arrested El Matatan. He was running the show back then. The cops put him away with the help of a judge who refused to be bought off. Those are rare in Mexico. Machado, who was El Matatan's top lieutenant at the time, stepped up. In retaliation for El Matatan's incarceration, Machado murdered the judge and his entire family."

"Let me guess," Noble said, "with an axe?"

"A hatchet, to be precise," said Burke. "Then he burnt the judge's house to the ground. Since then, Machado has been eliminating the competition and consolidating the drug trade under one roof. DHS sees the Los Zetas cartel as a significant threat to national security. Used to be these guys just shipped blow across the border. Now they smuggle munitions and radical Islamists as well."

"Where does Torres come in?" Noble asked, making rings with his coffee cup on the table.

"Eighteen months ago, we laid in an operation codenamed RIPTIDE. The objective was to gather intel on Los Zetas. That information would then be used by the DHS in a joint operation with Mexican authorities to take down the cartel and stem the tide of drugs flooding the United States."

"And Torres was the tip of the spear," Noble said.

Burke inclined his head. "He infiltrated the gang posing

as a pilot. We were getting good intel but it was all surface level stuff. About six months ago, Torres developed an asset by the name of Alejandra Domingo and put her in Machado's bed. We were getting everything: names, dates, shipments, even the location of the refining facilities. Two weeks ago, the information pipeline suddenly stopped. We don't know if Torres is alive or dead."

Noble's brow pinched. When an operation goes sideways, agents are trained to "go dark." Standard procedure is to stay off radar until it's safe to make contact, but two weeks is more than enough time to make it across the border from Mexico. If Torres hadn't turned up by now...

Noble didn't want to think about that. He said, "Who's leading the search and rescue?"

Burke picked up a half-eaten fry, examined it, tossed it back on the plate. "No one at CIA seems interested in finding out what happened. Foster tied the operation off."

"A field officer goes missing and no one wants to know what happened to him?"

Burke bared his teeth in a humorless grin. "I've been *ordered* to leave it alone."

Noble swore under his breath. It was bad enough the CIA had destroyed his career over the death of a crooked politician. Now they had left one of his brothers out in the cold.

Burke said, "We think Torres mailed a package shortly after he dropped off radar. We don't know where he sent it or what was inside."

Noble went back to staring out the window. The Cessna had taken wing and another small plane was coming in for a landing. It touched down with a shriek of tires, then taxied toward the gate. "Is that why Boy Wonder is following me?"

"Foster is afraid if you got a package from Torres you might run down to Mexico to help your friend."

"And if I did?" Noble asked.

"Foster would send someone to intercept you."

"Guess it's a good thing I didn't get any packages."

"Good thing," Burke said. He checked his watch. "I'd better go. I've got to catch a flight back to D.C."

"How was Torres passing information?" Noble asked.

"Through a local cut out at the Santa Ana Mission in Mexico City." Burke dropped several crumpled bills on the table and then levered his bulk out of the booth. "A priest by the name of Cordero. Watch your six, pilgrim."

Noble stared into his coffee cup. When he was nine or ten, his dad had taken him to the carnival. They had gone through the hall of mirrors together. In one mirror, ten-year-old Jake and his father were extremely tall and thin. In the next they were short and fat. In another they were shaped like Dali's clocks, bent and strange.

The intelligence community is a lot like a wilderness of mirrors. Nothing is what it seems. Burke might be operating off the reservation—feeding Noble info out of loyalty to the old unit—or this could be part of some deeper plot. Maybe the spymasters in the Clandestine Service were manipulating him into doing their dirty work. In the end, it didn't really matter. His friend was missing and Noble was going to find him. He owed Torres that much.

He drained his coffee, left a tip, and slid out of the booth.

CHAPTER THIRTEEN

Noble walked east to 4th Street and then turned north, staying in the shade as much as possible to escape the heat. College kids with tattoos and nose rings were collecting votes for the democratic candidate on one side of the street. Working class stiffs, tired of government corruption, campaigned for the insurgent on the other side. The two opposing forces were close to open warfare. A third group was collecting signatures to legalize pot. They looked a lot like the first group.

Noble stepped inside a secondhand record store with a picture window and a good view of the street. Vinyl shops were cropping up all over downtown Saint Pete. Noble couldn't figure out the craze. Why buy vinyl when he could keep all his music on a device that fit in his pocket?

This one had Bob Marley posters tacked to the walls and stank of incense. Music, some indie label that Noble didn't recognize, piped through the speakers. He pretended to flip through a collection of old jazz records near the door and watched the sidewalk for tails. After the record shop, he crossed the street to a craft beer garden. He asked to use the toilet and left through a back door which opened onto a trash-strewn alley. He continued north, taking turns at random and doubling back to throw off pursuit, until he reached a towering block of pink concrete called the Wyndham Arms.

It was promoted as an assisted living facility for "active seniors." Noble owed a bill roughly half the size of Bill Gates' fortune to the medical establishment for their work putting his mother's cancer into remission, and the second half of that fortune in rent to the Wyndham Arms.

The double doors hissed open and blast of cold air chilled the sweat on his forehead. The lobby could have passed for a plush hotel with leather armchairs and deep-piled carpet. A fake fire danced in a hearth. In the winter, it actually emitted heat. An old-timer with rheumy eyes sat in a wheelchair, gazing out the window. Noble scrawled his name on a sign-in sheet at the front desk and went in search of his mother.

He found her in the recreation room, playing gin rummy with three other women. Her gray hair was falling out in places—a result of the chemotherapy—and her skin was like parchment. A thick cable knit sweater swaddled her wasted frame. The battle with cancer had been too close to call, but Mary Elise Noble was a stubborn woman with a will of iron.

She picked up a card, laid down two runs and a discard. "Gin!"

The other ladies crowed.

Noble walked over. "You ever let anybody else win, mom?"

"Not if I can help it." Her eyes lit up at the sight of him. A weak smile hitched the corners of her mouth. It was good to see her smile. The last two months at the Wyndham Arms had been good for her. She had gotten some of her old strength back and made a few friends. She introduced Noble to her card buddies. He would never remember their names and didn't try. They spent thirty minutes telling him what a great son he was for visiting his mother.

"Feel up to a walk?" Noble asked.

"After two years in a hospital bed? I'm ready to run, but I'll settle for a walk."

She excused herself from the game.

Jake offered his arm. She slipped her frail hand through the crook of his elbow. He led her away from the card table to a pair of doors that opened onto a garden. She closed her eyes and turned her face up to the sun. "Sure does feel good."

It felt like walking into an oven, but Noble didn't tell her that. "How are you feeling?"

"Better," she said. "Every day is a little better."

They shuffled along a sidewalk which wound its way through a manicured garden. A snail could have kept pace.

"So you met Shawn Hennessey?" his mother asked.

"Sure did," Jake said.

"What's he like?"

"Shorter than I thought."

"You're tense," she said. "Is it the money?"

"Isn't it always?"

"God will provide."

Wish he'd provide a little faster, Noble thought to

himself. He didn't dare say it out loud though. Not in front of Mary Elise Noble. It would only start an argument.

"I'm going to be out of town for a couple of days," he told her.

Her grip on his forearm tightened. "For a man who doesn't have a job, you stay awful busy."

"Will you be alright while I'm gone?"

"If the food in here doesn't kill me."

Jake laughed. "I have some money coming in from Hennessey," he told her. "You should be set for a while."

Her thin lips pressed together in a tight line. The sidewalk had brought them in a large loop back to the double doors. She paused in the sunlight. "Thought you were done working for the Company."

"This isn't for the Company," he said. "A friend needs my help."

She locked eyes with him.

"Nothing dangerous," he told her.

Her expression said she didn't buy it. "Want to try that line again?"

He held up three fingers in the boy scout salute. "Honest Injun."

They shuffled through the doors into the recreation room. "Promise me you'll be careful."

"I always am," Jake said. "In the meantime, you take it easy and get your strength back."

"Lord willing," she said.

He grunted. Over that last several weeks they had reached an uneasy truce on the subject of God and the afterlife. Both realized their difference in opinion would tear them apart if they let it.

They passed a seating area where the television was tuned to CNN. Noble glanced at the screen. He was already tired of election coverage, but something registered at the back of his mind and he did a double take.

A moment later, he was fighting his way past the maze of walkers to get at the controller. The residents balked at the sudden intrusion. Noble ignored them, grabbed the remote, and started jabbing buttons.

"Jake?" his mother said. "What's gotten into you?"

"How do you go back?" Noble asked, pushing buttons to no effect.

"Lemme see it." An elderly black man in a wheelchair with tuffs of white hair over his ears held out an arthritic hand.

Noble passed over the remote. The last television show he had watched with any enthusiasm was *Firefly,* and that was long before the invention of the DVR.

The old man keyed a command into the remote and the image on the screen raced backwards. Noble felt foolish getting tech help from a ninety-year-old in a wheelchair. Maybe he should revisit those record stores? He watched people speeding around in reverse. "There!" he barked. "Stop. Play."

The old man triggered the remote. On screen, Secretary of State Helen Rhodes was stepping off a tour bus outside a convention center in New Hampshire. Cameras flashed. Rhodes waved and smiled. A crowd pushed against blue police barricades. But Noble wasn't interested in Rhodes. He was watching the entourage of aides exiting the bus.

He pointed. "Pause! Pause!"

The old man froze the screen.

Noble was staring at a still image of Samantha Gunn getting out of Helen Rhodes' tour bus. She was dressed in a pinstripe jacket and skirt with her hair pulled back in a ponytail. The image was blurry, the camera was focused on the Secretary of State, but there was no mistake.

"What the hell..." Noble muttered to himself.

Six months ago, Sam had been running a shelter for abused women in the Philippines. When her best friend was kidnapped by a ruthless kingpin, she had taken the law into her own hands and proved her courage in a firefight that would have reduced most grown men to Jell-O. Noble never would have figured her for a political aide, especially not for the likes of Helen Rhodes.

At least now he knew why she wasn't returning his calls.

"You done?" the old man asked with a hint of annoyance. "Mind if we get on with the news?"

Noble muttered an apology and fought his way back through the sea of walkers, still trying to make sense of it. Why would Sam go to work for Helen Rhodes?

His mother said, "Friend of yours?"

"Huh?"

She thrust her chin at the screen. "That girl getting out of the bus," she said. "Do you know her?"

"Yes," Noble said. "Er... no. No, I guess I didn't know her as well as I thought I did."

He said goodbye to his mother, waved to her card table buddies, and then legged it south toward the marina. The surveillance van was still slotted next to Pioneer Park under the shade of an oak tree. An angry line of black clouds was crawling in from the west. It was summer and just after four o'clock in Florida, which meant it was time for the afternoon thunder shower. You can practically set your watch by it. A strong breeze stirred the tree limbs. Leaves murmured to each other in their secret language. The air smelled like rain. Noble hurried along the docks to the *Yeoman*. The first heavy drop landed on his shoulder as he stepped on deck. A moment later the skies opened up. He hauled the cabin door shut. Rain hammered the roof. A fork of lightning blazed across the sky outside the galley windows. Thunder followed.

The *Yeoman* rolled on the choppy swell. With one hand on the bulkhead for support, Noble climbed into the hold, took a screwdriver from the tool chest and then went to his cabin. A Remington 870 shotgun leaned against the wall next to his bunk. His underwater camera sat atop a chest of drawers next to a photo of Sam. The picture was a reproduction of her college I.D. printed at a local Kinko's. Noble had cashed in a favor with a friend still working at the Directorate of Support who had managed to hack the Yale database and forward Noble the photograph. It was a little grainy, but Sam smiled at him from a cheap Walmart frame.

What was she doing working a political campaign for Helen Rhodes? Politics is a dirty game, but Rhodes took corruption to a new level. She had sat in the Situation Room at the White House and watched Islamic terrorists overrun an American embassy in Libya, killing four Americans. When questioned about it she had blurted out, "What difference does it make now?" Noble couldn't believe that Sam would knowingly go to work for anyone as blatantly corrupt as Rhodes.

He left the cabin door open and removed the screw

plate from the door hinge. Underneath was a small recess in the wood known in the intelligence community as a *slip*. He reached inside and pulled out the key. All he had to do now was shake the CIA watchdogs and get to Mexico.

Rain still pounded the roof. He wasn't going anywhere for the next fifteen or twenty minutes, so he used the time to fry up a tripletail from the icebox and boil rice. By the time he finished eating, the storm had spent its fury and the sun poked its head out. The air turned muggy hot.

Noble fired up the engines and motored out of South Yacht Basin, headed due east toward Tampa. He was about to cross a line and there was no going back. Once in Mexico City, he would be on his own, operating off the reservation.

CHAPTER FOURTEEN

Machado was a hulking figure in a red Puma track suit, pacing around like a caged lion. He had a shaved head and a neck the size of a normal man's thigh. Blood dripped from his knuckles.

The room was bare concrete walls in the basement of his mansion. A naked bulb hung from the ceiling and there was a drain in the middle of the floor. Juan Busto Esparza—a high ranking agent in Mexico's PFM, the *Policía Federal Ministerial*—was lashed to a chair by razor wire. He was naked and covered in his own blood. They had ripped out his fingernails and toenails before starting in on his face.

Machado stopped pacing long enough to slam a fist into Esparza's face. The impact made a meaty crack.

Ten years ago, a major heart attack had nearly killed Machado. The experience changed him. He gave up excess eating and drinking and found he actually liked working out. Machado had shed nearly a hundred pounds of fat. Now he was an impressive two-hundred and twenty pounds of solid muscle. He never took steroids. He prided himself on being a natural bodybuilder. His results were the product of lean proteins, healthy fats and heavy lifting. The musclebound physique had become a symbol of his indomitable will and when he punched, he put all two-hundred and twenty pounds into it.

He shook blood from his knuckles. "Where is the girl?"

Esparza turned his head to the side and spat out a broken tooth. "I don't know."

Machado flattened Esparza's nose and followed up with body shots until Esparza vomited blood, splashing Machado's track suit.

Finding out his pilot was working for the *Norteamericanos* was bad enough—Diaz had been a good soldier—but that pain paled in comparison to learning his mistress was working for the PFM. Worse, she had stolen recordings that could bring all of Machado's carefully laid plans crashing down.

"You are going to tell me what I want to know," Machado said.

"Go to hell," Esparza shrieked.

Machado clutched Esparza's skull between his hands and squeezed. Esparza's lips peeled back from clenched teeth. His arms jerked at the razor wire and his fingers danced on the air like a pianist looking for keys. A scream ripped from his throat. His skull creaked under the pressure. Machado continued to squeeze and Esparza's screams turned to a blood curdling warble.

"*El Jefe*!" Santiago stepped forward. "He can't tell us anything if he is dead."

Machado let go and took a step back, breathing heavy. He ran a hand over his face, smearing himself with Esparza's blood. "Get him to talk, *amigo*, or I start in with the hatchet."

Machado walked away, giving Santiago room to work. The lieutenant took a clean handkerchief from his pocket, squatted in front of the PFM Captain, and dabbed his forehead. "Why not tell him what he wants to know?" Santiago said. "We will find the girl sooner or later. Why suffer?"

Esparza shook his head, flinging droplets of blood and sweat. "I don't know where she is."

"This can all be over," Santiago prompted. "Tell us where the recordings are and I promise you a quick death. You won't feel a thing."

Crying now, Esparza said, "I don't know about any recordings. Six months ago, Alejandra filed for an extended leave of absence, something about a family emergency, and I haven't heard from her since. I had no idea she infiltrated your organization. I swear."

Santiago stood up, looked at Machado and shrugged.

Machado grabbed a hatchet from a table near the door and brought it down on Esparza's kneecap. The PFM Captain shrieked. Bright red blood pissed from his leg in arterial squirts.

Santiago skipped backwards to avoid the spray.

Machado felt the warm blood soak through his track suit. He brought the hatchet down again. "Tell me!" He bellowed. "Tell me what I want to know!"

Esparza screamed until his vocal cords ruptured and the only thing coming out was a thin exhalation of air.

Santiago turned away.

In his rage, Machado hacked off both of Esparza's legs and then buried the hatchet in his chest. When it was over, Machado stormed out of the basement and up the stairs to the first floor, followed by Santiago.

Henry Pennyworth Blythe, a middle-aged Brit with thinning hair and a paunch, was sitting in an armchair looking over a copy of yesterday's *Daily Telegraph*. He looked up as they entered. "No luck, I take it?"

Santiago shook his head.

Blythe folded his newspaper, stood up, and smoothed his slacks. "If those recordings get out..."

"I am well aware," Machado told him. He looked at Santiago. "Find Alejandra and we find the recordings."

Santiago said. "She may be dead, *el Jefe*."

"Then go find her body," Machado said.

"I'll put my best men on it," Santiago said.

Machado jabbed a thumb over his shoulder. "And get some men in here to clean that up."

"*Sí, el Jefe.*"

When Santiago had gone, Blythe said, "Maybe I should make a call?"

"And say what? That we secretly recorded our business dealings?" He shook his head. "We will find Alejandra and when we do, I'll make her tell me where the recordings are."

"It may all be for nothing." Blythe took off his glasses and cleaned them on his sweater vest. "Those recordings do not guarantee an ROI."

"There is one thing I am sure of," Machado said.

Blythe raised his eyebrows. "What's that?"

"Power corrupts," Machado told him. "Once you have it, you'll do anything to hold onto it."

"I hope you're right," Blythe said.

Machado clapped a hand on his shoulder, leaving a bloody handprint. "You worry about the money. I'll worry about our friend."

CHAPTER FIFTEEN

By seven o'clock the next morning, Gregory Hunt was back in D.C. He had showered, shaved, and was running on less than four hours' sleep. He pulled into Langley at 7:27 a.m., stopped his BMW at the yellow- and white-striped barricades and buzzed his window down. A guard in dark blue fatigues compared Hunt to his photo ID while another guard ran a mirror on a stick under the vehicle, checking for explosive devices. When they were satisfied, the guard stepped back inside his shed and pressed a button. The barricades swung up.

The Directorate of Intelligence is headquartered on the second floor and takes up most of the northwest corner. Hunt passed a sea of cubicles to a frosted glass door marked *Deputy Director Intelligence.* The room beyond was paneled in blonde wood with deep-piled carpet and a leather sofa for people to sit while they wait.

Foster's secretary, Ginny Farnham, reminded Hunt of his grammar teacher at Thayer Academy. A pair of reading spectacles rode low on her nose, her red hair was pulled up in a bun and crow's feet were starting around her eyes. Dark eye shadow and lipstick did a decent job hiding her age. God only knew how long she had been with the Company. Probably since the Clinton administration. Directors come and go, but good secretaries last forever. She looked up at the sound of the door, saw who it was, and pulled off her glasses.

"Mr. Hunt," she said with a smile. "Always a pleasure. How was Florida?"

"Overrated." Hunt perched himself on the edge of the desk, crossed his arms over his chest and turned on his smile. "Did you miss me?"

"I counted the hours." One hand toyed with the collar of her button-down blouse.

Hunt leaned in just enough to invade her personal space and caught a whiff of jasmine. Something about a woman's perfume got Hunt's motor running. Old or young, it didn't matter. He just liked it when they smelled nice. "Forget Florida," he said. "Ever been to Aruba? White sands. Crystal clear water. All the piña coladas you can drink. You and I could be sitting on the beach this time tomorrow."

Pink colored her cheeks. "Careful Mr. Hunt. Some people would call that sexual harassment in the workplace."

He laughed and tipped a nod at the inner door. "Is he in?"

"He's waiting for you."

"Duty calls."

The Deputy Director of Intelligence sat behind roughly an acre of cherry wood with a phone pressed to his ear. He pointed Hunt to an empty chair.

Before sitting down, Hunt unbuttoned his jacket and hiked up the legs of his trousers to avoid ruining the creases. He took special care in the way he dressed. Clothes make the man, after all. Hunt lived by the motto, "Dress for the job you want, not the job you have." If that were true, Foster must be angling for a job teaching history to undergrads.

The walls were covered in awards and commendations. A picture of a yellow lab stood on one corner of the massive desk. Foster had no wife and no girlfriend. Hunt figured a guy had to be pretty desperate to put a picture of a dog on his desk. But Hunt was smart enough to keep observations like that to himself. He wouldn't tell Foster it was pathetic to keep a picture of a dog on his desk any more than he would tell him to shave off the wispy strands of hair around his ears. *Why keep a few loose gray strands?* Like anybody was fooled? Just shave it off, Hunt thought. Shave it off and be bald with some damn dignity, for crying out loud.

He uncrossed and re-crossed his legs while he waited. Foster dragged the conversation out, a subtle way of letting Hunt know his place in the world. That was okay, let Foster have his day in the sun. This office would be Hunt's one day. He wondered if he would be bald by then and some younger man would be sitting across from him thinking the same things.

Hunt smoothed a hand over his hair. It wouldn't happen to him. His father was sixty-seven and still had a full head of hair. Besides, Hunt told himself, if he started to go bald, he would have the good sense to shave it off. Or maybe adopt a hat. A fedora, like Frank Sinatra used to wear.

"Keep me in the loop," Foster said and hung up. He

turned his attention to Hunt. "What happened? Where is Noble?"

Hunt felt like he was back at Thayer, sitting in the headmaster's study. "We're not sure."

"I thought you put a listening device on his boat?" said Foster.

"I did," Hunt told him.

"And?"

"Those microdots were never intended to be used as tracking devices," Hunt said. "They send audio over a short distance. Once Noble left the harbor, we lost the signal."

Hunt laid out the whole operation from beginning to end.

Foster propped his elbows on the desk and formed a steeple with his fingers. "So Burke walked into your op unannounced and Noble disappeared for approximately two-and-a-half hours? Have I got that right?"

"That's accurate," Hunt said, happy to shift the focus away from his failure and onto Burke's unexplained appearance.

"Those two are thick as thieves," Foster remarked. "Burke recruited Noble, trained him. Taught him everything he knows."

"Do you think Burke is working with Noble off the reservation?"

Foster shook his head. "That's a line Burke would never willingly cross, but he's right up against it. Close enough to get burned. We have to assume he's feeding Noble information."

"The unauthorized dissemination of classified information is a federal offence," Hunt said, reciting from the textbook.

Foster dismissed that with a wave of his hand. "You'll never make that stick. Burke has been with the Company a long time. Longer than me. He and Wizard are on a first name basis. Thankfully Burke doesn't have any political sense, or he'd be sitting in my chair."

"May I ask what's going on?" Hunt asked.

Foster leaned back, sized up Hunt and then said, "One of Noble's old Army buddies went missing in Mexico."

"And you think Noble will go to Mexico to look for him?"

"He's probably already on his way," Foster said.

"Say the word. I can be in Mexico before sundown." Hunt kept his expression carefully neutral. Inside, he felt like a dog pulling at a leash. He was dying for another crack at Noble. Taking down a rogue operative would be the perfect addition to his resume. It was just the sort of thing upper management likes to see when it comes time for promotion.

Foster frowned and shook his head. "No. Unless Noble obtained new passports through back channels, we know all of his legends. Flag his identities. Let the Mexican authorities do the heavy lifting. If they pick him up entering their country on a fake passport, Noble will spend the next ten years in a Mexican jail. That should keep him out of our hair."

It was an effort to hide his disappointment, but Hunt nodded. "I'll get right on it."

CHAPTER SIXTEEN

Sam met Taggart at McCormick and Schmick's on K Street a few minutes before eleven o'clock. The smell of sizzling beef made her stomach rumble. A long bar of polished mahogany dominated one wall. There was a cold fireplace on her left as she entered. Square tables covered in crisp white linen crowded the floor. Two dozen customers were already seated, filling the restaurant with friendly chatter and the clink of silverware. A waiter leaned against the bar, chatting with the bartender. Taggart was by himself at a table in the corner. He lifted a hand in greeting.

They had spent half the night going through the FBI Director's life with a fine-tooth comb. Secretary of State Rhodes had pulled strings and gotten them a complete copy of every FBI case file with Standish's name attached. It was a thick stack. Standish had been with the Bureau for thirty-two years and investigated everything from serial killers and organized crime to government corruption. Sam had studied the first dozen folders with interest. It was a rare glimpse into the inner workings of the FBI. America's alphabet soup of law enforcement agencies are not known for sharing. It was a rare chance to see how the FBI ran their shop and a look into the life of the FBI director himself. From what Sam could gather, he was by the book, methodical and dogged in his pursuit of justice. He was, as Taggart had already suggested, a *real* boy scout. And that wasn't hyperbole. James Standish had been a decorated Eagle Scout in his youth.

The files didn't turn up anything incriminating however, or even shady. Sam and Taggart had called it quits sometime after two in the morning. She hadn't even made it to bed when Taggart sent a text asking her to meet at McCormick and Schmick's for an early lunch.

Now, exhausted and running on a few hours' sleep, Sam cut her way across the dining room to Taggart's table in the corner. "I didn't figure you for a steak guy."

"I'm a vegetarian," Taggart said. He sipped from a glass of water garnished with lemon.

The waiter appeared. Sam ordered a cappuccino.

"So what are we doing here?"

"Taking a meeting," Taggart said.

"With who?"

Taggart thrust his chin at the door.

Senator Randal Dodd had just waddled in. He was a portly man in an ill-fitting suit with knees that buckled under his own ponderous weight. Broken blood vessels spread across his bulbous nose, from decades of alcohol abuse.

"Recognize him?" Taggart asked under his breath.

"I watch the news," Sam muttered, flashing the senator a polite smile.

Dodd had been serving in congress since the early nineties. He shuffled over and planted his bulk in a chair. The spindly wood legs groaned ominously. He spoke with a Daffy Duck lisp that sent droplets of spittle sailing across the table. "Always nice to see you, Guy. I haven't heard from anyone in Rhodes' camp since the start of campaign season."

Sam casually repositioned her cappuccino to avoid spit.

"Working for the Ice Queen doesn't leave much time for a social life," Taggart said.

Dodd turned his attention on Sam. "And who's this lovely young lady?"

"Senator Dodd, meet Vanessa Klein," Guy said. "Vanessa's a constitutional lawyer." The lie came off his lips so easily it was impossible to tell if he had thought it up in advance or if lying was second nature. Either way, Sam decided, he had the makings of a first-rate politician.

"Nice to meet you, Vanessa."

Dodd ordered a coffee with brandy, the clam chowder, wild Alaskan halibut, crab cakes, steamed mussels, and a mushroom spinach sauté. It was enough to feed seven.

Sam ordered the Mahi Mahi and Taggart had a salad.

"To what do I owe the pleasure?" Dodd asked after the food had arrived and he had tucked a napkin into his collar. He spoke around a mouthful of halibut. Small bits of fish flew from his lips like shell casings launched from the breech of an automatic rifle. "I assume you didn't bring me here to introduce your latest conquest."

Sam arched a brow.

"I suppose you've heard about the FBI director's remarks?" Taggart asked.

Dodd mopped his mouth with his napkin and bobbed his head. "Who hasn't? It's a serious accusation. Is it true?"

"Completely unfounded," Taggart said.

Dodd barked a laugh. "Then our girl has nothing to worry about."

Taggart shot him a flat look. "This is serious, Dodd. A scandal like this right before the election could ruin us and put the Republicans back in the White House."

"No one wants that," Dodd said.

"You went to school with Standish. We were hoping..." Taggart trailed off.

"That he's secretly queer?" Senator Dodd shook his head with a rueful grin. "No such luck, old boy. Standish bleeds red, white and blue. I doubt if he cheats on his taxes, much less his wife."

Taggart bared his teeth in frustration. "There has to be something. What about his kids? They ever been in trouble? Did the wife belong to any radical groups in college?"

"I can't help you, Guy. Believe me, I wish I could. No one wants to see an outsider in the driver's seat, but you're wasting your time digging into Standish." Dodd put down his fork and spread his hands. "He's one of those rarest of Washington specimens."

Sam questioned him with a look.

"He's honest," Dodd said.

Taggart hadn't even touched his salad. Sam couldn't blame him. It was full of spit and bits of clam chowder. He sat scowling, lost in thought.

Dodd cut off a piece of crab cake and shoveled it in his mouth. "Want my advice?"

Taggart nodded.

"Make sure you aren't the one left standing when the music stops." Dodd motioned for the waiter and ordered another brandy.

Taggart picked an invisible piece of lint from his powder blue tie. "Thanks for the advice."

"My pleasure."

After lunch, standing on the sidewalk in front of McCormack and Schmick's in the sweltering heat of the Foggy Bottom, Taggart hailed a cab and said, "On to plan B."

"Which is?" Sam asked.

Taggart opened the back door and climbed in without waiting for Sam.

She was forced to scramble in after him and pretended not to notice.

"The State Department," Taggart told their Pakistani driver, then turned to Sam. "If the FBI Director hasn't got anything to hide, we'll have to create something."

"I'm not sure I like where this is going," Sam said.

Taggart snorted and gave her a disapproving glance. "All part of the game, Vanessa. There's no place for truth in politics. We do what it takes to win. If that means planting evidence on a fed, that's what we'll do."

He motioned out the window to the traffic on K Street. "Take a look around. You honestly think John Q Public has any idea what it takes to run this country? Americans are knuckle-dragging Neanderthals, clinging to the antiquated notion that a genie in the sky is running the show."

Taggart jabbed himself in the chest with a finger. "*We* run the show. We always have. Elections are a dog and pony show. The power structure in Washington decides who gets to be president. We just let the people think they have a choice."

"How do you explain an independent in the election?" Sam asked.

"A fluke," Taggart said. "People rallied behind him because he talks tough and doesn't play by the rules, but don't be fooled. He hasn't got the backing of anybody on the Hill."

"So the Washington machine calls the shots," Sam said. "Is that it?"

Taggart inclined his head.

"So much for democracy," Sam muttered.

"Democracy is overrated," Taggart told her. "People need a ruling class, whether they realize it or not. Provide them with fast food, football and cable television, and they'll keep forking over tax money and voting us into power."

"The illusion of freedom," Sam said.

"That's right."

"To be clear," Sam said. "You're asking me to help plant false evidence against the Director of the FBI?"

"Think of this as an opportunity," Taggart told her. "What you have here is a chance to collect a few chips in the big game—to ingratiate yourself with the *real* power in Washington."

"I'm listening," Sam said.

CHAPTER SEVENTEEN

Burke arrived at the office exhausted, feeling like he hadn't slept. He had been up most of the night arguing with his wife. They did that a lot lately. Kowalski handed him a cable out of Southeast Asia as he passed by the sea of cubicles. The front of the manila folder was stamped *URGENT—EYES ONLY*.

Burke's secretary, Dana, was at her desk. Carefully manicured nails flew over the keys and her breasts strained against blue silk. Her blonde hair was up in a ponytail this morning. Burke caught a whiff of warm vanilla and imagined Dana in tub full of soapy water.

She glanced up as he entered. A playful smile twitched the corners of her red lips. "You look like hell, boss."

"Good morning to you too." He dropped Kowalski's file on her desk and passed through into his own office. There were no accolades on the walls, no pictures, and nothing personal. His desk was utilitarian: a computer and a phone. A safe was built into the wall behind the desk. Cardboard boxes were stacked in one corner, next to a rubber plant that

Burke had inherited along with the office. The only excess he allowed himself was a top-of-the-line swivel chair with memory foam. If he was going to be sitting all day, he might as well be comfortable.

Dana poured coffee, mixed in just the right amount of cream and sugar, and followed Burke into his office. "Boy Wonder had a meeting with Foster first thing this morning," she informed him.

Burke dropped into his chair and rocked a few times. "Hunt on his way to Mexico?"

"Not yet." She handed him the coffee.

Burke accepted the mug with a nod. "Only a matter of time," he said. "Before the end of the day, would be my guess."

Dana spotted a wadded-up bag of potato chips half-buried under paperwork. She pulled it out and gave him a stern look.

He hitched his shoulders.

She tossed the crumpled bag, overhand, into the waste-basket. The movement strained her blouse. Burke caught a tantalizing glimpse of black lace between the buttons. The potato chip bag hit the rim and went in.

"Two points," Burke said.

She perched on the corner of his desk and crossed her legs. Her skirt rode up, revealing a pair of tan thighs. "Think Noble will go to Mexico?"

Burke woke up his computer with a nudge of the mouse and logged in using his passcode. "He's probably there already."

"How can you be so sure?"

"I been playing this game a lot longer than you, kid."

“Hope you’ve thought this through,” Dana said. “A lot is riding on it.”

“Noble is our best bet.”

“You put a lot of faith in this guy.”

“He’s one of the best I ever trained,” Burke said. “You’d like him. He’s about your age.”

“Is that right?”

He inclined his head. “You could do worse.”

She arched one sculpted brow. “Maybe I like my men a little older.”

Their eyes met. Burke felt a stirring deep in his gut. He said, “Find out what Kowalski thinks is so urgent, will you?”

She slipped off his desk and adjusted her skirt. “Anything else?”

“See if the vending machine has any cheddar cheese chips.”

“I’ll get you a fruit salad from the cafeteria,” Dana told him.

He watched her walk to the door.

CHAPTER EIGHTEEN

Delta flight 7202 touched down at Mexico City International Airport just after 2pm. Tires screamed on the tarmac, jerking Noble from a fitful sleep. A yawn nearly dislocated his jaw. He rubbed his eyes while the jet taxied to the gate, then collected his carry-on from the overhead, and shuffled for the exit along with the rest of the passengers.

At customs, he handed over his real passport. He was hoping the CIA had flagged his fake IDs and forgotten to flag his real name. It was a good bet. Hunt had, in fact, overlooked Noble's real name when he alerted Mexican authorities to a potential terrorist threat.

The agent scrutinized Noble's passport and recognized his face from the pictures tacked to a board in the break room. His eyes went to Noble and back to the passport. His hand slipped under the desk and Noble knew he was blown. A knot formed in his gut. From the corner of his eye, he spotted a pair of airport cops moving in his direction.

The customs agent said, "Would you follow these men, please? They have a few questions they would like to ask."

"Is there a problem?"

"No problem, sir." The agent hitched a smile onto his face. "Routine questions. That's all."

Airport security officers flanked him. One took his bag. The other gripped his elbow. It was all done in a very polite but firm manner. They steered him away from customs, past whispering crowds, and ushered him through a side door marked SÓLO EL PERSONAL DEL AEROPUERTO.

Noble found himself in an uncarpeted hallway with bare walls and stark lighting. The smell reminded him of a FedEx store, the scent of cardboard boxes and fresh printer paper permeating the air. A door on his right had a sign marked PORTERO. To the left was twenty meters of blank hall that ended with a right turn. The officers, still flanking him, steered Noble down the hallway.

He hadn't committed any crimes in Mexico—that they knew of—so they couldn't arrest him, but they could deny him entry and put him on the first flight back to America where Hunt would be waiting to pick him up. Noble couldn't let that happen.

The heavy door clomped shut behind them, sealing out the noise from the terminal. The guard on Noble's right had his arm in a vice grip. The guard on his left held Noble's carry-on, leaving his holstered weapon unguarded. Noble grabbed the gun on the guard's hip using his left hand and swung it in an arc, catching the other guard a blow to the face. The man's nose broke with a snap. Blood spurted from his nostrils. He covered his face with both hands and staggered backwards.

The other guard tried to wrap Noble up in a bear hug. Noble reached over his shoulder, grabbed the officer's uniform collar and used a judo throw, sprawling the officer out on the concrete floor in a semi-conscious daze.

The first officer recovered and tried to draw his weapon.

Noble swept his legs out from under him with a kick. The officer sat down hard and lost his grip on his gun. Noble kicked at the pistol. The Berretta skittered across the floor.

The officer put his hands up, bloody palms out. Droplets of blood flew when he spoke. "Please don't kill me. I have a wife."

"Ever want to see her again?" Noble asked in Spanish.

The officer nodded.

"Take your radio off your belt and toss it," Noble ordered.

He hurried to comply.

"Now his," Noble said, pointing to the semiconscious partner.

The cop scrambled over on his hands and knees, pulled the radio off his partner's belt with trembling fingers, and tossed it.

"You're doing good," Noble reassured him. "Now, carry him into the closet."

The officer got both hands under his partner's armpits and hauled him to the janitor's closet. He used his elbow to operate the latch. It was full of mops and cleaning agents, but the guard managed to squeeze into the space next to his partner, who was starting to come around.

A quick inspection of the door handle showed it only opened from the outside. Noble trapped both officers in the broom closet, took a moment to re-tuck his shirt and then retrieved his carry-on bag. He stuffed both firearms and radios inside before hurrying to the end of the hall. He followed the access corridor, navigating by instinct and hoping he didn't run into any airport personnel, until he found a stairwell.

He took the steps two at a time, reached the ground floor and cracked the door for a peek. He was facing the luggage carousels and the exit. No one was watching the Employees Only door. Noble slipped out and strolled past the travelers waiting on their luggage.

He was halfway to the exit when alarm bells started. A pair of airport security people, milling around the luggage carousels, turned and hurried toward the nearest escalator. A few people looked up in surprise, but the alarm was too distant to cause panic.

Noble ignored it and kept moving.

A concrete overhang shaded the unloading zone where cars jockeyed for position at the curb. A balding man got out of a Nissan Tsuru to hug his wife and four-year-old daughter, leaving the driver's side door open. The Tsuru is the Mexican equivalent of a 1992 Sentra. They are still manufactured in Mexico and, other than a transmission upgrade, built with all the original parts. For Noble that meant no modern bells and whistles, like On Star. He didn't have to worry about the vehicle being shut down remotely.

While the man was busy making funny faces for his daughter, Noble slid into the driver's seat and put the Nissan in gear. The sedan leapt forward. Noble cramped the wheel hard to miss the bumper of a parked SUV and then he straightened out as he merged into the passing lane. The father shouted and ran after the car. Noble put the accelerator down, swerving around slower vehicles, following signs for the freeway.

CHAPTER NINETEEN

HUNT AND HIS TEAM OF JUNIOR ANALYSTS HAD SET UP shop in one of the Situation Rooms on the second floor. Unlike the dimly lit rooms made popular by Hollywood, this one was bathed in bright fluorescent light. The carpet was gray and worn through in places. The coffee maker was crusted with hard water and computer fans gave off the smell of warm circuit boards. The Op had been designated Task Force Gringo, a name Gwen had come up with.

Ezra and Gwen were in their element, hunched over their terminals like a pair of nearsighted turtles. The rattle of keyboards broke the steady hum of the computers. Hunt paced while the tech nerds worked their magic.

Foster was the only other person with access to the temporary Op Center. There was a lot of scuttlebutt on the second floor about what Hunt was working on; several people speculated that he was running down a rogue officer, but no one knew for sure. Hunt liked it that way. Let them wonder. Cryptic rumors about black on black missions would bolster his reputation inside the Company.

So far, they had located Noble's boat on the opposite side of Tampa Bay, docked and paid through the month. A thorough search of the vessel had failed to turn up anything useful. They had put out BOLOs in all the major airports and transit stations in Central and South America. They had even flagged his fake passports in Texas and Nevada on the off chance he would fly into Dallas and drive south.

At 3:55 p.m., just when Hunt was thinking about finding a couch to sneak a nap, Gwen pulled off her headphones and said, "An American matching Noble's description just beat up two cops and escaped from Mexico City International Airport."

Hunt swore. "Get me on the phone with airport security."

Gwen rapped the keys and then handed the headset to Hunt. He put one headphone against his ear, adjusted the mic and waited for someone to answer.

"*Hola...*"

Before the phone operator could go any further, Hunt said, "This is officer Chuck Dixon with the United States Federal Bureau of Investigations. I'm calling about the American that just escaped custody."

The operator transferred him to security. Hunt listened while an airport cop explained how Noble had disarmed a pair of officers and escaped. The suspect had been travelling under the name Jacob Noble. Hunt bit back another curse. "He's wanted for questioning in connection to terrorism inside the United States. He should be considered armed and dangerous. You need to put out an A.P.B."

"*Qué?*" the airport cop asked. "What is A.P.B., *señor?*"

Hunt covered the microphone with one hand. "What's Spanish for 'all points bulletin?'"

Ezra shrugged.

Gwen shook her head.

"Find out!"

Ezra opened a web browser. Gwen reached for an operations binder. Ezra was faster.

Hunt relayed the unfamiliar Spanish and waited.

The guy on the other end still didn't understand what Hunt wanted. He threw the headphones down on the console and leaned over Gwen's chair. "Get on the horn with Mexican law enforcement. Release Noble's real name and photos. Make sure they know he's armed and extremely dangerous. And one of you, *for the love of God*, find out how to say 'all points bulletin.'"

Deputy Director Foster chose that moment to sweep into the Situation Room, demanding an update. He had a knack for catching employees at the worst possible moments.

"Airport security tried to apprehend him, but he got away," Hunt said.

A vein throbbed in the center of Foster's pale forehead. "How did he manage that?"

"He disarmed two cops."

"Is anyone dead?"

Hunt shook his head.

"That's a lucky break," Foster said.

"He's been in Mexico less than an hour and two cops are in the hospital," Hunt said, exaggerating the seriousness of the officers' injuries. "Imagine what he'll do before the day is out. Put me on a plane to Mexico. I'll nail this guy."

Foster shook his head. "Track him from here. Alert the authorities in Mexico. I want Noble neutralized before sundown."

"We are trying to put out an A.P.B.," Hunt said. "If we can figure out how to say it in Spanish."

He gave Ezra a significant look.

Ezra pointed to the screen in front of him. "That's what it says right here."

"Find Noble," Foster said. "Before he does any more damage."

"Um, pardon me, sir..." Gwen pushed her glasses up her nose. "Any idea what he's up to? It would make it easier for us to track him."

"You aren't paid to ask questions," Foster told her. "Noble's a loose cannon. Always has been. He needs to be found. *Find him.*"

Gwen turned back to her computer with her shoulders up around her ears and her head down, like a scolded puppy.

"We are doing everything we can *from here,*" Hunt said.

Foster disappeared through the door.

Hunt went back to pacing.

CHAPTER TWENTY

Noble ditched the stolen car in a crowded lot. Even without OnStar, the local police would have a bulletin out on the stolen Tsuru. He left the keys in the ignition and walked west on Andrade Avenue with the afternoon sun beating down. The mercury was topping one hundred degrees. People walked with their eyes narrowed against the heat. At least Saint Petersburg got a breeze off the Gulf. Mexico City is landlocked. Noble could feel the asphalt burning through the soles of his shoes.

It had been seven years since he had been in Mexico City. His team had pulled a successful sneak and peek in Chile and then spent three days in Mexico drinking cheap booze and chasing skirts. The capital hadn't changed much. It was still a sun-drenched metropolis surrounded by slums in the middle of a desert—an urban nerve center working hard to make a place for itself on the world stage, struggling somewhere between the first world and the third.

Noble hailed a motorcycle cab. Enterprising young Mexicans in need of work used cheap motorbikes as unlicensed taxi services. The kid driving looked fifteen or sixteen. Noble asked if he was familiar with the Santa Ana Mission.

"*Sí, señor.*"

Noble threw a leg over the seat. The kid eased off the clutch, twisted the throttle and zig-zagged through the ever-present traffic that jammed up the city center. Noble leaned back, gripping the chrome luggage rack, and enjoyed the wind in his hair. The air was a chemical soup that had to be swallowed instead of inhaled. Noble shuddered to think what it was doing to his lungs.

The Santa Ana Mission occupied a corner lot. It was two stories, built from sandstone with red clay shingles. A massive wooden cross was nailed to the front of the building. Pigeons roosted in the bell tower.

The kid charged twice the going rate and then roared off in search of another sucker. Noble pushed through a pair of large oak doors into a candle-lit cloister. The thick stink of incense sucker punched his sinuses. He felt like an interloper here. Noble was on the fence when it came to the whole "hereafter" business. If there was a God, He and Noble weren't on speaking terms.

Noble made his way into the nave. His steps echoed. Rows of wooden pews marched toward a simple pulpit. Light struggled in through stained glass windows. A sculpture of Christ was nailed to a cross. Blood dribbled from his wrists and feet. His eyes were turned up to heaven.

Hell of a way to go out, Noble thought to himself.

A young priest threaded his way between the pews. He had thinning hair and delicate features. In perfect English he said, "Have you come for confession?"

"We'd be here all day," Noble said. "Where I can find Father Cordero?"

The priest faltered. "I am Father Cordero."

Noble glanced around to be sure they were alone. "I understand you've been passing information for the CIA, Father."

A nervous smile flitted across Cordero's face. He started to shake his head.

Noble cut him off. "Don't lie. I know you've been acting as a cutout. I'm not here to hurt you, father. My friend is missing. I'm here to find him."

"Who is your friend?"

Noble took out a seven-year-old photograph of him and Torres in the Plaza de la Constitución.

Cordero hesitated, then nodded. He motioned to a pew. They sat.

"Your CIA approached me two years ago about helping them gather intelligence against the Los Zetas cartel. They told me all I would have to do was accept packages from one person and give them to another. Your friend would come once, sometimes twice a week, and give me a thumb drive. He called himself Diaz."

"How did he give you the information?" Noble asked.

Cordero pointed to the collection box. "He would put it in the tithes and offerings. A few days later another man would come for confession. I would pass the thumb drive through the partition."

"Keep going," Noble said.

Father Cordero shrugged. "Two weeks ago, Diaz stops coming. I do not know why."

"What about the other man, the one picking up the information? What happened to him?"

"He came the next week but I had nothing for him. I told him I had not seen Diaz. That was the last I have seen of him."

The story sounded okay, but Cordero was holding something back. "What aren't you telling me?"

Another nervous smile flashed across his face. "I don't know what you are talking about."

Noble leaned back, crossed his arms, and fixed the priest with a look. "I'm going to find out sooner or later. Make it easy on both of us."

Beads of sweat collected on Cordero's forehead. He wiped his face on his sleeve. "I only agreed to pass information, you understand? I thought I was helping my country. The cartels are a blight on Mexico. But now..."

"Spill," Noble ordered.

Cordero massaged his temples. The struggle was plain on his face. He wasn't cut out for spy work. Finally, he turned to Noble and asked, "Are you a good man?"

Noble shook his head. "No."

Cordero sighed. "At least you are honest."

Noble shrugged.

"Come with me."

They passed through an alcove and up a narrow flight of steps to the second floor. It was ten degrees hotter up here. Noble's toes squished inside his socks. They entered a hall with arches that opened onto a cloistered garden in the courtyard below. A dry stone fountain stood at the center and a few stunted rose bushes struggled to survive the heat.

"Not much of a garden, is it?" Cordero remarked.

"No," Noble agreed.

"Not much of a gardener either," Cordero said. "He did not come to work this morning. That is why I am forced to confide in you. There is no one else I can trust."

Before Noble could ask what the gardener had to do with anything, Cordero pushed open a door and motioned Noble inside.

CHAPTER TWENTY-ONE

Santiago sat with his back to the wall. His polished leather shoes were stacked on the table next to a backpack stuffed with pesos. His black shirt sleeves were rolled up to his elbows. Sweat glistened on his tattooed forearms. Overhead, three ceiling fans whipped around so fast they threatened to break free of their mounts.

He shook a cigarette from a pack, stuck it between his lips and flicked a gold-plated Zippo. Dust motes danced in the pale light filtering through windows layered with grime.

The bar was called *Paquita's* and was empty except for Santiago and his crew. Lorenzo and Esteban occupied a table near the door, playing cards. Jorge was throwing darts. Ramone was behind the bar, sipping tequila and cleaning his nickel-plated 410 Taurus, a miniature hand-cannon he called a revolver. Lucita, the only woman in the crew, sat on top of the bar in a miniskirt, thumbing a message into her phone.

Paquita's had once belonged to Santiago. He had turned

in his badge after fifteen years with the Mexico City police force, invested his entire savings in the bar, and gone into business for himself. It only took three years to go bankrupt. He was about to close up shop when Machado made him an offer; the drug lord would front the cash to keep Paquita's open and in return, Santiago would launder money through the till. One thing led to another, now Santiago worked for Machado full-time.

He took a drag and sent a cloud of smoke up to the ceiling where the fan whipped it apart. He supposed, looking back, he had known what he was getting into. The bar was a money pit. Cops in Mexico are either on the take or they don't live long enough to retire, and Santiago figured it was better to be a full-time gangster than a full-time cop, part-time crook. At least this way he didn't have to balance his loyalties.

Before he could give the matter any more thought, el Lobo—the Wolf—came in, followed by an old man in a dirt-stained chambray work shirt. The old man had a tanned face with deep lines from decades of work under the harsh Mexican sun. He tortured a straw hat between his hands and blinked in the dim light. His eyes lingered on Lucita for a moment and then fixed on Santiago and the backpack.

El Lobo led the old man over by the elbow. "Tell him what you told me."

The old man tortured the hat some more. "You are looking for the Domingo woman?"

Santiago inclined his chin.

The old man licked dry lips. "And the money? Five hundred thousand pesos?"

Santiago took the cigarette from his mouth and pointed the glowing tip at the backpack.

The lined face bent toward the pack like metal filaments drawn to a magnet.

Santiago uncrossed his ankles and dropped one leg over the pack. "First you tell me where the girl is."

A bead of sweat trailed down the old man's craggy cheek. He glanced around the room again. Ramone opened the cylinder on his nickel-plated revolver and spun it, letting the mechanical whir fill the silence. The old man swallowed hard. "She is at the Santa Ana Mission."

Santiago's eyes narrowed. "How did you come by this information?"

"I'm the gardener, *señor*."

Santiago took a deep drag and smoke trailed out through his nostrils. "If you are lying to me..."

Ramone snapped the cylinder on his revolver shut with a loud *clack*.

The gardener flinched. "It is no lie, *señor*. You will find her there. She is being treated by the nuns."

Santiago nudged the backpack with the toe of his dress shoe.

The old man stuffed the hat on his head and clutched the pack to his chest. "*Gracias, señor. Gracias*," he said as he backed out of the barroom.

Santiago watched him go, then turned his attention to el Lobo.

The Wolf gave a small nod, silent assurance that the old gardener was telling the truth.

So, Alejandra was alive after all. Santiago was sure she

had died from her wounds. Well, no matter. She would not live much longer. He flicked his cigarette butt at a garbage can across the room. It bounced off the wall in a shower of sparks. "Let's go, *mis amigos*." Santiago stood up and stretched. "It's time to confess our sins."

CHAPTER TWENTY-TWO

NOBLE STEPPED INTO A CRAMPED BEDROOM WITH shuttered windows. The copper stench of blood and offal attacked his senses. Alejandra Domingo lay on a narrow cot, clinging to life. Machado had done a real job on her. Blood-stained bandages hid the left side of her face completely. The other half was covered in angry purple welts. She sucked air through busted lips.

The sight turned Noble's blood to ice. Every counterintelligence officer knows the risks; swim with sharks and you might get eaten. Taking out an enemy agent is one thing, but cutting up a woman's face is different. This was barbaric.

A heavy-set nun in a wimple occupied a chair near the head of the bed. She started up when the door opened, her round face tight with fear. Father Cordero made a calming motion with both hands. She sank back down.

"Her name is Alejandra Domingo," Cordero said. "She was helping your friend extract information from Machado."

Noble nodded without taking his eyes off her. "I know."

The nun dipped a washcloth in a bucket and dabbed Alejandra's forehead. The semiconscious woman responded with a weak moan.

"She staggered into the nave two weeks ago," Cordero told him. "Naked and covered in blood. We couldn't take her to a hospital. Machado has people everywhere. We have been caring for her as best we can."

"Has she said anything?" Noble asked.

The nun shook her head. "She is delirious with fever."

Cordero said, "She cannot stay here any longer."

"Why?" Noble asked. "What happened?"

"Machado has offered a half million pesos to anyone who knows where she is."

Noble let out a low whistle. Half a million was a lot of money in Mexico. Enough to live like a king.

Cordero said, "I fear the gardener has been tempted by sin."

The nun made the sign of the cross.

Noble felt the first giddy rush of impending danger. "Did he know she was here?"

Cordero spread his hands. "The sisters and I did our best to keep it a secret, but..."

Noble nodded. Treating someone with severe injuries is hard to keep quiet. They need medicine and food, and throwing out wads of bloody bandages every day tends to raise suspicion. He asked, "Can she move?"

Cordero shook his head. "I'm surprised she made it here on her own. She had lost a lot of blood."

"How did she get here?" Noble asked.

"In a BMW."

"Where is it now?"

"In a parking garage four blocks away," Cordero said.

"Go get it," Noble ordered.

The priest hesitated and then said, "I don't have a license, *señor*."

Noble gave him a hard look.

Cordero backed out the door. "I will return as soon as I can."

Noble went to the side of the bed.

The nun shook her head. "She was such a beautiful girl."

Noble wasn't surprised. Torres had a knack for surrounding himself with beautiful women.

Alejandra stirred. Her cracked lips parted. She croaked out, "Water."

The nun pointed to a pitcher. Noble poured a cup and carefully tipped some into her open mouth. She coughed and spluttered. He slid an arm under her shoulders and sat her up. The sheet fell away. Cuts and bruises covered her entire body. Noble patted her back until she stopped coughing and then helped her take a drink. This time she managed to swallow.

Her right eye peeled opened. "You are American?"

"That's right." He took the key out of his pocket. "Do you know what this goes to?"

Recognition flashed in her eye, but she shook her head.

"You sure?" Noble asked.

"I've never seen it."

He took out the picture of him and Torres. "What about him? You know him?"

Her face crumbled. "Diaz..." The name trailed off into

broken sobs. The flood gates opened. Noble eased her back onto the mattress and pulled the sheet over her naked breasts.

"*Señor?*" The nun had gone to the window and was looking out through the slats.

Noble joined her.

A dust-covered Jeep Wrangler had pulled up and a team of hard cases, armed with pistols and sub-machine-guns, piled out.

"Are they here for the Tuesday night Bible study?" Noble asked.

The nun shook her head.

He frowned. "I didn't think so."

CHAPTER TWENTY-THREE

Four hard cases ran to the door of the mission while another man exited the Lexus. He was tall and well-dressed, in a dark button-down with his hair slicked back and his sleeves rolled up. Tattoos covered his forearms.

Noble was outnumbered and out-gunned. Hiding was out of the question. They'd tear the mission apart until they found the girl. He cursed and the nun gave him a reproving look.

Noble went to the cot and got an arm under Alejandra's shoulders. "Help me get her up!"

The nun swiveled Alejandra's feet off the bed onto the floor.

Alejandra's one good eye fluttered open. "Are we in danger?"

"We need to get out of here," Noble told her. "Can you walk?"

She nodded, but that alone took all of her strength. Walking was out of the question. Noble slipped an arm around her waist and hauled her to her feet. The sheet fell away. Her knees shook like a newborn filly.

The nun grabbed the sheet and tried to cover her up.

"No time," Noble barked. He hustled Alejandra, her bare feet trailing along the floor, into the upstairs hallway. "Is there a back way out?"

The nun nodded. "*Sí, señor.*" She led him along the passage. Noble's heart thrummed inside his chest. Alejandra did her best to keep her feet moving, but only succeeded in making it harder for Noble to carry her. He hugged her tight, probably causing her a lot of pain, but she bore the treatment in silence.

They turned a corner in the upstairs hall with open windows looking down on the inner courtyard. Two of the Los Zetas *sicarios* burst into the garden at the same time. Noble drew up short in the space between windows. He put his back against the wall and motioned for the nun to stop. She wasn't fast enough. One of the hard cases spotted her and pointed. "There!"

A hailstorm of bullets screamed through the arches, blasting chunks from the sandstone walls. The sound felt like a jackhammer in his ears. Dust clogged his nose and stung his eyes.

The nun got her back to the wall. Noble warned her to stay put. She nodded.

He shifted Alejandra's weight, pulled one of the Glocks he had taken from the airport cops and used his heel to rack the slide. He stuck the pistol around the window frame and squeezed off three rounds. He was firing blind, but it had the desired effect. The cartel killers high-stepped over dead shrubbery to the back wall for cover.

There was a closed door at the far end of the hall. Noble thrust his chin. "Stairs?"

The nun nodded.

Stuck in the middle of a passage was the worst possible place he could think to be in a firefight. There was no cover and nowhere to run. If the cartel thugs caught him here, they would cut him to ribbons. Noble dumped Alejandra into the nun's arms. "Stay put."

She struggled to keep Alejandra off the floor.

Noble ran to the end of the corridor and heard feet pounding up the steps. He stuffed his pistol into his waistband and flattened himself against the wall.

The door flew open. A bulldog of a man came through with a nickel-plated revolver clutched in one chubby paw. Noble caught the Bulldog's wrist in one hand and drove his elbow into the man's face, breaking his nose with a dull crunch. Blood gushed from both nostrils. Noble used the momentum to spin the bulldog around and lever his revolver at a second man coming up the steps—a rail-thin Mexican with a MAC-10.

Noble slipped a finger into the trigger guard, over the bulldog's finger, and squeezed. The revolver roared. Fire licked from the barrel. The blast hammered Noble's eardrums.

The skinny guy took .410 buckshot in the chest from less than two meters. Nine lead balls tore through him. He went backwards down the stairs and sprawled in a heap on the landing. The smell of spent gunpowder hung in the air.

The bulldog got his free arm around Noble's neck and choked off his air supply. Noble used his bodyweight to drive the bulldog into the door frame. The sandstone wall shuddered under the impact. Noble slammed him twice more. The bulldog lost his grip and Noble sent him tumbling down the steps.

The bulldog landed on top of his dead partner. Noble was hoping the fall would break his neck. No such luck. The bulldog was alive and full of adrenaline. He groped for the MAC-10. Noble aimed the revolver and squeezed the trigger. The bulldog rolled clear, and the shot hit the dead man instead. The bulldog staggered to his feet, retreating around the bend in the stairs before Noble could get off another shot.

The bulldog could sit at the bottom of the steps and keep them pinned until he was out of ammo. Noble ran back down the hall and pulled Alejandra's slender arm over his shoulder.

The nun breathed a sigh of relief. "What now?"

Noble carried Alejandra the other direction, back toward the staircase that Father Cordero had led him up when he entered. As he rounded the corner, a cartel gunman in a cowboy hat and snake-skin boots reached the top of the steps.

Noble raised the revolver and fired. Alejandra's weight pulled him off balance. The shotgun load ricocheted off the stone wall. The cowboy threw himself through an open door, stuck his pistol around the frame and fired blind. Angry lead hornets buzzed along the hall.

Noble retreated to the corner. His heart was beating so hard he could feel his pulse throbbing in his neck. His hearing was gone, replaced by a high-pitched ringing. The nun cowered at his side. They were trapped in the U-shaped hallway. The bulldog controlled one end. The cowboy controlled the other. Noble was stuck in the middle. He couldn't defend both sides at once.

He had to make a play. He could put Alejandra down and rush one of the gunmen, but it would give the other a chance to shoot him in the back. At the very least he would die on his feet. He was working up his courage to charge the cowboy when he heard a car horn blaring.

CHAPTER TWENTY-FOUR

Father Cordero mashed the horn and cramped the steering wheel to avoid a stalled bus. He swerved into the oncoming lane and, for one terrifying second, was staring directly at an oncoming pickup. He cut the wheel and slewed back into the flow of traffic.

The two vehicles in front of the mission belonged to the cartel, that much was obvious. None of Cordero's petitioners could afford a Lexus. Fearing he was already too late, Cordero weaved through traffic to the front of the mission and stamped the brake pedal with both feet. The wheels locked. The rear bumper humped up like a dog with its butt in the air. A spray of gravel peppered the back of the Lexus. Through the thick sandstone walls came the muffled pop of gunfire. Cordero cranked open the driver's side door and held down the horn.

Noble heard the horn and knew Cordero was outside with a

car. All he had to do was get to it. Directly across the hall was a room with windows facing the street, but it forced Noble to move straight through the cowboy's line of fire.

He slung Alejandra over his shoulder in a fireman carry. She croaked. Noble hated to cause her any more pain, but he needed to move fast. He couldn't do that while dragging her. With a deep breath to steady his nerves, he stepped across the hall and crashed his foot into the door. It popped open with a shriek of splintering wood.

The cowboy started shooting as soon as Noble moved. Bullets hissed past his head. He hustled through the open door into a cramped chamber. There was a colorful quilt on a narrow bed and a few picture frames atop a dresser. A rocking chair took up one corner.

The nun crowded in behind him, slammed the door shut and put her back to it. Her face pinched in pain. A dark stain had soaked through her black robes. She pressed both hands over the wound.

Noble saw it and hissed.

"Keep pressure on it," he said. "We'll get you to a hospital."

She slid down the door to a sitting position, leaving a dark red smear on the wood. "Go. Save the girl."

"I'll get you out of here," Noble said.

She shook her head. "Not unless you are going to carry us both."

"Give me a minute. I'll think of something."

"Go," she said. "I'll hold the door as long as I can." Her mouth was filling up with blood and it painted her lips crimson.

"You don't have to do this."

She managed a weak smile. "Hurry."

Noble felt like someone had rammed a rusty nail through his heart. He couldn't carry them both and the cartel soldiers would break down the door any minute. He said, "I'm sorry."

"Don't be," she said. "Not... your fault."

Indignant at the thought of leaving a nun to bleed out on the floor, he turned and threw open the window. The porch roof was only a few feet below. Noble lifted Alejandra over the sill and lowered her down.

"You have to use your legs," he told her.

She nodded. Her bare feet touched tiles. She clutched the window frame for support. As soon as she was stable, Noble climbed out onto the overhang. Shingles buckled under his weight. He looped his left arm around her slim waist and she winced. There was no time to be gentle. Thirty yards separated them from Father Cordero and the BMW.

People on the street ran for cover. Cartel battles are common in Mexico City. So are civilian casualties. A few brave—or stupid—people took video with their cellphones from a café across the street.

Noble carried Alejandra. Clay tiles cracked underfoot, threatening to send them sliding right off the overhang. It forced him to slow down. He expected to feel a bullet punch through his back any second. Time stretched as he struggled to haul Alejandra the last dozen yards. It was like a dream where the faster you run, the slower you go. The corner seemed to move further away with every step. He finally reached the edge and spotted a black BMW covered in dust. Cordero stood in the open door, pressing the horn like a wire operator tapping out Morse code.

"Head's up," Noble yelled as they rounded the corner.

Cordero's eyes went wide at the sight of Noble on the porch roof with Alejandra, naked, clinging to his side.

"Help me," Noble ordered. He tucked the revolver in his waistband, took Alejandra by her wrists and lowered her onto the roof of the BMW.

Cordero hesitated, his sense of propriety at odds with the desire to help.

Noble glared at him. "Help me!"

The young priest gave himself a shake and reached up. Noble let go. The roof buckled under Alejandra's weight. Cordero caught her and helped her down.

Noble dropped from the overhang, denting the roof under the impact. He leapt to the ground. The driver's seat was caked in dried blood. The keys were in the ignition and the engine was running. While Cordero carried Alejandra around the front bumper, Noble threw himself behind the wheel. The priest hauled open the passenger's side door and dumped Alejandra into the seat.

Noble was about to order the priest into the backseat when the driver of the Lexus burst through the front door of the mission.

Alejandra's right eye opened wide. "Drive!"

Noble shifted the BMW into reverse and stamped the gas. The engine revved and the car shot backwards with the passenger's side door still open.

The cartel thug stiff-armed Cordero out of his way and leveled a 9mm Glock at the retreating BMW. The gun thundered. Brass shell casings leapt from the breech. Bullets smacked the hood of the BMW and starred the windshield. Noble forced Alejandra's head down and craned around in his seat so he could see out the back window.

Santiago leapt behind the wheel of his Lexus, thumbed the starter and cut the wheel hard. The car swung around and knocked down a motorcyclist. The passenger tires mounted the opposite curb. People scrambled out of his way. A high school girl wasn't fast enough. She disappeared under the front grill. Santiago pushed the accelerator to the floor. The transmission growled through second, into third. He buzzed the window down, stuck his Glock out and triggered a volley at the BMW.

Noble reversed through oncoming traffic. The engine red-lined at forty miles an hour. A delivery truck clipped the open passenger's side door. It disappeared in a shriek of metal and exploding glass. Alejandra, only half conscious, almost rolled out of the car. Noble reached past her, snagged the safety belt and buckled her in.

The cartel assassin was gaining. Noble spotted an alley and cramped the wheel. The BMW screeched through a backwards turn. The wall sheared off the driver's side mirror. Noble steadied the wheel and pulled the revolver from his waistband.

The Lexus fishtailed into the alley, kissed the wall and gave off a shower of sparks. The engine roared and the

Lexus closed the gap. Noble stamped the gas pedal to the floor. The BMW screamed. The front bumpers met. Plastic crunched. Noble crouched behind the steering wheel and triggered the revolver, aiming for the driver. The cartel assassin ducked beneath the dash and returned fire. Bullets blew out the front windshields on both cars.

The alley ended and Noble held his breath as the BMW hurtled backwards across a busy boulevard. The back bumper got hit. Noble felt the BMW spin like a carnival ride. His heart tried to leap out through his throat. He turned into the spin, like a boxer rolling with a punch. The BMW howled to a stop, rocking on its springs. Thick white smoke billowed up from the tires. The back bumper was hanging off. The hood was buckled and pockmarked with bullet holes, but the engine was still running. Noble shifted into drive and pressed his foot to the floor. The car leapt forward.

A taxicab had slammed the front of the Lexus. The two vehicles came together in a loud crunch. The Los Zetas soldier stumbled out of his ruined car and emptied his weapon at the escaping BMW. Noble wove through traffic, putting as many vehicles between him and the cartel killer as possible. He didn't ease off the gas until the assassin was lost from sight.

CHAPTER TWENTY-FIVE

Burke had a phone to his ear. It was almost seven in the evening and every few minutes his belly gave a tortured rattle. He ignored the requests for food and said, "They actually talked about planting evidence? That's great. Did you get any of it on tape?"

"All of it, but we don't have jurisdiction inside the United States. None of it is admissible in court."

"This information will never see the inside of a court," Burke said.

"How do you want me to proceed?"

"Keep going down the rabbit hole. Let me know what turns up."

He placed the phone in the cradle and looked up to find Dana standing in his office door. She leaned in the frame with her arms crossed under her breasts and her head tipped to one side. "Quitting time, boss."

"Have a good night."

"I'm going for a drink. Care to join me?"

Burke leaned back in his seat and studied her. His pulse

raced. He could never go through with it. The remnants of his stalled marriage were still twitching, like a patient on an operating table, clinging to life. And workplace romance was strictly forbidden in the CIA. One or both of them would be fired if anyone even suspected. But the idea was enough to light the fires of his imagination.

Images flooded his mind. His mouth was suddenly dry. He cleared his throat and gestured to the stack of paperwork on his desk. "Duty calls."

"I'll be at the Smoke & Barrel if you change your mind."

He had to stop this before it started. Scratch that. It had already started. They had been flirting for months. He had to stop it before it got out of hand. He said, "Listen, Dana..."

The phone on his desk shrilled. It was Deputy Director Foster's internal line. Burke held up a finger for her to wait and picked it up. "This is Burke."

Foster's voice sounded more pinched than usual. "I need to see you in my office right away."

"I'm on my way." He hung up and told Dana, "We'll talk later. I've been *summoned*."

"Is it bad?"

"I can't imagine it's anything good."

"Our friend in Mexico?" she guessed.

"A likely bet."

"Do you need me to stay?" Dana asked.

He shook his head. "Have a drink for both of us."

"Don't lose your temper," she warned.

Burke crossed the building to the Directorate of Intelligence, like a man headed for the gallows. Two possibilities stood out. The first was that Foster had evidence Burke had given Company intel to Noble. The second, and worse, was that Foster had gotten wind of operation NAUTILUS. Burke waved to Foster's secretary and stuck his head in the inner office. "You wanted to see me?"

"Have a seat." A vein pulsed in Foster's temple.

Burke closed the door and took a chair. He wasn't nervous. He had seen combat all over the globe, received two Purple Hearts and the Army's Distinguished Service Cross. Waiting to get dressed down by a pencil-dick like Foster was laughable. He was more worried Foster would sideline him before operation NAUTILUS could provide actionable intel.

Foster picked up a television remote from his desk and pointed it at a flat screen on the wall. A Spanish news cast was reporting on a gun battle at a Catholic mission in the heart of downtown Mexico City. The subtitles at the bottom of the screen attributed the violence to the drug cartels. A nun had been killed. Eyewitnesses had taken cell-phone video. Burke's lips tightened as he recognized Noble climbing out a second story window with a naked woman clutched to his side. The camera was too far away to make out details, but Burke recognized Noble's angular silhouette and rebelliously long hair.

Foster paused as the two figures on screen were about to jump down onto the roof of a BMW. "Correct me if I'm wrong, but that looks a lot like Jake Noble."

Burke puffed out his cheeks. "That kid is unpredictable. You never know where he'll turn up."

"A member of his Special Operation Group goes missing in Mexico City and two weeks later Noble is trading bullets with cartel thugs," Foster said. "You're telling me that's coincidence?"

"I'm saying I don't know anything about it." Burke spread his hands. "I don't keep track of Jake Noble."

Foster jabbed the button on his intercom. His secretary came on the line. Foster said, "Is he here?"

"Yes. He just arrived."

"Send him in."

Gregory Hunt breezed through Foster's door with his boyish grin firmly in place. He took a seat, crossed his legs and nodded to the Deputy Director of Intelligence, ignoring Burke.

"Mr. Hunt was in Saint Petersburg yesterday," Foster said.

"What a coincidence," Burke said. "I was in Saint Pete yesterday."

"So you admit that you met with Noble?" Foster said.

"I paid him a visit." Burke shrugged. "Despite the way Noble's career turned out, I still consider him a friend. I was in town, so I went to see him. Nothing illegal about that."

Foster nodded the whole time Burke was speaking. His mouth worked into a humorless smile. "You have an answer for everything, don't you?"

"I don't have anything to hide, if that's what you mean."

Foster exploded out of his seat. "You had an op in Mexico. It went sideways. You lost an agent and instead of tying it off, you turned Noble onto it, so he could pick up the pieces."

"You got it all backwards," Burke said. "I was in Saint Pete catching up with an old friend."

"Yeah?" Hunt finally jumped into the conversation. "What did the two of you talk about?"

"The usual," Burke told him. "Weather, baseball, our favorite Taylor Swift song."

"Cut the crap, Burke," Hunt said.

Foster held up a hand. "You sent Noble to Mexico. I can't prove it yet, but when I do, I'm going to make sure you swing for it."

Burke crossed his arms and stared down the Deputy Director. He didn't bother defending himself. Foster would keep digging until he had found something he could use to scuttle Burke's career.

Foster waited. When it was clear Burke was done talking, he said, "Get the hell out of my office."

Burke stood and walked out, resisting the urge to slam the door.

Foster pulled off his glasses, wiped them on his shirt and hooked them back on his ears. He had a real situation unfolding in Mexico. One agent was missing, presumed dead, and a former field officer was killing cartel thugs on the evening news. All during an election year.

Hunt cleared his throat. "Should we read the Mexican authorities in on Noble?"

"Tell them a former spook is running around Mexico whacking drug dealers?" Foster dismissed that idea with a wave of his hand. "That's not how we do things at the Company, Mr. Hunt. We deal with our own. Gather your team. You're going to Mexico."

Hunt held back a grin. He had made discreet inquiries and found the name Jake Noble was legend. Crusty old spymasters, who dated back to the Cold War, whispered it in reverence. Noble had come along shortly after 9/11 and quickly risen to superstar status. The Company turned to him for black ops that no one else was crazy enough to take on. Noble had a reputation for pulling off the impossible. Taking him down would cement Hunt's reputation. "I don't need the tech nerds," he said. "I can deal with Noble on my own."

"I don't recall asking your opinion, Mr. Hunt."

"I'm just saying this will be easier without—"

Foster cut him off with a raised hand. "They are going with you. It's not up for debate."

"What's our cover?" Hunt asked.

Foster snatched the phone off the cradle. Hunt heard Ginny pick up in the other room. "Ginny, touch base with the boys at the Alibi Shop. I need Priority One legends for Hunt, Ezra Cook and Gwendolyn Witwicky. Destination Mexico City. It doesn't have to be pretty, but it had better hold up. And make it snappy."

The Alibi Shop is the unofficial name for the CIA's Directorate of Support. The experts who work there create false papers and passports that are indistinguishable from the real thing. They know the paper stock a passport—from any country in the world—should be printed on. They can reproduce theater tickets, with correct dates and times, for the Russian ballet dated six months ago. They know what kind of wool Chinese farmers use in winter coats and the exact farms where Italian shoemakers get their leather. During the Cold War, most of the American spies captured behind the Iron Curtain were blown because of minor inconsistencies, like the number and spacing of holes in a belt that did not match the belt maker's specifications.

Foster hung up. "Ginny will take care of your flight plans. I want you to peek in on the boys downstairs at the Alibi Shop. Make sure they hurry, but not so fast that they botch the job."

Hunt went to the door and paused with his hand on the knob. "One question, sir. What means am I authorized to use?"

Foster considered it. "Bring him back alive."

Hunt's handsome face twitched. "Yes sir."

Foster sat, pulled off his glasses, and pinched the bridge of his nose between thumb and forefinger. It was bad enough he had lost an agent. Now he had to deal with a vigilante running around killing drug dealers. He looked at the phone and considered making a call, then thought better of it. No point worrying her.

CHAPTER TWENTY-SIX

Noble checked into a rundown motel in San Rafael, paid cash and used a fake name. The neighborhood is unique for its French colonial architecture and low rent prices that, in recent years, have made it a haven for young artists. Before that, it was known for prostitution. In an effort to localize the sex trade, Mexican law enforcement allowed hookers to ply their trade in San Rafael without fear of being hassled by cops. Noble chose it because Mexican authorities generally turn a blind eye to that part of town.

Getting Alejandra into the motel unseen was a chore. He laid her across the backseat, parked in front of the door to the room and waited to make sure he wasn't going to be seen before carrying her inside. Then he drove the bullet-scarred BMW six blocks away and parked it on the street, keys in the ignition and the windows rolled down, before walking back.

Budget motels all seem to have the same décor: floral bed cover, beige carpet, television stand, and a bland painting of the beach. This one smelled like lemon-scented industrial cleaning agents.

Noble flicked on a light in the bathroom, ran the sink and splashed cold water on his face. His neck was tight from the crash. Tomorrow it would hurt like hell. Rubbing his aching muscles, he went back into the bedroom.

Alejandra was sprawled on the bed.

He went about inspecting her injuries. Every inch was covered in bruises. The cut on her face was the worst of it; the knife had gone right to the bone. Cordero and the nun had stitched it up as best they could. Two dozen jagged sutures ran in a sloppy line from her forehead to her jaw. The wound showed signs of infection, it was angry, swollen, and weeping puss. Noble gently replaced the bandage and laid a hand on her forehead. She was burning up.

He lifted the edge of the blanket, draped it over her naked body and sat down on the corner of the bed to think. He was holding onto the hope that Torres was still alive. Alejandra either knew where he was or what had happened to him. If she died, that information went to the grave with her. Besides, the CIA had a less than stellar reputation for taking care of assets. The espionage game leaves no room for sentimentality. If an asset gets captured or killed, you cut ties and move on. But Noble was a soldier at heart and taught to never leave a fallen comrade behind. Alejandra had put her life on the line for Torres. That made her a fellow soldier in Noble's book.

He got up, stretched, and rummaged through drawers until he found a paperclip. He wedged the paper clip in the door jamb as he left, and walked until he found a taxi.

Twenty minutes of bumper-to-bumper traffic put him

in the heart of the financial district. It took another ten minutes to find a car rental. Noble walked in and saw a grainy video of himself on a television screen, jumping from the roof the Santa Ana Mission. Authorities considered him armed and extremely dangerous. A cold hand gripped his heart. His first instinct was to turn around and walk out, but that would be a dead giveaway. The clerk hadn't seen the report yet. He was too absorbed in his smartphone. Thank God for social media.

Noble rapped the counter, flashed a friendly smile and asked for a car. He used one of his fake passports to rent a dark sedan under the name of Charles Parker.

The desk clerk put down his smartphone and keyed information into the computer. "Would you like the optional insurance, *señor?*"

"I'll be extra careful," Noble said.

The news broadcast switched to coverage of the heat wave, predicting temperatures in the upper nineties for the rest of the week, then a report about a ten-foot-long python in someone's swimming pool. The clerk handed Noble a set of keys, bid him safe travels and went back to his smartphone.

With a clean set of wheels, Noble used his phone to pull up a list of animal hospitals in Mexico City. Alejandra would need antibiotics to fight off the infection and cat antibiotics are the same stuff they give humans, only in smaller doses. He thumbed through the results until he located a pet clinic in a quiet neighborhood.

He passed an electronics store on his way and pulled in. A bell chimed as he opened the door. The shelves were full of unlocked iPhones, secondhand laptops and pirated movies. A fat Mexican was perched on a stool, a video game controller clutched in his chubby hands, playing the latest Call of Duty. The sound of digital machine guns and explosions filled the shop. He paused his game when Noble entered. "You need something, gringo?"

"I'm looking for a signal amplifier that I can tether to my cell."

The fat proprietor gave him a sidelong glance. "Whatchu you need that for?"

"I think my girlfriend is cheating on me," Noble said. "I'm trying to catch her in the act."

"Your face is all over the news, *Americano*. Wanted by the police. Armed and dangerous, they say." His hand started to creep along the counter.

Noble gave him a hard stare. "Don't."

The fat man paled. His hand went back to his side. "You going to kill me?"

Noble took out a wad of cash.

"What do you want with a signal amplifier?"

"I have business with the cartel."

"People who do business with the cartel usually end up dead, *amigo*."

"The cartel never dealt with me before," Noble told him.

He snorted and shook his head. "They eat white boys like you for breakfast. Take my advice and go home, gringo."

"Do you have a signal amplifier?"

The fat man considered it for a moment. "Sure you aren't going to kill me?"

Noble peeled a pair of hundred dollar bills off the wad.

"Sure you aren't going to call the police the second I walk out?"

He reached under the counter, came up with a small box about the size of a deck of playing cards and pushed it across the counter. "Good luck, *Americano*."

Noble put the bills on the counter and took the amplifier. The fat man would probably call the cops as soon as the door closed. Noble would be long gone by the time they arrived. He went back to the rental sedan, turned south and cut over two blocks before turning north again.

The animal clinic had a large, red neon cross and a cartoon of a happy doggy out front. The parking lot was empty. Office hours were 8 a.m. to 6 p.m.

Noble turned on the radio, filling the car with the generic beats and clichéd lyrics synonymous with Spanish pop. He attached the signal amplifier to his cellphone and set it up to broadcast white noise. The music was replaced by hissing static.

Over the last decade, alarm companies have been moving to Wi-Fi-based signals. These are even easier to defeat than Shawn Hennessey's home alarm. All a thief needs is a signal amplifier and a cellphone that can broadcast enough white noise to drown out the Wi-Fi signal. Right now, people in the apartments across the street were wondering what had gone wrong with their television sets.

Noble left the engine running, got out and took a set of lock picks from the lining of his wallet. The commercial-grade deadbolt on the front door gave him some trouble. Using the illumination from the car's headlights, he worked slowly and methodically, setting one pin at a time until he felt the lock open.

The reception area was dark except for the light from an emergency exit sign. Posters warned of heartworms and the importance of regular checkups. Faded pet magazines cluttered a coffee table.

Noble let himself into the examining offices. A wall of cages housed sick cats and dogs. They raised an alarm of their own. The overpowering stench of cat urine brought tears to his eyes. Noble stopped and poked a finger into the cage of one forlorn kitty with a name tag that read Cali. He scratched between her ears and then rifled cabinets for antibiotics. He pocketed bottles of doxycycline and ciprofloxacin before loading up on bandages and medical tape.

Robbing clinics was getting to be a habit. It wasn't too long ago he had been raiding another medical clinic, this one in Hong Kong. Noble wondered if it was just bad luck or if it said something about his life choices. With an armful of medical supplies, he was headed for the front door when he heard movement behind him.

CHAPTER TWENTY-SEVEN

Burke had Kowalski's file open and a mug of cold coffee on his desk. A crumpled potato chip bag winked under the stark fluorescents. The hands on the clock pointed to 7:25. With a few phone calls he had learned Hunt was scheduled to fly out of Dulles on a direct flight to Mexico City first thing in the morning. He didn't want to think about what would happen when Noble and Hunt crossed paths. And they were bound to cross paths. Burke pinched the bridge of his nose between thumb and forefinger. The die had been cast, for better or worse. Now all he could do was wait and see how it all played out.

He returned his attention to Kowalski's file. A high-ranking spymaster in the Kiddon—called the Rabbi—was laying in the pipeline for the defection of an Iranian nuclear physicist. Burke paged through the briefing and scrawled notes. There was a split over how to handle it. President Sotoro, a Columbia grad who had changed his name from Barry Palmer to Barat Sotoro, was sympathetic to the Palestinians. He had given Iran the green light to develop nuclear centrifuges and enrich uranium. In exchange, they promised not to use the technology to build weapons, a promise worth about as much as the paper it was written on.

While no one in the CIA wanted to see the Iranians get the bomb, they also didn't want to directly oppose the President of the United States. It put the Clandestine Service in a tricky spot. With the election only months away, Burke was holding his breath. If Helen Rhodes got the nomination, Israel would be on its own, surrounded by hostile Muslim nations that wanted to see it wiped off the map.

Burke wondered if he would even have a job by the time the election rolled around. He and Foster rarely saw eye to eye. Their relationship had always been one of polite hostility. With the current Director ready to retire and Foster in line to take over, Burke's days were numbered. He had a choice: He could slip quietly into retirement ahead of the DCI, or go out with a bang.

As he closed the Kowalski file and locked it in his safe, his thoughts turned to Dana. Their flirtatious banter had started out innocently enough. He had made a few off-the-cuff remarks about what he would do if he was twenty years younger. She made quips about older men. Over the last several months, as Burke's marriage continued to self-destruct, innocent flirtation had turned into something more.

He checked his watch. It was 7:30. Plenty of time to make it across the river into the city.

Going home was like walking through a minefield. He and Madeline rarely talked and when they did, they argued. Acid comments flew from their lips, like poison darts. It was a bitter war with no clear beginning and no end.

Burke took out his cellphone and keyed in a text message, saying he would be late. He hesitated before hitting send. Lust and loyalty battled for possession of his soul. With his career circling the drain and only the promise of a spiteful shouting match waiting for him at home, he pressed send.

He locked his office and rode the elevator down to the parking garage with a tight knot of fear and anticipation forming in his gut. The sun was slouching toward the horizon. Burke turned the air conditioner on full as he crossed the Francis Scott Key bridge toward Georgetown. He kept telling himself to turn around. In an hour or two she would get tired of waiting and go home, and that would be the end of their office romance. But he didn't turn around.

The Smoke & Barrel is a cozy bar advertising BEER, BBQ & BOURBON, nestled in a strip of trendy night spots. It was a few doors down from a blazing electric marquee that read, appropriately enough, *Tryst*. The Smoke & Barrel's only signage is a barrel lid with the name burned into the wood. It was an anonymous saloon in a city famous for clandestine meetings.

Burke silenced the voice of reason, parked the car and jogged across the boulevard. A cabbie blared his horn. Burke made the safety of the sidewalk and pushed past a group of college kids clogging up the entrance. A short flight of steps led down to a handsomely furnished bar. Beltway insiders gathered around high top tables, laughing at their own jokes, whisky in hand.

Dana was at a corner booth. She caught his eye and smiled. She wore a raincoat cinched tight around her narrow waist, despite the heat. A glass of bourbon was on the table in front of her.

Burke slipped into the booth.

"I didn't think you would come," Dana said.

"I didn't think I would either." Burke flagged a server and ordered scotch over ice.

"Should I ask how it went with Foster?" Dana asked.

"He's looking for an excuse to fire me."

"That bad?"

Burke shrugged.

She reached across the table and took his hand. "Anything I can do?"

"I wouldn't have laid in RIPTIDE and NAUTILUS if I wasn't prepared for the fallout."

The server came back with his drink. Their hands parted.

Dana lifted her glass. "To rebels."

They clinked glasses and drank. She had her hair down and a warm flush in her cheeks. One hand kept toying with the collar of her raincoat. "If Noble fails?"

Burke took a long swallow. He didn't want to think about that.

She waved the question away and changed the subject. "So are we colleagues having a drink after work, or something more?"

"You tell me."

She sipped her bourbon and said, "Maybe I'm a sleeper agent trying to seduce you."

"In that case I would be *forced* to go to bed with you," Burke said, "in an effort to flip you."

They shared a laugh. The conversation wandered onto

more pleasant topics. Talking with Dana was easy. Their glasses emptied and they ordered more. It was close to ten when she said, "I'd better go. I've got an early day tomorrow. Care to walk me home?"

"Where do you live?"

"Around the corner on Calvert," she told him.

They finished their drinks and he walked her three blocks to the door of a two-story row house painted yellow. She threaded her arm through his as they climbed the steps to the front door. The smell of her shampoo toyed with his imagination.

"Nice place," Burke told her.

She dug a set of keys out of her pocket and unlocked the door. "Can I give you the tour?"

Burke made one last desperate attempt to save himself. "We both know what will happen if I come inside."

She turned to face him and opened her raincoat. Underneath, she had on thigh-high nylons and nothing else. Her face turned up to his. Their lips met. Her body pressed against him. It was all the convincing Burke needed. The last of his defenses crumbled as she took his hand and pulled him inside.

CHAPTER TWENTY-EIGHT

Sam paced around her rented flat with a burner phone pressed against her ear. The digital clock on her dresser said 8:15 p.m. A sodden towel was draped over a chair. She was shirtless, in dark denims and hiking boots. Her hair hung in damp tangles around her naked shoulders. Over the past six months, she had packed on fifteen pounds of muscle. Rather than making her look bigger, as she had feared, she was now sleeker and more angular.

She listened to the phone ringing and said, "Come on, Burke. Pick up."

It went to voicemail. She hung up and stashed the burner phone in a slip behind the bathroom door. She was already running late. There was nothing left to do but forge ahead. She picked up a black bra from the bed, one of several fitted with tiny recording devices. The microphones were voice-activated and operated on a seventy-two hour battery. Each bra could record up to 750 MB. It wasn't a whole lot of memory, but only so much information could be stored in the space where underwire would normally cup a woman's breast.

There was a honk from outside. Sam shrugged into the bra, chose a black button-down from the closet and pulled her wet hair back into a ponytail. It would have to air dry, and she'd have tangles tomorrow. After clipping her sidearm into her belt, she scooped up her house keys and cellphone and hurried downstairs.

She was living on the second floor of a Georgetown apartment that butted up to the C&O Canal. A black Lincoln Town Car idled at the curb, blocking traffic. Sam slid into the backseat.

Taggart was dressed in a somber grey suit. There was a plastic shaker cup full of vile-looking green sludge in the cup holder next to him.

"You're late," she said and showed Taggart her wristwatch.

He waved it away. "I had a meeting."

"Standish is due home at nine," Sam reminded him.

The driver swung out into traffic.

"Relax," Taggart said. "All you have to do is slip in, plant the files on his laptop, and get out."

"You realize what will happen if we're caught," Sam said.

"If *you* are caught," Taggart corrected.

Sam turned in the seat to face him. "You aren't going in with me?"

He snorted. "Clandestine entries are not my line of work."

"Me neither," Sam said. "I'm paid to protect people. Not break into houses."

"You'll do fine," Taggart assured her. He held up the flash drive. The idea was to plant child porn on Standish's computer. When it was discovered that the FBI director had a hard drive full of kiddie porn, his career would be over. It would be enough to make John Q Public forget all about his allegations against Secretary Rhodes.

Sam said, "So I take all the risks and Rhodes gets all the rewards?"

Taggart smiled, but his reptile eyes were flat and emotionless. "That's no way to look at it, Vanessa. Do this for Secretary Rhodes and she'll make sure you get a spot on the Presidential Detail. Screw it up and she'll make sure you get assigned to a foreign diplomat in a third world hell-hole. We clear?"

Sam nodded, secretly relieved Taggart would not be tagging along. She could take the flash drive, break into the house, come back out a few minutes later and claim she had done as she was told. Who could say otherwise?

"Did you just shower?" Taggart asked.

The question rattled her. "Um... Yes."

"You smell nice," he said.

From anyone else it would be a compliment. Coming from Taggart, the comment made her want to crawl out of her skin. She muttered thanks and turned to look out the window.

Twenty minutes later, they pulled to a stop in a suburban neighborhood across the street from a park with a baseball diamond. Arc sodium lamps bathed the empty field in artificial daylight. Even at 8:35 p.m. the temperature hovered close to ninety degrees. A jogger made her way around the park, slick with sweat. They heard the soft tread of her sneakers and heavy breathing as she passed the car.

Taggart said, "You're up, kid. Standish's house is two blocks up on the corner. Big house surrounded by a brick wall. Can't miss it."

"I know which house it is." She had used back channels inside the Secret Service to dig up the floor plans and security measures. The idea was to get in and out without anyone knowing she had ever been there. She tucked the thumb drive into her pocket and climbed out of the car.

"Oh, and that thumb drive keeps an activity log every time it's used," Taggart said.

Her plan to botch the job circled the drain. They would be able to tell if she had plugged the drive into a computer. A tight knot formed in her chest.

Taggart leaned across the seat. "We'll meet you back here in ten minutes."

She stared at him in disbelief. "You're leaving?"

"We're just going to circle the block," Taggart said. "We can't afford to be seen hanging around. This is a rich neighborhood. The residents get suspicious of strange cars idling at the park. Can't have the police asking questions. We'll take a couple laps around the neighborhood and pick you up when it's done."

Sam chewed her bottom lip. It was getting late and she didn't have time to argue. "Ten minutes," she said. "Don't be late."

She closed the door and started north, keeping her head down, avoiding the street lamps as much as possible. The FBI Director's property was set back off the road, surrounded by a shoulder-high wall of old brick topped with decorative iron spikes. A flying dragon tree wilted in the summer heat, giving off a sour stench. Flies buzzed around the fallen fruit.

After a quick look to be sure no one was watching, Sam leapt the garden wall and landed in the soft grass. Standish was allergic to all forms of pet dander so there weren't any dogs to deal with. Sam made her way across the side yard to a pair of French doors on a small patio.

A combination of intimidation and backroom deals had provided Taggart with the code to Standish's home alarm. All Sam had to do was pick the lock. She drew a pair of picks from her back pocket and set to work. Sweat formed on her brow. Jake made it look easy, but then, he had a lot more practice. It took three minutes and twenty-seven seconds to set the pins and release the cylinder. The lock opened. Sam let herself in and hurried through the dark house to the front entryway where she punched the code into the keypad.

Now for the hard part.

She needed to make it look like she had planted the files without actually setting the FBI director up for a fall. She glanced at her watch. It was 8:50. With ten minutes to go, she hurried up the stairs. There were three bedrooms on the second floor. One was the master, where the FBI director and his wife slept. It was a spacious room, with a bed and a television. The other two rooms had been converted. One was a home office with dark mahogany bookshelves, an antique desk and a leather sofa. There was a map of the United States with sticky notes in a masculine hand and a framed copy of the Constitution next to the Gadsden Flag. A laptop computer sat on the desk.

The third room was decorated in white and blue. A collection of scrapbooking material littered the shelves. An old wood bench, painted white, was parked against the far wall and on it rested a laptop with a floral protective case. Sam stabbed the space bar to wake the machine from sleep mode, then slotted the USB drive and watched a spinning hourglass.

While the thumb drive downloaded onto the wife's computer, Sam raced back across the hall to the FBI director's home office. She yanked open drawers until she found pen and paper. Tearing a sheet from a yellow legal pad, she scrawled,

You are being set up!
Clean your wife's computer!

She heard the sound of a car in the drive. Her heart leapt. She uttered an oath, went to the window and parted the curtains enough for a peak. A silver Audi stopped in front of the garage. The headlights splayed across the front of the house. The garage door motor came to life.

CHAPTER TWENTY-NINE

FOSTER ARRIVED HOME AT 8:42 P.M. HE LIVED IN A two story Colonial less than five miles from the FBI director where Sam was breaking in. As DDI, Foster warranted the highest protection the Company had to offer. There was a panic room in the basement, twenty-four-hour surveillance, and a gated drive. A QRF team could be on his front lawn in less than ten minutes. Foster parked his Mercedes in the garage and entered through the kitchen where he was greeted by a yellow lab.

Chief wagged his tail and pawed at his empty food dish. Foster poured a bowl of dog chow and stood there watching the dog eat. Early in his career, Foster decided he didn't have time for a wife. There would be time, he told himself, to find a nice girl just as soon as he had made Director and things settled down a bit. That idea was laughable now. It had taken twenty-three years of kowtowing, back-stabbing and backroom deals to make Deputy Director Intelligence. With each new promotion, life got more complicated instead of less. There had been prospects. There always were. More than one young woman had recognized his as a rising star, but Foster fended off all advances. Truth was, deep down, he didn't like women very much.

He wasn't gay. No sir. He enjoyed sex with women, but he had never met a woman he actually *liked*. But there were times, like tonight, standing in the kitchen watching Chief eat, that he regretted the decision. It would be nice to have someone to come home to. Instead, his evenings consisted of a glass of wine and the History Channel.

Chief finished dinner, went to his leash hanging by the front door, sat down and whined.

"Later," Foster told him. He poured a tall glass of merlot.

Chief laid down in front of the door with disappointment on his doggy face.

Foster started for the sofa, wine in hand, when his phone vibrated. He dug it out of his pocket and found a text message.

We need to meet.

He put his glass down. "Maybe we'll take that walk after all, boy."

Chief came off the floor with his tailing wagging and his tongue lolling from his mouth.

Night had chased away the last of the daylight. Stars were coming out, but the air was still muggy hot. Foster loosened his tie and opened his top button. They strolled to the end of the drive, Chief tugging at his lead. The dog was panting like he had already run a mile. They passed through a small gate in the stone wall that surrounded the property and turned north.

A black Lincoln with tinted windows idled on the

corner of Tennyson and Longfellow. Foster tied Chief's leash to a lamp post and climbed into the backseat. Guy Taggart sipped from a plastic cup full of lawn clippings. He drank two a day, claiming the foul-smelling brew kept his heart healthy, his colon clean and gave him extra energy.

"What's so important?" Foster asked.

"Rhodes wants to know what's going on in Mexico." Taggart took a swig. It left bits of green between his teeth.

"I'm taking care of it," Foster assured him.

"Doesn't look that way to me," Taggart said.

"Watch your tone." Foster turned to face him. "I don't answer to you."

Taggart took another drink. "You answer to her, and she wants to know what's going on in Mexico. Or maybe she needs a better choice for Director?"

"Don't threaten me, you little cockroach. Tell her I've got it under control."

"We both know she's not going to like that answer."

Foster sat there hating the arrogant punk in his bespoke suits and his disgusting elixirs. Taggart was a slippery little eel. He always seemed to come out on the winning side, no matter which way the political winds shifted. Much as Foster disliked him, Taggart was the power behind the throne. Pissing him off was bad for business. Foster took a deep breath. "One of Mathew Burke's pet assassins blew a gasket. He went to Mexico to avenge his friend. I've got people on their way right now to intercept him."

"That's problematic," Taggart said.

"Yeah, well, it won't be a problem for long."

"What's his name?" Taggart asked.

"Excuse me?" Foster said. He had heard the question; just couldn't believe Taggart had the stones to ask.

"What is the agent's name?" Taggart said with perfect calm.

"Are you asking me to unmask the identity of a former CIA operative?"

Taggart sipped his drink and waited.

Foster shifted in his seat. The car felt like it was shrinking around him. Giving up Noble would put him even deeper into Rhodes' pocket. If it ever came to light that he had exposed the identity of a CIA officer, even a disavowed officer, Foster would go to jail. On the other hand, if Rhodes got elected, and that was looking more and more likely, his cooperation would guarantee his appointment as the next Director of the CIA.

Taggart seemed perfectly content to wait him out.

"His name is Jake Noble," Foster said. "He's a former Special Operations Group team leader. I've got some of my best people on their way to intercept him. Let them handle it."

"That's up to her." Taggart saw the look on Foster's face and said, "Don't come apart on us now. Keep up your end of the deal and you'll be sitting in the Director's chair by February."

"You don't have to worry about me." Foster got out of the car before Taggart could ask any more questions that he didn't want to answer. He slammed the door, grabbed Chief's leash and started for home.

CHAPTER THIRTY

SAM FELT THE BREATH FREEZE IN HER LUNGS. THE first rule of intelligence is *Don't get caught*. Being found inside the FBI director's house was a one-way ticket to Leavenworth. She wouldn't even get the dignity of a trial. She would simply disappear.

She rushed across the hall. The little hour glass was still tipping end over end. The files had not completely downloaded yet. Sam snatched the drive out of the laptop and stuffed it in her pocket as she bounded down stairs. She heard the garage door roll shut and the soft sound of car doors opening.

She remembered the alarm was disabled and sprinted through the dark house to the front entryway. In her haste, she keyed in the wrong number. The pad squawked at her, warning her that she had two more tries. She heard the muffled voices of Director Standish and his wife coming from the garage.

With her pulse jackhammering in her ears and her fingers trembling so bad she could barely connect with the numbers, Sam keyed the alarm code a second time. The digital display flashed *ARMED* in red. A second later, the FBI director and his wife entered through the garage door.

The system chirped.

Sam put her back to the wall separating the entryway from the living room.

Director Standish stopped at the garage door to disable the alarm which Sam had just activated. His wife, Becky, went to the kitchen. If she had looked to the right, she would have seen Sam pressed up against the front hall. But she didn't and the kitchen light snapped on.

"Do you want one?" the wife called.

"A small one, thanks," Standish said.

"White?"

"Red." The FBI director crossed into the kitchen and Sam held her breath. He stopped in the hall and, for one terrible second, Sam thought he would turn and look right at her. Then he moved into the kitchen. When he was out of sight, she checked the alarm pad, saw the word *DISABLED*, and reached for the door knob.

The wife said, "Can we at least discuss it?"

Sam paused.

"It's not up for debate," Director Standish said.

"She's going to be the next president."

"That may be," Standish said. "But I swore an oath to this country."

Sam hesitated. Slipping out the front door was the smart thing to do. Then she thought of Jake. How would he handle it? *He'd get the job done, even if it meant putting himself at risk.* She crept to the kitchen door and prayed the recording device in her underwire was strong enough to pick up the conversation.

"That idealism is why I married you," Mrs. Standish was saying. "But we have to be realistic. If you go through with this and she wins in November, you'll be out of a job."

"We've got money," Standish said.

"That's not what I'm talking about, David, and you know it."

"I'm not going to be bullied."

"Rhodes is dangerous."

Standish said. "No one is going to hurt you. I'm here to protect you."

"What about the children, David?"

There was a pause. Standish asked, "Did something happen? Did someone threaten Charlie or Beth?"

More silence while Mrs. Standish took a long gulp from her wine glass. "Beth got an envelope in the mail a few days ago. I wasn't going to tell you about it."

"What was it?"

"Pictures. Someone took them through her bedroom window."

Standish's voice was a growl. "They can't get away with this."

"Beth wasn't the only one," Standish's wife said in a small voice. "I got a call on my way into work yesterday. It was a man. He said I should be careful. Next thing I know a Lincoln with tinted windows came out of nowhere. Nearly ran me off the road."

Standish snarled a curse.

"Please listen to me, David." Mrs. Standish was panicked now. "You need to be smart about this. I know you swore to uphold the law, but this is bigger than you. It's bigger than *us*. She'll bury us. Please, I'm asking you for the sake of our children, let this one go."

Sam had heard enough. She treaded back down the hall and eased the front door open. Outside, she sprinted across the lawn and scaled the fence. A rusty iron spike raked her thigh. She closed her mouth around a scream. Pain raced up her leg. She dropped down on the other side of the wall, wincing at the noise, but the street was empty. She paused to check the extent of her injury when she was two blocks away. The spike had ripped her pant leg open and dug a shallow, two-inch-long cut along the outside of her left thigh.

"Probably have tetanus," Sam muttered.

At the park, she sat down on the swings, waited fifteen minutes and when Taggart didn't show, she started the long walk back to D.C.

CHAPTER THIRTY-ONE

MACHADO STACKED PLATES ONTO A BARBELL, BRINGING the total weight up to three hundred and fifteen pounds. A bib of sweat had soaked through the front of his Puma track suit. His home gym had everything a serious lifter could need, including a series of ellipticals and a mechanized rock climbing wall with adjustable speeds. In one corner, there was a smoothie bar stocked with fresh fruits, protein and creatine powders for that all-important shake after a heavy workout. Dean Martin slurred his way through *Bye, Bye Blackbird* on state-of-the-art speakers.

Machado scooped up a water bottle from the floor and took a sip before settling himself onto the bench. He took a moment to adjust; locked his shoulder blades behind him, gripped the bar in both hands and filled his lungs with air. With a powerful exhalation, he exploded the bar up off the pins. The steel rod bowed under the weight. Veins bulged in his neck. He pumped out eight reps and racked the weight. It landed on the pins with a loud clang.

The gymnasium door swung in on silent hinges.

Santiago entered wearing his customary black. He crossed his arms over his chest and waited.

Machado sat up, breathing heavy. "What the hell happened? You are all over the news."

"She got away," Santiago stated.

Dean Martin had been replaced by Frank Sinatra singing "*Fly Me to the Moon*." Machado brought his smart phone out of his pocket and muted the music. "I can see that. Where did she go?"

"I'm still working on that."

"What about the priest? Did you question him?"

"By the time I got back the police were all over the church, *el Jefe*."

Machado wanted to wrap his hands around Santiago's throat and break his neck. "So you lost her, again?"

"I have every man at my disposal out there looking for her," Santiago said. "She's wounded. She can't get far."

"I heard this story before. The first time she escaped." Machado laid back down and pumped out another eight reps. He sat up, toweled off his face and drank water.

Santiago said, "I'm doing everything I can, *el Jefe*."

Machado went to the smoothie bar, picked up a file and handed it to Santiago. "His name is Jacob Noble. He works for the American Central Intelligence Agency."

"How did you get this?" Santiago asked as he leafed through the file.

"Reach out to your friends in the police department," Machado said. "I want the gringo dead—I don't care what it costs—but bring the girl back alive. Is that clear?"

"*Sí, el Jefe*."

Machado watched him go, ran both hands over his bald

head, cursed. He wanted to kill the girl with his own two hands, wanted to watch her suffer, but more than that, he wanted those recordings. They were his insurance deposit.

Santiago took the file and walked down the hall to Machado's private home theater. He would have to throw around some money, but Noble would be in a body bag before the end of the week. He went to the bar, poured a drink and placed a phone call to the Chief of Police.

"*Cómo estás, mi amigo?*" Santiago said.

"*Muy bien,*" the Chief said. "How is the private sector?"

"Some days are better than others," Santiago admitted. "I need a favor."

"Tell me what you need. I'll see what I can do."

Santiago rattled off Noble's vital statistics from the file.

"We are already looking for this man," the Chief told him. "He escaped police at the airport earlier today and stole a car."

Santiago drained his drink and refilled the empty glass. "Tell your officers that Machado is offering fifty thousand pesos to the man who pulls the trigger."

The Chief said, "That should motivate them."

"One more thing. He has a girl with him," said Santiago. "Machado wants her alive."

"Anything else?"

"He's American, so it has to look clean. Understand?"

"No problem. He is armed and dangerous. No one will question the kill. Give my regards to your employer," the Chief of Police said and they rung off.

CHAPTER THIRTY-TWO

NOBLE DROPPED THE SUPPLIES AND PULLED HIS GUN. A forlorn-looking puppy had escaped his cage and knocked over a bottle in his search for food.

"I almost plugged you," Noble told the pup.

The dog responded with a whine.

Noble holstered the weapon and started to pick up his collection of stolen goods, then stopped. "You hungry, fella?"

The puppy looked up with hopeful eyes. A face like that would make a good television ad for pet adoption. It said, *I'm pitiful. Give me treats.* Who can resist a look like that?

Noble found a can of dog food and an electric opener. The puppy licked his chops in anticipation. There were no dishes or bowls so Noble emptied the food onto the floor. The dog didn't seem to mind. He attacked the glop. Noble scratched behind the little guy's ears while he ate. When he had finished, Noble gently lifted him into an empty cage.

His good deed done for the day, Noble gathered up the

medicine and bandages and returned to the waiting rental car. He dumped his haul in the passenger seat, shifted into drive and pulled out of the lot. His cellphone was still putting out white noise. As soon as he was out of range, the clinic's alarm system would signal the monitoring company, but Noble would be long gone by then.

He threaded his way through back streets to the rundown heap of bricks and mortar calling itself a motel. A sedan with dark tint idled on the corner. The pair of hard cases in the front seat could be cops, cartel thugs or just a couple of guys waiting on friends, but Noble didn't believe in coincidences.

He parked in the back lot, out of sight of the road, close to the stairs. The bundle of medical supplies would have to stay with the car. He stuffed the antibiotic in his pockets and left the rest. He could come back if there was time.

From the second floor landing, he could see the sedan on the corner. The pair of hard cases in the front seat were watching passing cars. Hugging the wall, Noble crept to the door. The paperclip was on the ground. He heard the sound of a scuffle inside.

CHAPTER THIRTY-THREE

Noble yanked the gun from his waistband and kicked the door. A pair of thugs had Alejandra pinned to the mattress. One was holding her down while the other tried to inject a syringe full of clear liquid. She was awake and fighting with all the strength she had, flailing her arms and legs, but it was a losing battle.

Noble drilled a pair of rounds through the guy holding the syringe. The bullets slammed him into the wall. The needle hit the carpet. He slid down to a sitting position, leaving a bright red smear on white paint.

The second man pulled a handgun. Alejandra rolled off the bed onto the floor with a thud. Noble sidestepped into the room, swung his sights onto the second killer and they both fired at the same time. A deafening drumroll filled the room. Bullets sizzled past Noble's ear, ripping chunks from the plaster wall. The side of the thug's head disappeared in a red mist. He toppled over onto the bed. Brain matter spilled across the mattress.

The whole thing was over in less than five seconds. A

cloud of blue smoke hung in the air, filling the room with the cloying stench of cordite. The first man was still alive, sitting with his back to the wall. His eyes were open and fear was written across his face in capital letters. He knew he was dying. One of Noble's bullets had ripped through his lung. Pink bubbles formed around the wound.

Noble kicked him over onto his side and used his toe to lift the man's shirt. He found a Glock 19—the weapon of choice for law enforcement agencies the world over—and a shield clipped to the man's belt. Noble bared his teeth. Killing cops, even dirty cops, is bad business.

Alejandra lay on the floor. Her mouth worked but no words came out. She made sounds like a baby first learning to talk. Noble hauled her up.

"We have to go," he told her.

Her knees buckled. He looped an arm around her waist to keep her from falling. He had to carry her down the stairs. The sedan with the tinted windows roared into the parking lot as they reached the bottom step. Noble changed directions and ran for an opening in the cinderblock wall surrounding the property.

The driver braked hard. The wheels locked. The passenger's side door flew open before the car finished its slide. A man leapt out with a pistol in his hand. "Police! Don't move!"

Noble hustled Alejandra to the gap in the wall. The plain clothes officer snapped off a pair of shots. Bullets impacted the cinderblock with hard *thwaks*. Noble hunched his shoulders and ducked his head, like a turtle trying to crawl inside his shell.

The opening let onto a weed-choked alley that ran

between industrial lots. Chain link fences topped with barbed wire hemmed them in. A pit bull strained at his leash, barking madly. One of the warehouses was still open. The bay door was rolled up. Workers in blue coveralls stood in the delivery bay, smoking cigarettes. Noble couldn't go over the fence without doing Alejandra serious injury, but he could make it harder for the cops to murder them in cold blood. He tossed his weapon over a fence into the back of a dump truck.

Alejandra's strength gave out. Her knees buckled. Noble tightened his grip around her narrow waist and stumbled along the alley. They didn't get far. The unmarked sedan cut off their escape and the plain clothes officer entered the alley behind them with his weapon drawn.

Noble threw one hand up in the air, struggling to hold Alejandra with the other. He yelled loud enough for the factory workers to hear. "Hold your fire. I'm unarmed. We surrender."

The officers closed in on them, shouting directions. Noble went down to his knees. Alejandra sagged against him. He had to let her go when they ordered his hands behind his head. She fell in the weeds. Noble laced his fingers together behind his head. A weight crashed into him from behind. He let out a breath and went face down in the dirt. A knee pinned Noble's head to the ground while his hands were wrenched behind his back. Steel cuffs bit into his wrist.

The warehouse workers ventured out to the fence for a better look. One of the cops ordered them back. Noble was hauled to his feet and herded to the waiting car. He allowed himself to be wrestled into the backseat. Alejandra was tossed in beside him. The officers climbed in front and the doors locked with a thump.

The passenger took out a phone and dialed. "We have them in custody."

They either didn't know or didn't care that Noble spoke Spanish. He could hear someone on the other end, yelling into the phone.

"There were witnesses," the officer said. He listened in silence, then he said, "Understood."

He put the cell away and gave his partner a significant look. The driver put the car in gear. They drove through the heart of the city, past ramshackle neighborhoods. Fifteen minutes later, they were rumbling over an unpaved road through barren desert, a plume of dust trailing the car.

CHAPTER THIRTY-FOUR

NOBLE SAT IN THE BACKSEAT OF THE SQUAD CAR, HIS hands cuffed behind him, listening to the tires on hard-packed earth. Mexico City was a pale glow in the rear view. The headlights picked out a rutted dirt lane cutting through scrub brush. A few stars struggled to shine through layers of smog. The rest was darkness.

The cop riding shotgun kept turning to leer at Alejandra.

Noble said, "Don't even think about it."

He thrust his service pistol over the back of the seat. "Worry about your own skin, gringo."

They rode another ten minutes in silence.

The driver pulled off the dirt road and shifted into park. The headlights blazed across a barren patch of sand and thorny bushes. Both officers got out, left the engine running, and opened the back doors. The driver put his gun under Noble's chin. "Slowly."

Noble obeyed. The driver gripped his elbow and marched him to the back bumper. "On your knees."

Dying on his knees was out of the question. Noble turned his head and spat. The cop hammered a blow to Noble's solar plexus. Pain lit up his brain like a Christmas tree. All the air went out of his lungs. His legs folded. Gravel bit into his knees. He gasped for breath.

While Noble tried to get his lungs working again, the lead officer pulled out his cell and dialed. The cops spent the next several minutes trying to figure out how to initiate video chat. Noble, still on his knees with his back against the bumper, rolled his eyes. "Hey, you guys need help with that?"

They finally figured out Skype and then Noble was looking at a roided-up Mexican. It didn't take a genius to put a name to the face. "Hello, Mr. Noble," Machado said. "You have something of mine. I would like it back."

"Are you with the library?" Noble said. "Is this about my overdue books—"

The partner cracked Noble across the face. Knuckles connected with the side of his head. His vision scrambled. He pitched over into the dirt. The officer took a fistful of hair and hauled him back to his knees. Noble's temple throbbed from the impact. He forced his eyelids open. For a second, he was looking at three Machados. He blinked and the images merged into one.

"I am not a man for games, Mr. Noble. Your friend Diaz took something from me. Either you have it, in which case we can come to some arrangement for its safe return, or you do not. In which case these men will kill you."

Noble clamped his teeth together. The muscle at the corner of his jaw bunched. His silence earned him another punch to the side of his head. A buzzer went off inside his skull.

"Nothing to say?" Machado asked. "Why are you in Mexico, Mr. Noble? The CIA did not send you. Did you come to avenge the death of your friend?"

Machado's words hit him like another sucker punch. Any hope that Torres was still alive winked out. A loss so deep it was a physical pain assailed him. His throat clamped shut.

"He died like a coward," Machado said, "begging for mercy."

One of the cops snorted.

Noble's voice came out raw. "I'm going to kill you."

Machado laughed. "A threat I have heard hundreds of times before, Mr. Noble. Yet here I am. I will ask you one more time. Do you have what I want?"

"That depends."

"On?" Machado asked.

"Whether you want your teeth kicked in."

Machado took a breath, closed his eyes and held it. He let it out slowly. "Show me the girl."

The officer holding the phone said, "She's half dead, *el Jefe*."

"*Do as you are told!*"

The cop turned the phone on Alejandra, who was still sprawled naked in the dirt.

"Anna, my dear, can you hear me?" Machado said. "Or should I call you Alejandra. That is your real name. Alejandra Domingo. I had a very interesting discussion with your boss, *Señor* Esparza."

Her face pinched in pain. She let out a low moan.

"I would kill your family for this betrayal," Machado said, "but I already did that."

Her lips moved. No sound came out. She swallowed and tried again. "Go to hell."

His lips peeled back in a humorless grin. "I'm going to *show* you hell, Alejandra."

She whimpered in fear.

Machado said, "Kill the *Americano*. Bring the girl to me."

"*Sí, el Jefe*." The officer pocketed his phone. "Time to die, American."

Noble was hauled to his feet and herded deeper into the desert, high-stepping over thorny underbrush. He said, "You know who I am? I'm CIA. Think you can kill a CIA officer and they aren't going to notice? There won't be anywhere for you to run. Nowhere to hide. They'll kill you."

The cop gave him a shove. "Shut up."

Noble stumbled but managed to keep his feet. "Listen, we can make a deal. Let me go and I'll disappear. No one has to know."

He wanted to sound like a man begging for his life. It didn't take much acting.

"Too late for that, gringo."

The cop grabbed his shirt collar, like a man yanking a dog's leash.

Noble stopped. He felt the muzzle against the back of his head. "Wait a minute," he said. It was an effort to keep his voice steady. "Don't shoot me in the back. I want to die like a man. At least give me that dignity."

The cop snorted. "Have it your way, *Americano*."

He grabbed Noble's arm and turned him around. Noble used the momentum to drive his shoulder into the cop's abdomen. The attack knocked the air from the officer's lungs. The pistol slipped from his fingers. Noble followed up with a kick to his kneecap. The cop's leg bent the wrong way with a *snap*. He opened his mouth to scream.

With his hands cuffed behind his back, Noble looped an arm over the officer's head, putting him in a choke hold, and they both went to the ground. The officer struggled to pry himself loose. When that didn't work, he groped around for his fallen pistol. Noble increased the pressure. The cop's face turned purple. His fingers clawed the sand. One finger touched the pistol grip and slipped off. Noble rolled over, pulling the cop away from the Glock and wrenching his head to one side. His eyes bulged. His heels beat out a tattoo on the desert sand. Noble rolled again and heard vertebrae pop. The cop went limp. His eyes rolled up. Noble held him another sixty seconds to be sure he was dead, then sat up and looped his wrists down under his shoes.

With his hands now in front of him, Noble crawled through the sand to the Glock and did a press check to be sure it had a round in the chamber. In the light from the car's headlamps, he saw the copper gleam of a hollow-point bullet.

The second officer had Alejandra pinned to the trunk of the idling police cruiser. He held her wrists together over her head with one hand and worked his zipper with the other. She kicked and shrieked, but she didn't have the strength to throw him off. Noble walked up behind him, leveled the pistol at the back of his head and pulled the trigger. Thunder rolled across the barren landscape and echoed off distant mountains. The officer pitched over into the dirt with his eyes open and half of his face missing.

Alejandra tried to push herself up but slithered down off the car. Silent sobs shook her naked shoulders.

Noble asked, "You okay?"

She spat in the dead cop's face and cursed.

He knelt and relieved the dead man of his service pistol and spare magazines. "Every cop and criminal in Mexico is looking for us," Noble said more to himself than Alejandra. "We need a place to lay low. Some place no one would think to look."

She pushed hair out of her face with one trembling hand. "I know a place."

CHAPTER THIRTY-FIVE

Burke switched off the headlamps before pulling into the driveway. All the windows in his two-story brownstone were dark. Stars winked overhead. He parked, got out and closed the driver's side door gently, before climbing the steps. He fumbled his house keys. They hit the step. Burke winced at the sound. He scooped them up with a muttered curse and fitted the door key silently into the lock.

His eyes were still adjusting to the dark when a lamp clicked on in the living room. Burke's right hand moved to the small of his back. The reaction was hardwired from thirty years in Special Forces and counterespionage. He managed to check the motion halfway. He hadn't worn a gun in over fifteen years.

Madeline was sitting on the sofa, wrapped in a cornflower blue dressing gown. Her legs were folded beneath her. Her eyes were flat, emotionless orbs, masking the hurt below the surface. "Where you been, Matt?"

"Work." The excuse sounded hollow even to him.

A tear welled up in the corner of one eye. Madeline dashed it away. "Don't lie to me, Matt. I want the truth. You owe me that much."

He hitched up his shoulders. "What do you want me to say, Maddie?"

"What's her name?"

"Dana."

Madeline nodded slowly. "How long?"

"This was the first time," Burke told her. "I swear."

Her face pinched. She covered her mouth with one hand.

"Maddie, I'm sorry—"

"Don't." She shook her head.

Burke inspected the floor. The silence stretched out and Burke didn't know what the hell to do with himself.

"We used to be happy once," Madeline said. "What happened? When did it all go bad?"

"Things haven't been good for a while," Burke said.

"No," she agreed. She stared at the lamp so she wouldn't have to look at him. "So it's come to this?"

He stood there, not sure what to say. His legs felt disconnected from his body. His brain was stuck. In the end, Madeline decided for him.

She said, "Find someplace else tonight."

"Maddie—"

She held up a hand. "Just go."

Burke's feet finally reconnected with the rest of his body. He turned, took his keys and walked out of the house. He wasn't sure where he was going and he suddenly wasn't sure he wanted his marriage to be over. For months he had been looking for a solution, praying for something to put an end to the charade. Now it had finally happened and Burke couldn't shake the feeling that something precious had been destroyed forever.

CHAPTER THIRTY-SIX

THE CRUMBLING VILLA HUNKERED IN THE SHADOW OF the Sierra Madre Oriental range. A crumbling stone wall overgrown with ivy surrounded the property. There was a dry fountain full of dead leaves in the courtyard. Weeds grew up between the paving stones. The house was two floors with arched windows and a red-shingled roof that had been bleached by the sun.

Fire had gutted one entire wing of the villa. The walls were blackened timbers. The roof had collapsed. The rest of the place was untouched. Clothes still hung in closets and the furniture was collecting dust. Cobwebs hung in the doorframes.

Noble spent the first few days on high alert, only allowing himself a few hours of sleep each night. If Alejandra knew about this place, there was a good chance someone else did too. But three days had passed without incident and Noble told himself to relax. The nearest town was seven miles away. It was a one-stoplight village called Tolantongo where he went for food and supplies.

Alejandra was recovering with the help of the antibiotics. Yesterday she had managed to sit up and eat solid food.

Now, four days after their escape from the mission, Noble climbed the stairs to the master bedroom with a tray of food, bottled water, and pills. Alejandra stood on the balcony, wrapped in a sheet, staring across the neglected garden to the tropical forest looming beyond a crumbling stone wall.

He put the tray of food on a dresser furred with dust, took the antibiotic and a bottle of water and joined her on the balcony. The air was still and oppressively hot. Mosquitoes buzzed around their ears.

Noble handed her the pill and the bottle.

She chased the antibiotic with a long swallow and handed the bottle back.

He took a swig. "What is this place?"

"Home." She pulled the sheet tight around her shoulders.

"Machado killed your parents?"

"My father was a judge. Machado tried to buy him off. When he would not be bribed, Machado sent his butchers. They killed my father and my mother and set fire to the house. I was fourteen."

A pack of bloodthirsty killers and a fourteen-year-old girl. Noble didn't need details. It was bad. He leaned on the stone balustrade. "How did you link up with Torres?"

"Who?"

"Diaz."

A shadow of pain crossed her face. "I'm *Policia Federal Ministerial.* Diaz contacted me nine months ago. He already had an information pipeline in place. All he needed was someone willing to climb into Machado's bed."

"So you slept with the man who killed your parents." It was more statement than question.

"You must think that's strange."

Noble shook his head. "You've got nerves of steel."

"I had tried all the legal channels," she said. "Machado is untouchable. He owns half the police force and kills anyone he can't bribe."

"And Torres promised you revenge," Noble said.

She nodded. "Every night while he laid next to me snoring, I wanted to put a gun in his mouth and blow his brains out. Diaz kept me sane. He helped me see the big picture. Killing Machado wasn't enough. He wanted to dismantle the whole organization from top to bottom."

"How did it all go sideways?"

"Machado has an informant in the CIA."

Noble made a skeptical face.

"We did it right," Alejandra insisted. "The first two months before I infiltrated, Diaz taught me tradecraft: cutouts, dead drops, ciphers, blinds. We set up multiple channels and firewalls. We never made a move unless we were clean. Someone on your end blew our cover."

"You'll have to do better if you want to convince me."

She turned to face him. "Machado got a call one night. We were watching one of those ridiculous American gangster films he loves so much. I could tell something was wrong by the way he was looking at me. I went to the bathroom and locked myself in."

"Who was Machado talking to?" Noble asked.

"I don't know." She shook her head. "But he called

Santiago right after and said there was a leak. I heard it all through the bathroom door."

"He said Diaz was CIA?" Noble asked.

She nodded. "I called Diaz on my cell and warned him before Machado could break the bathroom door down."

"How did you get away?"

"Diaz traded himself for me."

"And you're sure the leak was on *our* side?" Noble asked.

She nodded. "It's a woman, that's all I know. She usually talks with Machado's accountant, an Englishman by the name of Blythe."

The muscles in Noble's jaw bunched and released. If someone in the CIA had exposed Torres, Noble would find out who and make them pay. He took the key from his pocket. "What's this go to?"

Alejandra shook her head. "I don't know."

"Torres sent it to me," Noble told her. "It's important. You sure you don't know what it unlocks?"

"I've never seen it before." Alejandra insisted.

He clenched the key in his fist. She was lying. He didn't know why, and he wasn't going to force the truth from her, yet. He changed subject. "Who's Santiago?"

"Machado's top lieutenant. You met him at the Santa Ana Mission. He killed Diaz." She pointed to the bandage on her face. "He's the one who did this."

"Keep talking," Noble said.

"Santiago used to be a cop. Now he works for the cartel. He's smart and ruthless. If Machado dies, Santiago is next in line. I'm surprised he hasn't tried to take over already. The other members of his crew are hired muscle, except for el Lobo. He's pretty crafty. They'll want payback for Ramone, the one you killed."

"Good," Noble said. "We can use that to our advantage."

"Diaz was your friend?" Alejandra asked.

"Yeah."

"You will avenge him?"

"That's right."

"I'll help."

Noble motioned to the tray of food sitting on the dresser. "Eat. You'll need your strength."

CHAPTER THIRTY-SEVEN

Hunt and his team set up shop in the American Embassy on Paseo de la Reforma. They secured an unused office on the second floor that smelled like cigarettes and stale coffee and they turned it into their command post. Folding tables were loaded down with computers, printers, fax machines, encrypted modems and secure telephones. The room was so cramped they had to climb over one another. Carry-out boxes littered every unused surface. A flat-screen television hung in one corner, showing Noble's escape from the Santa Ana Mission on repeat. A map of Mexico was tacked to the wall with a map of the capital next to it.

For three days, they watched and waited. They monitored airplanes, busses and trains all the way from Texas to Colombia without sign of their prey. Gwen and Ezra translated intercepts and napped in shifts on a threadbare sofa crawling with dust mites. Hunt spent most of his time pacing. Inaction and spicy local cuisine were taking a toll. His eyes kept returning to the television screen. He wanted to know who the girl was. *Why was she so important?* Noble had shot up a church and led a bunch of gang bangers on a high-speed chase through the city to rescue her. *Why?*

Hunt had gone to the mission and questioned the priest. All he got was a name, Alejandra: a common Spanish name and useless without a family name. Hunt sipped coffee from a Styrofoam cup and pulled a face. He was ready to kill for a decent mocha latte. He put the cup down and asked, "Where are we on the girl?"

Gwen had headphones against one ear, monitoring local police bands. "She hasn't shown up in any hospitals. It's like they just disappeared."

"They didn't disappear," Hunt growled. "They're in Mexico somewhere. Find them."

Gwen turned back to her computer with her head sunk between her shoulders.

Hunt immediately regretted the outburst. He was still trying to get in Gwen's pants—what better time than on assignment in a foreign city—and losing his temper wouldn't help. He pinched the bridge of his nose between thumb and forefinger. Find the girl. She was the key. Find the girl and they would find Noble.

"Here's something interesting," Ezra said. He was stretched out on the sofa, leafing through a stack of mission files with Noble's name attached. "Gwen, do you remember Samantha Gunn? She was in our training class. Asian, dark hair, *super* cute."

"I remember. What about her?"

Hunt's ears perked up at Sam's name.

"I just came across her name in an operation report." Ezra sat up and swung his legs off the sofa. "It's heavily redacted but it looks like Samantha Gunn helped Noble rescue a diplomat's daughter from a human trafficking ring in Hong Kong."

Hunt said, "That can't be right. Noble was blacklisted before any of you joined the Company."

"It gets weirder," Ezra told him. "This operation report is almost seven months old. That's *before* Sam was at the Farm and *after* Noble was blacklisted."

"That is weird," Gwen agreed.

"Right?" Ezra turned to Hunt. "You probably don't remember her."

Hunt remembered her alright. He had been tasked with teaching a hand-to-hand combat class at the Farm between field assignments. It was an easy posting and afforded him opportunities to meet cute female recruits. He had made sure to get plenty of "hands-on" experience with Sam. She was Ivy League, smart, and ambitious. They hit it off right from the start. She had never mentioned Jake Noble, or Hong Kong.

Hunt took out his cell and dialed.

Sam came on the line after three rings. "Well, well. Mr. Hunt. I thought you were on assignment in some far-flung corner of the globe, making the world safe for democracy?"

"I am," Hunt told her. "I need a favor."

"I don't hear from you for two months and now you need a favor?" She asked, but her tone was playful.

"I would have called sooner but the DDI is keeping me on the run. I haven't slept in my own bed more than two nights in a row."

"Whose bed *have* you been sleeping in?" Sam asked.

"Jealous?" Hunt asked.

"I'd be lying if I said no," Sam told him.

Gwen and Ezra exchanged glances.

Hunt leaned his hips against the window sill. "Tell you what, I'll have some personal time when I wrap things up here. Why don't we spend a few days at my family's cabin? Just you and me, no distractions."

He could hear the smile in her voice. "You know my policy on sex before marriage."

"I promise to be a perfect gentleman," Hunt lied.

"I'm listening," Sam said.

"I need any info you have on a guy named Jacob Noble."

There was a pause on the other end. "Why are you asking about Jake?"

"So you *do* know him?"

"I know him," she admitted. "What's going on?"

Hunt knew he would have to embellish a little if he wanted to enlist her help. He said, "He's blown a gasket. He's totally off the reservation. He killed several people. I need to find him before he does any more damage."

"There's been some kind of mistake," Sam said. "I know Jake. He wouldn't do that."

"Listen, Sam, it's important I find him," Hunt said. "Do you know any safe houses he might use in Mexico? Any friends?"

"Safe houses? No. He never mentioned Mexico."

"Did he ever talk about a girl named Alejandra?" Hunt asked.

"What? No. I've never heard that name. Greg, what's going on?"

"Listen, Noble's on the run. He might try to contact

you. If he does, you need to call me right away, do you understand?"

When he didn't get a response, Hunt said, "Sam, this is important."

"I understand," she said. "I'll let you know if I hear anything, but I'm telling you, there's been some kind of mix up."

Gwen stood half way up from her chair, her face flush with excitement. "I found her! Alejandra Domingo!" She pointed at the computer screen.

Hunt covered the phone and shot her a hard look.

She sat back down and said more softly, "I found her."

"Hey, Sam?" Hunt said into the phone, "I've got to go. Call me if you hear anything, okay?"

"Okay, but you have to do something for me."

"Name it," Hunt said.

She said, "Promise me you'll give Jake the benefit of the doubt."

"I'll do what I can," Hunt said and hung up. He turned to Gwen who was looking apologetic. "What did you find?"

There was a color surveillance photo on Gwen's monitor of a Mexican woman coming out of an office building, wearing a jacket and a skirt with her hair up.

Hunt leaned over Gwen's shoulder for a closer look. "You sure?"

"That's her." Gwen tapped away at the keyboard. "Her name is Alejandra Domingo. She was part of an operation called RIPTIDE. It was set up to gather intel on an organization called Los Zetas. Apparently they're a drug outfit."

All three of them gathered around Gwen's computer for a look at Alejandra Domingo without the bandages.

Ezra said, "She's hot."

"What happened?" Hunt asked.

Gwen consulted the operation file. "The op went bad. The officer running it disappeared. Suspected dead. Ms. Domingo disappeared as well. The information channel dried up and we tied it off."

"Who was the field officer?" Hunt asked.

Gwen brought up the file. There was a black-and-white headshot of Torres with a devilish grin on his face. Next to his headshot, in red letters, his status: DECEASED.

"They don't even know if he's really dead," Ezra said. "They just abandoned him?"

"One of the job hazards," Hunt said, but something about operation RIPTIDE didn't feel right. In fact, this whole mess had a stench to it.

Ezra and Gwen exchanged looks. This was their first real assignment and the cold hard truth of intelligence work was hitting home. A field officer works deep behind enemy lines and if anything goes wrong, no one was coming to the rescue.

Hunt said, "Let's find out more about Ms. Domingo."

It took some digging. They went to work compiling everything they could find on Alejandra Domingo, tracing her life from grade school all the way through college. After that, Gwen had to penetrate the Mexican law enforcement database.

"She's PFM," Gwen said at last.

"What's that?" Ezra asked.

"*Policia Federal Ministerial,*" Gwen explained. "It's the Mexican equivalent of the FBI. It was created in 2006 by

President Vicente Fox Quesada in an effort to combat the cartels and corruption in Mexico."

Hunt was more interested in Alejandra's family history. He said, "Her father was a judge. He was killed by the Los Zetas cartel."

"That explains her motives," said Gwen.

"Pull up everything you can on the father," Hunt said.

Gwen pecked at the keys. A moment later they had a file on Judge Domingo. Near the end was an old news report and a series of photos of a burned-out villa in the countryside north of Mexico City. Hunt jabbed a finger at the pictures on the screen. "Where is that?"

CHAPTER THIRTY-EIGHT

After confirming the information on the thumb drive had been used, Taggart had put in a call to the DHS. The next morning, the FBI director had investigators crawling through his personal life. The investigation made national headlines. Media pundits convicted Standish in the court of public opinion and insisted he was a misogynist pedophile using his position in the FBI to ruin Rhodes' shot at the White House. Forty-eight hours later, when the investigators came up empty-handed, the DHS was forced to issue an apology. Then it came out that they had acted on an anonymous tip, the media surrounding the whole affair turned into a full-blown circus. It dominated every news cycle. Shawn Hennessey was making passionate pleas for an investigation into the DHS and the anonymous tipster, but a snowball in hell stood a better chance.

Rhodes was getting dragged through the mud, Standish had become something of a minor celebrity—a Robin Hood figure fighting a corrupt system—and Sam, well, she had a tough couple of days.

When the files didn't turn up on Standish's computer, she had been chewed out, first by Taggart and then by Helen Rhodes herself. The old battle axe had summoned Sam to her office on Capitol Hill and screamed herself hoarse. At one point, Sam thought Rhodes might actually give herself an aneurism. No such luck. Sam stood there and bore the insults in silence until Rhodes shrieked a dismissal.

When Rhodes had finished with her, Sam's boss in the Secret Service placed her on administrative leave. Sam had never been fired from a job before. It stung.

The call from Hunt was the only bright spot to her day, and that had been marred by disturbing questions about Jake Noble. He was the last person Sam wanted to discuss with Hunt.

She was wading through a confusing tangle of emotion when she arrived home that evening and found an X drawn in chalk on a blue mail box outside her flat. Instead of looking for a spot to park, she hung a left at the corner and headed downtown to the E Street cinema. She had put a pink mark on the box before leaving that morning. It was a prearranged signal. Burke had added the other half of the X to indicate he was ready for a meet.

Sam paid for parking in a garage and crossed E Street to the theater, still dressed in the secret service blazer with a white button-down and slacks. She had her hair up in a ponytail. A few damp tangles framed her face. She examined the collection of movie posters outside the theater. One of the polished brass frames bore a small chalk mark in the bottom corner. The show was *To Have and to Have Not.* Sam consulted her watch. The mark was on the bottom left corner, which meant the showing closest to seven o'clock. She waited through the line and paid for the 7:15 showing.

A teenager with braces behind the ticket window said, "It already started."

"It doesn't get good until the second half," Sam told him.

She handed her stub to another teenager, this one with a face like melting wax. The cinema seemed to be run exclusively by post-pubescent high school students. He ripped the ticket and mumbled a theater number. Sam passed the concession stand for an elevator located at the end of the hall next to the restrooms. She rode it to the second floor. The doors opened and she was face to face with another teenager. This one had a nose ring. He was busy typing a message into his phone.

Sam squared her shoulders, hoping the business attire would be enough to sell the lie. "We don't pay you to text, young man."

The phone disappeared with the efficiency of a three-card Monte dealer collecting bets. He started to ask, "Who..."

"The concession stand is backed up," Sam cut him off. "See if you can make yourself useful."

"Yes ma'am." He stepped into the elevator and punched the button for the ground floor.

Sam breathed a sigh of relief, located Theater 7's projection booth and knocked five times. Two fast, three slow. Burke opened the door. Sam stepped inside and closed it behind her.

The projection machine filled the small space with a steady hum. Gone are the days when an actual person had to change reels. Now, the projectionist can simply load a disc, press play and come back when the movie is over. Which meant they had the place to themselves for the next hour and a half.

Sam said, "I nearly got caught by the puberty patrol."

Burke should have cracked a grin—Sam knew his sense of humor—instead he perched himself on a stool and scooped up a tub of buttered popcorn. A whiff of booze added to her sense of foreboding. Burke stuffed a handful in his mouth and asked, "Did you get anything useful?"

"I can prove Rhodes is using the Secret Service as her own personal gestapo, but that's about it." Sam said.

"Keep digging," Burke said.

"I'm on administrative leave," Sam told him. "Are you drunk?"

"I'm getting there," Burke admitted.

"You want to talk about it?"

He thrust his hand into the tub of popcorn but lost motivation. His large black fist lay half buried in the yellow pile. "Madeline and me are split up."

Sam laid a hand on his massive shoulder. "I'm so sorry. What happened?"

"I screwed up."

"What did you do?"

"You know Dana?"

"Your secretary?" Sam said.

He nodded.

"She's half your age, Matt."

"You think I don't know that?" Burke put the popcorn down and picked up a cola, big enough to be classified a bucket. He drank until the straw gurgled.

"What did Maddie do when she found out?" Sam asked. Burke was a good man and his wife was a sweet lady but the relationship had been rocky for a while now. Sam had been wondering if they would pull out of the nose dive or end up in the side of a mountain.

"She kicked me out," he said. "It's less than I deserve. I was never the best husband. I was never there for her the way I should have been. It's this job. It takes no prisoners when it comes to relationships." Burke tossed the empty drink at a garbage can but missed.

"Tell me about it," Sam muttered to herself.

Burke said, "Maddie knew the stakes going in. We did alright at first. We made it work. But somewhere along the line I think we both stopped trying. Lately it's been worse than usual and Dana, well, she was there. You know?"

"I know," said Sam, thinking of Hunt. He had been there when Jake was not. She put her back to the wall and stuffed her hands in the pockets of her blazer. "What are you going to do?"

"Too early to say." Burke admitted. "Slip out of that bra."

"Turn around," Sam said.

Burke directed his attention through the square opening to the movie screen where Bogie and Bacall were exchanging witty repartees. While his back was turned, Sam shrugged out of her blazer, unbuttoned her shirt and took off her bra. She put the shirt and blazer back on and held the bra out for Burke. "At least we can prove Rhodes planted false evidence against Standish."

"Which we facilitated," Burke pointed out. "That would put us in jail right along with her. It's not enough."

"It's the best we have until I get reinstated," Sam said.

Burke grimaced, showing the gap between his front teeth. "The election is right around the corner."

"What's going on in Mexico?" Sam asked.

Burke glanced up at her with the unspoken question written on his face.

"I got a call from Greg Hunt earlier today," she said by way of explanation.

"Mexico is where my worst fears were realized," Burke told her.

Sam turned a plastic milk crate over and sat. "Want to read me in?"

"This could end my career," Burke said. "The less you know the better."

Sam raked a hand through her hair. "My first official job for the Company is a black on black intelligence gathering operation against a United States politician, on *American soil*. That's illegal, in case you forgot. My career could be over before it begins. If this is going to go any further, you need to read me in."

He sized her up. Being half in the tank probably helped. He said, "It started a decade ago. I was still overseeing Special Operations in the War on Terror back then. American was fighting the Taliban and no one was afraid to put the word *Islamic* in front of *terrorist*.

"One morning I woke up convinced we had a leak. The idea formed so gradually I was hardly aware of it until it was full and staring me in the face. I couldn't point to anything specific, you know? It was gut instinct, really. The occasional operation went sideways, but that was nothing out of the ordinary. Still, I was certain there was a mole inside the Company.

"At first I tried to ignore it," Burke said. "Paranoia is a job requirement in this business. But there's a fine line between healthy suspicion and paranoid schizophrenia."

"I remember the lecture." Sam said. "*You* gave it my second week at the Farm."

"Yeah, well, I left some parts out," Burke told her. "Constant suspicion puts a lot of stress on a person. Over the years, I've watched brilliant agents lose the battle with paranoia. The lucky ones get to retire. The unlucky ones end up in a mental institution run by the Pickle Farm."

"I'd heard rumors we had our own nut house," Sam said.

"It's true," Burke said. "I didn't want anyone thinking I had scrambled my noodle, so I kept my suspicions to myself. I buried the idea for as long as I could, but it kept floating back up to the surface anytime an operation went off the wire, or an agent ended up dead."

"What'd you do?" Sam asked.

"A few years ago, I started keeping detailed notes on all of the failed operations. I tracked every officer, every asset, every analyst. I eventually compiled a list of probable suspects. Then I fed out a series of barium meals."

"Barium meals?" Sam asked. "I've never heard the term."

"You wouldn't," Burke said. "Your generation is all about high tech espionage. But back in the Cold War, a barium meal was one of our best tools for weeding out Reds who had infiltrated as double agents."

"How does it work?" Sam asked.

"It's simple really." Burke slipped into the tone he used

when he taught counterintelligence classes at the Farm. "Let's say you have eight possible traitors. You set up eight different operations and then you feed key bits of intelligence back to your suspect pool. Then you wait to see which op goes bad."

"What about the officer running the operation?" Sam asked.

Burke's lips pressed into a thin line.

"You gambled with people's lives," Sam said.

"We do that every day."

Sam leaned back against the wall, crossed her arms over her chest and let the pieces come together in her mind. "One of your barium meals was in Mexico?"

Burke inclined his head. "God help me. It was the last one I suspected would go bad. I included it just to cover all my bases."

"Who is it?" Sam asked. "Who's the leak?"

"Helen Rhodes."

CHAPTER THIRTY-NINE

Sam said, "That's a hell of an accusation, Burke."

"That's why I need irrefutable proof," he told her.

Someone was passing by the projection booth. Burke held up a hand for silence. They waited until the footsteps retreated down the hall.

"If you are wrong about this, we're *both* finished," Sam said.

"I wish I were," Burke told her. "Torres, the field officer in Mexico, found evidence she's been taking campaign funds from the Los Zetas cartel."

Sam whistled.

"That's not the worst of it," Burke said. "I did some digging into her financials. Over the last two decades, she's received over a hundred million dollars in payouts from Saudi Arabia, Libya, Colombia, and a half dozen other countries on America's naughty list. It turns out the Secretary of State has been getting large infusions of cash from the Muslim Brotherhood and various Middle East groups with ties to radical Islam."

"All groups that want to see America destroyed," Sam said.

Burke nodded.

She stood up and paced. "If she gets elected, her campaign donors will be holding her leash."

"Too bad I can't prove it."

"What about the information Torres uncovered?" Sam asked.

"Missing," Burke said.

"How did Rhodes even find out about a CIA operation against the cartels?" Sam asked.

A spiteful grin formed on Burke's face. "She and Foster are thick as thieves. They went to Columbia Law together. She's the reason he's Deputy Director of Intelligence. It certainly has nothing to do with talent."

The ramifications left a sick feeling in Sam's stomach. "Once she's elected, she'll appoint Foster as Director. She'll have open access to every operation the Company lays in the works."

Burke nodded. "And she's beholden to the various terrorist and criminal organizations funneling cash into her war chest. Any operations that threaten her donors will go sideways. A lot of innocent people will die."

Sam said, "We need to take this information to the Wizard."

Burke spread his hands. "And tell him what? I know she's bent, but I can't prove it. And I don't know if Foster is on the take or just plain stupid."

"I can't decide which would be worse," Sam said. "Who else knows about this?"

"Just you, me and Dana."

Sam threw her hands in the air. "Is there anything you haven't shared with your secretary?"

Burke pulled a face.

"Sorry," Sam muttered. "That was a low blow."

He waved it away. "What did you learn from your conversation with Hunt?

"Noble's in Mexico and he's in trouble," Sam said. "Greg's there now with a team trying to hunt Jake down. I caught some crosstalk before we hung up, it sounds like they've got a lead on his location."

Burke pinched the bridge of his nose between thumb and forefinger. "Damn, that kid is resilient."

"Which one?" Sam asked.

He smiled. "Both."

"I'm worried," Sam said.

"Me too," Burke admitted. "Noble embarrassed Hunt once already. He'll be looking for payback and that kid has a chip on his shoulder the size of Gibraltar."

Sam felt a quick stab of panic and wasn't sure who she was worried about, Greg or Jake. Or both. She said, "Greg wouldn't kill Jake."

Burke gave her a sidelong look that said he wasn't so sure.

"What should we do?" Sam asked.

"Go home."

"You can't be serious?"

"Right now, the most important thing you can do is stay in character," Burke told her. "Rhodes might have people watching you. Remember, you're a recent graduate of the Secret Service and you're already on administrative leave. Act accordingly."

"What about Jake?"

"He's a big boy," Burke said. "He can handle himself."

Sam followed orders and went home, tired and emotionally wrung out. Perspiration had soaked through her button-down blouse. She poured a tall glass of chianti—in keeping with her cover story—and then drew a hot bath. She kicked off her heels and stripped out of her slacks. She hung her clothes from a hook on the bathroom door. Her gun went on the toilet lid within easy reach and her panties went on the floor. She eased into the steamy embrace of the tub with a long sigh.

What a day.

She sipped wine and picked up a hardback copy of *Cold Fury*, the latest thriller from William Miller. She read a few pages, shook her head and snorted. Spy novelists never get the details right. But this one wasn't *too* bad. Sam tried to get lost in the book, but her conversation with Hunt kept intruding on the narrative.

She felt guilty for giving Noble the brush off. They had a good thing going. Then she had been forced to choose between Jake and the Company. Meeting Hunt her second week at the Farm had only made the decision that much harder. In the end she decided to cut him off, go cold turkey. A clean break.

She put the book aside and waded into the confusing tangle of emotions. On the one hand, there was Hunt: handsome, well-spoken with an easy smile and a promising career. But Hunt had a reputation. Then there was Noble:

silent, taciturn and a little rough around the edges. He was a former spy with no direction and no future. And despite all of the strikes against him, Sam couldn't manage to banish Jake from her thoughts.

Now both men were on a collision course in Mexico.

The idea started a quiet panic in her gut. For all she knew, they could be trading bullets already. But there was still a chance to warn Noble and maybe defuse the situation. She scrubbed her face with both hands. *How hard could it be?* All she needed was a 24-hour superstore and a prepaid burner phone. She chewed her bottom lip. Before she had time to think it through, Sam was out of the tub and toweling off.

CHAPTER FORTY

AFTER SUPPER, ALEJANDRA FELT UP FOR A WALK SO they strolled around the garden. Dead rose bushes lined the path. Weeds ran riot. The sun had dipped below the horizon, leeching most of the light from the sky, but sweat still soaked though their clothes. Alejandra had on a moth-eaten floral print dress that she had found in one of the upstairs closets. Wearing her dead mother's clothing must have been heart-wrenching, but she never let it show and Noble didn't ask. She plucked a slender vine and tortured it between her fingers as they walked. "Tell me about Diaz."

"Torres," Noble corrected her. "He was a good man."

"Tell me something I don't know."

"He saved my life," Noble said, "On several occasions." A sad smile crept over his face. "During the opening days of America's War on Terror, we were training guerilla fighters in the mountains of Afghanistan. The locals had a knack for horseback riding, so joint special operation command gave us the task of teaching them to fight in the saddle.

"But Torres grew up in L.A. The only horses he had ever seen were on television." Noble chuckled. "The Afghans gave him this giant dappled grey. The beast was seventeen hands high. Torres barely came up to the saddle."

Alejandra cracked a smile. "What happened?"

"He grabs hold of the pommel, vaults himself into the saddle and the horse bucks. Torres lands flat on his back in the dirt. We all thought he broke his neck."

"Was he hurt?"

Noble shook his head. "No. He jumped up and cold-cocked that horse right in the head."

"He punched it?"

Noble nodded. "From that day on, Torres and that horse had an understanding. For a kid from L.A., he turned out to be one of the best riders on the team."

Alejandra laughed and threaded her arm through his. They walked arm in arm. A strange sense of displacement came over Noble, like he was filling in for his dead friend. He wondered if Alejandra felt the same. It was sad and sweet all at the same time.

"The Taliban had been hammering a firebase in the Korengal Valley," he said to fill the silence. "U.S. troops were taking heavy causalities. We were patrolling the area, trying to make contact, riding our horses through a shallow wash when a mortar round came whistling down. I was riding point. The explosion killed my horse and I was trapped beneath him. While everyone else rushed forward to engage the enemy, Torres stayed behind to protect me. The jihadists lobbed one mortar round after another. Explosions were going off all around us. I told Torres to find some cover, but he refused. He shielded me with his own body until our guys could engage the mortar team."

"That sounds like Diaz," Alejandra said. "Did he... have anyone..."

"No." Noble shook his head. "No wife. No kids. Our unit was the closest thing he had to a family."

They did two more laps around the neglected garden, sweating through their clothes and ignoring the stink of rotting vegetation, before Alejandra turned her steps toward the veranda doors.

Noble had taken up residence in a room with a window that looked out across the courtyard to the front gate. Generic furnishings suggested a guest bedroom, which suited Noble just fine. He didn't like the idea of sleeping in a dead man's bed. The smell was another matter. It smelled like an attic, even with all the windows open. Outside, cicada buzzed in the night.

It was after midnight when his ears caught the sound of bare feet outside his bedroom door. His eyes snapped open. His heart jogged in his chest. He slipped a hand under the pillow and brought out one of the Glocks he had taken from the Mexican police officers.

There was a soft knock. The door swung open on worn hinges. Alejandra stood in the frame. The lines of her naked body were silhouetted against the darkness of the hall. Traces of soft moonlight caressed her curves.

Noble sat up. "Something wrong?"

She hovered in the doorframe, caught by indecision.

He placed the Glock on the bedside table. "You should be in bed. You need your..."

She crossed the room and silenced him with a kiss. It was warm, soft and eager. Noble's hormones rallied and his body responded to her touch. Their lips melded together. Her naked flesh pressed against him. Her breath came out in trembling bursts. Noble wanted to enjoy this, but thoughts of Torres kept crowding his mind. He gripped her shoulders and gently pushed.

Their lips parted.

Noble said, "I'm not him."

It was several seconds before she spoke. "I'm sorry," she whispered.

"Don't be," Noble said.

She slipped off the bed and went quietly to the door.

Noble relaxed into the pillows and let out a long breath. He wasn't in the habit of turning down sex and it had been a long time. Too long. His God-fearing mother would be proud, but his libido was screaming in revolt at this unprecedented turn of events.

He consulted the luminous dial on his TAG Heuer. It was 12:47am. Noble closed his eyes. Tomorrow he would start making plans. He had been on hold while Alejandra healed, but if she was well enough for sex, she was well enough to plot an assassination. He still wanted to know what the key unlocked and why Torres had sent it to him, but that could wait until Machado was dead.

He was drifting on the edge of sleep when he realized the cicadas had stopped buzzing. Alarm bells jangled inside his skull. He sat up and swung his legs over the side of the bed, listening intently.

His phone vibrated on the bedside table and Noble's heart tried to climb out though his throat. He checked and found a text message from an unknown number.

You've got company.

CHAPTER FORTY-ONE

Hunt parked a rented pickup a half kilometer from the abandoned villa. He climbed out, left the door open and checked the magazine on a nickel plated .45 caliber Kimber Custom. It was a beautiful weapon with a five-inch barrel, tritium night sights and mother-of-pearl grips. He had bought it after graduating the Farm as a gift to himself. It was his signature accessory. Some guys had a wristwatch they favored, others had cufflinks or a tie tack. Hunt had his Kimber Custom, like Dirty Harry's famous .44 Magnum. He even had his initials engraved in the slide.

He took a moment to disable the overhead dome in the pickup so the light wouldn't give him away, then crept along the wooded road toward the property, keeping his eyes open for movement and his ears alert to the smallest sound.

It had taken Gwen most of the day, but she finally managed to locate the address of the estate nestled in the foothills of the Sierra Madres. Miles from the nearest farm and hidden from prying eyes by a festering jungle, it was the perfect place to lay low.

Hunt paused at the entrance. Pale light from a half moon showed him a stone wall covered in thick ivy and an open gate. He had waited until the early morning, to catch Noble at the low point in his circadian rhythm, but walking in through the front door was an option of last resort. Instead, he threaded his way through the trees, working around the perimeter toward the back of the property and found a spot where the wall had surrendered to age. The stones had spilled outwards like a child's toy chest turned on its side.

Hunt climbed carefully over the fallen stones to the inner courtyard. This side of the house had been completely gutted by fire. He entered through a charred gap in the masonry that had once been a set of French doors but was now a yawning cavity. In the main hall, a chandelier lay in the middle of a terrazzo floor. The arms were bent at crazy angles and the crystals were chips of shattered diamonds winking in the darkness. Decades of dust muffled his footfalls. He took a sweeping staircase to the second floor and started checking bedrooms and parlors.

He went slow, working his way methodically through the house in search of his prey. He had nearly exhausted the second floor when he heard a rattle, like wire hangers on a closet rack. There was a soft creak as someone crept over sagging wood floors. Hunt followed it to a room near the front of the house which overlooked the upstairs balcony.

There was another rattle. Now that he was closer it sounded like a shower curtain. Hunt nudged the door with his foot. He was in a master bedroom with a four-poster bed and an ancient oak armoire standing in one corner. A pair of French doors let onto a balcony. Moth-eaten drapes stirred in the breeze. Another door led to a private bathroom. Hunt moved on silent feet to the bathroom and stepped inside with his gun up, looking for targets.

Alejandra Domingo sat on the toilet, a silk bathrobe gathered around her hips and her knees pressed together. One side of her face was still covered in medical gauze. She stared at him with her good eye. "Do you mind?"

The scene caught Hunt completely off-guard. The barrel of his weapon drooped. He opened his mouth to stammer out an apology before his training caught up with years of social protocol. The gun came back up. "Let me see your hands!"

CHAPTER FORTY-TWO

Noble didn't need the text message. Six years in Special Forces had taught him to heed the sounds of nature. Birds and snakes are an ever-present threat to cicadas. When they stopped buzzing, Noble had known something was wrong. He had thrown off the sheets and raced upstairs to Alejandra's room.

From the balcony overlooking the garden, he had watched a figure slip through the gap in the wall and recognized Foster's fair haired golden boy. Noble let Hunt make his way across the lawn to the house while he and Alejandra threw together a hasty plan.

She had played her part to perfection. All of Hunt's attention was focused on her. He had failed to sweep the rest of the room and didn't see Noble standing behind the bathroom door with a rolled-up hand towel.

When Hunt leveled his pistol at Alejandra and ordered her hands up, Noble looped the hand towel around Hunt's wrist in one quick motion. The gun clapped thunder. The pedestal sink exploded in a shower of porcelain.

The two men struggled for control of the weapon. Hunt was young and strong, but Noble had more experience. He had been through the same hand-to-hand combat training and could predict Hunt's moves. He used the knowledge to counter the more dangerous attacks before they could do any real damage.

The gun barrel was wrenched back and forth in the fight. Hunt pulled the trigger out of desperation. The gun barked. The mirror shattered. Alejandra covered her ears with both hands and screamed.

Noble yelled, "Tub! Now!"

She took two long strides and launched herself into an alabaster bathtub. A bullet destroyed the toilet tank a second later. Brackish water flooded the floor.

Noble groped for the magazine eject. His fingers found the small raised knob. The magazine clattered across the tiles. That left one round in the chamber.

Hunt hammered a fist into Noble's shoulder blade. A lance of blinding pain raced up his back into his brain. Six months ago, a shotgun ricochet had bounced off the hull of a cargo ship and lodged in Noble's shoulder. Hunt must have familiarized himself with Noble's file, because he pummeled the old wound repeatedly.

Noble used his legs and shoulders to drive Hunt into the wall. Tiles crunched under the impact. Hunt returned the favor, slamming Noble into the opposite wall. He followed up with a well-placed knee to Noble's almost-healed ribs.

Noble stomped down on Hunt's foot and drove him out of the bathroom, into the bedroom where he had more room to fight. Knuckles impacted the side of Noble's head, causing fairy lights to dance in his vision. He ducked a second haymaker and elbowed Hunt's jaw. They staggered through the bedroom, trading knees and elbows, still wrestling for control of the weapon. The fight carried them out the bedroom onto the upstairs landing. Their bodies crashed into the railing. Wood splintered, and their weight carried them over.

Noble felt the terrifying helplessness of falling. A scream jerked from his throat. The terrazzo floor came up to meet him. He landed on top of Hunt and the lights went out.

Noble's brain tried to make sense of fragmented information. Every joint in his body hurt. He was lying on a cold floor, covered in dust and grit. He twitched his left hand and felt a layer of dirt under his fingernails. He knew he had to get up, had to move, but couldn't remember why. His brain trumpeted a warning klaxon until his eyes snapped open. He was on his back, staring up at the ceiling. Pain pulsed in every fiber of his being. He curled his toes and then his fingers. No broken bones.

The fight, the fall: it all came back in a flash.

He turned his head, hearing tendons creak, and saw Hunt on the floor next to him.

Alejandra appeared at the broken railing. "Noble? Are you okay?"

"Think so," he croaked out.

She looked at Hunt. "Is he dead?"

Noble pressed two fingers against Hunt's throat and found a pulse.

"He's alive," Noble said. He turned over and spotted the handgun. It had come to rest amid the broken arms of the fallen chandelier. Noble pulled himself across the floor. Chips of broken crystal dug into his skin. Every inch was torture. He reached the gun as Hunt was coming around.

By the time Hunt regained consciousness, Noble had pushed himself into a sitting position and thumbed back the hammer. The sound echoed around the spacious hall. Hunt blinked a few times before his eyes focused on Noble. He groaned.

Noble said, "Alejandra, find something to tie him up with."

CHAPTER FORTY-THREE

HUNT FELT LIKE SOMEONE HAD TAKEN A SLEDGE hammer to his spine. He could still move his toes—that was a good sign, but a whole bottle of aspirin wouldn't put a dent in his headache. The pain was only half of it. A thirty-three year-old man had beaten him twice now. That fact tasted like a mouth full of turpentine. He told himself it was the fall. If not for the tumble from the balcony, he would have taken Noble down.

They had him lashed to a wooden chair with electrical cords in an empty parlor on the first floor. Wire bit into his wrists. His fingers were pins and needles.

Noble had handed his gun to Alejandra with instructions to shoot Hunt in the knee if he tried anything, before limping out of the room. She kept the pistol trained on his chest and watched him with her good eye. Her bathrobe was loosely tied, revealing one naked thigh.

Hunt said, "Your friend Noble is in a lot of trouble. You know that?"

"Who said he was my friend?"

"He came all the way to Mexico to rescue you."

Alejandra lifted one shoulder. "He rescued me for his own reasons."

"Do the right thing," Hunt told her. "Cut me loose. I can protect you, get you a new identity. You can go to America. Maybe I can even arrange for plastic surgery. You could have your face back."

A humorless laugh worked its way up from her chest. "I don't want your protection."

"What do you want?"

"Machado dead," she said. "Can you give me that?"

Hunt didn't know what to say to that.

She snorted. "Then we've got nothing to talk about."

He gave up trying to reason with her. Hell hath no fury like a woman scorned.

Noble returned ten minutes later with a car battery and jumper cables. He touched the connectors together. Electricity crackled. Sparks flashed. The sound left a sick feeling in Hunt's stomach. It was an effort to control his bladder. He said, "You wouldn't."

Noble touched the jumper cables to Hunt's shoulder.

Every muscle in his body convulsed. His eyes tried to leap right out of his skull. He used every curse word he knew and then made a few up. Spittle flew from his lips.

"Two ways we can do this," Noble told him. "I can torture you. Or you can tell me what I want to know."

One jolt was enough to convince Hunt. Any more and he would crap his pants. He spoke through clenched teeth. "Ask me anything you like."

"Discretion is the better part of valor," Noble

commented. He took a chair from the corner, turned it around, straddled it. "You work directly for Foster?"

"*Deputy Director* Foster," Hunt corrected him.

Noble didn't look impressed. "What are your orders?"

"Neutralize you before you do any more damage."

"Alive?" Noble asked.

"Unfortunately."

Noble took a brass key from his pocket. "What's this open?"

"I have no idea."

He rapped the key against Hunt's forehead, causing him to wince. "Try harder."

"*I don't know*."

Noble nodded, satisfied, and pocketed the key. Then he waited.

Hunt tried not to let the silence unnerve him. It was an old interrogation trick. Don't ask any questions, just sit there and stare at the subject until they start talking to fill the void. Hunt had used it himself. He pressed his lips together and studied the wall.

"What do you know about Operation RIPTIDE?" Noble asked.

"I know your Army buddy was down here on assignment, the op went sideways, and he's missing. Instead of tying it off, Burke sent you to find him."

"He's not missing," Noble said. "He's dead. Someone on your end blew his cover."

Hunt shook his head. "Bull crap."

"Is it?" Noble said. "Then why is Foster hell-bent on sweeping the whole thing under the rug?"

"Ops go bad. Agents get killed. It's a job hazard."

"You're awful young to be so jaded," Noble said.

"You're awful old to be so sentimental."

"Careful," Noble told him. "Torres was my friend."

"Even the best officers make mistakes," Hunt said.

"Something about it doesn't add up," Noble said.

"You're letting your emotions cloud your judgment," Hunt said. "You're not seeing the big picture."

"The big picture?" Noble snorted. "Here's the picture I see. The Company puts a man in the cartel. He sets up a pipeline and he's collecting actionable intel. Before that information can be used, his cover is blown and he ends up dead. No one at Langley seems interested in how or why. How's that picture strike you, hot shot?"

"It doesn't always have to make sense," Hunt said, "Field officers follow orders. You, of all people, should know that."

Noble shook his head. "Something stinks and you know it."

"Look, Noble, I'm sorry about your friend," Hunt said. "It doesn't give you an excuse to wage a one-man war on the cartel."

"Who's going to stop me?" Noble leaned in. "You?"

Hunt boiled with impotent rage.

Noble glanced at his watch. "How long have I got before your team starts to worry?"

Hunt made a show of ignoring the question.

Noble picked up the jumper cables and arced electricity off the connections.

"My check-in is five o'clock."

CHAPTER FORTY-FOUR

GWEN PACED THE SMALL OFFICE ON THE SECOND FLOOR of the embassy, willing the secure line to ring. Ezra was in a chair clicking a ballpoint pen, staring into nothing. *Click-click-click.* Every couple of clicks he would spin the pen around and then go back to clicking. *Click-click-click.* When she couldn't take any more, Gwen blurted, "Would you stop that?"

He put the pen down, muttered an apology and started tapping a foot, which was almost as bad.

After four days in Mexico City, both analysts were ready to get back to their own beds and familiar food. Covert operations in exotic locales sounded good in training; the reality had turned out far different. All they had seen of Mexico was the airport and the embassy. Instead of world-class resorts and cocktails, they were sleeping on a flea-infested sofa and drinking canned soda to avoid dysentery.

Both had been excited for their first overseas assignment. Mexico wasn't exactly the other side of the globe, but it was further from a desk than most analysts got in a lifetime. They had secretly relished the idea of going back to Langley with war stories. Instead, the only stories they would have to tell would be about the long hours cooped up in an office on the second floor of an embassy, sifting through police reports and news bulletins.

Now they were just waiting for Hunt to call and say they could go home. It had been a long night. The sun was coming up, throwing an angry orange glow over the rooftops of Mexico City. The hands on the clock pointed to five-fifteen. Hunt's check-in window had come and gone.

Gwen paced with her hands clasped together, like a woman in prayer. She let out a shaky breath. "This is really happening."

"He'll call," Ezra said. "He's just late. That's all. Probably lost track of time."

Gwen shook her head. "We have to go to the villa," she said. "That was the plan."

"And do what?" Ezra spread his hands. "We're not field officers. We're analysts. My training is in MASINT, for crying out loud."

"Doesn't matter," Gwen stated flatly. "We're his backup."

Ezra swallowed, reached under one of the desks and pulled a plastic case from the side pocket of his duffle bag. A Sig Saur P229 was nestled in the gray foam lining.

Gwen pulled an identical case from a purple backpack.

Ezra checked the action on his weapon and exhaled, puffing out his cheeks. "I haven't fired this thing since training."

"Me neither," Gwen admitted.

They looked at each other. Butterflies zipped around inside their bellies. This was it. This was the real thing. They had wanted war stories. It looked like they were going to get more than they had bargained for.

They stuffed their weapons into their waistbands and went downstairs to a rented sedan parked in the embassy garage. Ezra drove. They rode in silence. Neither wanted to talk about what they would do if they got to the villa and Hunt was dead. Worse, they might get to the villa and find Noble there, still very much alive. There was no telling what he was capable of. He was a former Green Beret. They were computer jockeys.

Ezra stopped in the middle of a dusty lane hemmed in by towering oaks bearded with Spanish moss. Hunt's rented pickup was twenty yards up the road, parked on the shoulder with the hood up.

Gwen's face brightened. "Maybe he just had engine trouble."

"Maybe," Ezra said.

They sat watching the pickup for several minutes. When nothing happened, Ezra said, "I guess we should check it out."

Gwen nodded. "Should we take our guns out?"

Ezra thought about it. "Yeah. Yeah, I think so."

They pulled out their weapons and performed one last check before getting out of the car. They stood in the open doors for a moment, ready to dive back in if bullets started flying. Ezra was the first to work up his courage. He left the relative safety of the open car door and took a few steps in the direction of the pickup. Gwen followed. They had covered half the distance when someone said, "That's far enough."

Ezra froze in his tracks. Gwen let out a small squeak, like chalk on a blackboard.

"Drop your guns in the dirt and turn around slowly."

Neither analyst even considered anything other than complete co-operation. They dropped their weapons and lifted their hands over their heads, before turning around.

Noble exited the trees with a pistol aimed at them—Hunt's prized .45 caliber Kimber Custom. Alejandra Domingo emerged from the other side of the road, holding a pair of 9mm Glocks. She was dressed in oversized denims cinched tight around her waist, a baggy tank top, and bandages covering half her face.

"Take three big steps back," Noble ordered. "My associate is going to collect your weapons. Either of you tries to be a hero and you'll join Hunt."

Ezra and Gwen stepped back, keeping their hands up. His comment about joining Hunt left a lump in Gwen's throat. Tears filled her eyes. Her chin trembled. Ezra was too scared for words. This was *not* how he had envisioned his career at the CIA.

Alejandra took their guns and stuffed them in her pockets before rejoining Noble at the car.

"You'll find Hunt in a parlor on the first floor," Noble told them. He and Alejandra climbed in the sedan, fired it up, and roared backwards down the dirt road, leaving a cloud of dust in their wake.

Ezra let out a breath, bent over and put his hands on his knees. "I thought we were dead."

"I think Greg *is* dead," Gwen said.

She grabbed Ezra's elbow and hauled him toward the house. They passed the pickup truck and saw the battery was missing. There was a second car in the driveway, but the battery was gone from that one as well. Fearing booby-traps, they entered the house cautiously, going room by room, and found Hunt tied to a chair with a gag in his mouth. His blonde hair was disheveled. One eye was swollen shut. Dried blood rimmed both nostrils.

Gwen pulled the gag out. "Are you okay?"

He nodded. "Noble?"

"He got away," Ezra said.

Hunt shouted a curse.

"Along with our only transportation," Gwen pointed out.

"And our weapons," Ezra added.

"You two did a real bang-up job," Hunt said. "Remind me to put both of you in for commendations."

They started to stumble out apologies.

"Cut me loose!"

CHAPTER FORTY-FIVE

NOBLE PULLED INTO A FILLING STATION ON A STRIP OF barren highway running through cactus country. Alejandra went inside for snacks. Noble slotted the nozzle, set the handle and then redialed the unknown number. He had been too busy dealing with Hunt to follow up on his mystery friend earlier. Now, he leaned his hips against the car and listed to the dial tone. He was about to give up when Sam's voice came on the line.

"Hi, Jake. Been a while."

"Sam?"

"Surprise," she said without inflection.

Noble felt the bottom drop out of his universe. It was like waking up from a deep nap and not knowing what day it is. Had he slept an hour? Or all day? He cleared his throat. "I'm going to need some context."

"Matt Burke recruited me about six months ago," she said, explaining her sudden disappearance. "I would have called sooner. I wanted to, but..."

"But you were instructed to sever all ties," Noble

finished for her. A sense of loss so profound it was a physical weight settled on his shoulders. He closed his eyes. His face pinched. He had lost Torres and now Sam.

"Please understand, Jake, I didn't know," she said to fill the silence. "They didn't tell me until *after* I was at the Farm. By then it was too late. I was already in."

He buried the hurt in that cold dark place where he put all the other things he would never have in life. Love, marriage, kids, a regular job. It all went into the vault. He said, "You don't have to explain."

"I'm sorry, Jake. Really I am."

"Don't be," he said. "Are you part of Hunt's team in Mexico?"

"No," she said. "I'm in D.C., between assignments. Is he alive?"

"He's alive," Noble told her. "How did you get onto his operation?"

There was a pause. "He and I have history."

The pump clicked off, echoing the full stop in Noble's brain. He tried to make sense of the statement. Sam and Hunt? The guy was a complete tool. What the hell did she see in him? He racked the nozzle and threaded the gas cap back on. "You and Hunt?"

"Not exactly," she said.

"What's that mean?"

"It's complicated," she said.

"Does he make you happy?" Noble asked.

"Sometimes," she said.

"But not all the time?"

"When I'm with him, it's like I'm the only girl in the world."

"And when you're not?" he asked.

There was another long pause. "He can be a bit much, I admit that, but he's not a bad guy."

"He tried to kill me," Noble said.

"Is he okay?" she asked.

"He's fine," Noble told her. "I'm fine too, thanks for asking."

She muttered an apology. "Did either of you try *talking* before knocking each other's teeth out?"

"We talked some." Noble said, thinking of car batteries and jumper cables. *I should have fried him.*

"And?" Sam asked.

"We didn't see eye to eye."

She gave an exasperated sigh. "Listen, Jake..."

Noble didn't have the time or energy to hash out relationship problems. He changed subjects. "How much do you know about RIPTIDE?"

"I know Torres was gathering intel against the Los Zetas," she said. "I know someone talked and it got him killed."

"We're on the same page so far." Noble switched ears with the phone. "I've got a source that seems to think there's a leak on your end."

"Your source might be right," Sam admitted. "Certain people here feel the same."

"A mutual friend of ours?" Noble asked.

"He's a big cuddly bear. And that's all I'm saying. I've said too much already. I'm *way* out on a limb here."

"That makes two of us," Noble told her.

Alejandra came out of the gas station, dressed in a

cheap tourist sweatshirt. She had the hood up to hide the bandages and a plastic bag in one hand.

"I gotta go," Noble said.

"Before you do," she said. "I really am sorry about the way things turned out."

"Me too," he said. "You'd better ditch that phone as soon as you can. They'll be monitoring my calls."

"I will," she said, and then, "Jake?"

"Yeah?"

"Be careful."

"I will."

She hung up.

Alejandra looked at him over roof of the car. "Who was that?"

"A friend."

"Someone you trust?"

"With my life," he told her.

Ten minutes later they were back on the highway headed south towards Mexico City. Noble said, "Operating on the premise that Machado has an informant in the CIA, who else in his organization would know?"

"Blythe," Alejandra said without pause.

Noble twirled his hand for her to continue.

"Machado's accountant." Alejandra said. "He's got a thing for little boys. He did three years on child pornography charges in England. After that, he couldn't land a job in the U.K.—no one wants to hire a pedophile—so he moved to Mexico."

"Drug dealers aren't too particular about the company they keep," Noble commented.

Alejandra nodded. "A pervert like Blythe is custom made for the drug trade. Machado turns a blind eye to his sexual proclivities and offers protection from the law. Blythe provides creative accounting and tax shelters. The two are practically joined at the hip. Where Machado goes, Blythe follows."

"They can't be together all the time," Noble said. "Where does Blythe get his boys?"

"The meetings are arranged through the internet, but Diaz—Torres," she corrected herself, "tracked the source to an apartment in Zona Rosa. Once or twice a week, Blythe goes to a five-star hotel in the city. A courier drops off the boys."

The idea left a sour taste in Noble's mouth. Raping children plumbs the very depths of human depravity. People like that deserve a special place in hell, if it existed, and a very nasty death if it didn't. Noble had a score to settle with Machado, he'd ice Blythe for free. He said, "Let's go pay a visit to Blythe's pimp."

CHAPTER FORTY-SIX

It was a long walk back for Hunt and his team. They had spent the better part of the morning turning the villa inside out trying to find the missing car batteries. Wherever Noble hid them, he did a good job. By the time the sun reached its zenith, they abandoned the search and started the grueling march to the highway and eventually Mexico City.

Hunt spent the first half of the walk thinking of new and inventive ways to hurt Noble, but nothing he imagined was painful enough. Noble deserved to suffer. Pain fueled Hunt's dark fantasies. He had been beat up, thrown off a balcony, and electrocuted by car battery. His joints ached. His head pounded, and it felt like someone had replaced his spine with broken glass. Every step hurt.

By the time they reached the highway, Hunt had walked off most of his rage and his thoughts turned to his strange talk with Noble. Hunt had been expecting a man on the edge, unhinged, someone driven by rage. Noble was in control. Worse, his questions nagged at Hunt. Shelving his deep-seated loathing of Noble, Hunt wrestled with questions and didn't like the answers he came up with. There were too many pieces that didn't fit.

Gwen had been walking with her thumb out for the better part of a mile when a beat up El Camino pulled over. The driver, a fat Mexican with a toothy grin, offered them a lift into town. The three agents climbed into the bed and the driver took them all the way to the American embassy.

They grabbed lunch from the cafeteria and then rode the elevator to their cubby hole on the second floor. Ezra and Gwen dug into their food while Hunt put in a call to the DDI.

"This is Clark S. Foster."

"It's Hunt." He eased himself down on the ratty sofa with a sigh. Pain marched up his spine, but at least he was off his feet.

"Have you neutralized Noble?"

"We had a bit of a setback."

"I'm listening."

Hunt picked up a bottled water and pressed the cold plastic against his swollen eye. "We tracked him to a burned-out villa on the outskirts of town..."

"And?"

"He disarmed us and got away."

"He disarmed all three of you?"

"Yes sir," Hunt said.

There was silence on the other end.

Hunt cleared his throat and forged ahead. "About the missing field officer, Torres. Noble made some allegations..."

Foster interrupted him. "His cover was blown. End of story. Your mission is Noble. Am I making myself clear?"

"Sir, Noble implied—"

"I don't care what Noble said!" Foster's voice distorted the tiny phone speaker. "He's off the reservation. He needs to be stopped."

Hunt kicked his shoes off and pinched the bridge of his nose. "I'll need to rearm before I take another go at him, sir."

Foster's voice was a dangerous whisper. "Gregory, I want you to listen to me *very* carefully. Don't come back to Virginia until Jake Noble is in a body bag. Is that clear?"

"Perfectly clear, sir. About our weaponry..."

The line went dead.

Four days ago, he would have turned summersaults at the order to kill Noble. Now, it didn't sit too well. Hunt relaxed deeper into the sofa. His body begged him to stretch out and drift off to sleep, but he couldn't afford to rest.

Ezra and Gwen watched him with identical expressions.

Gwen said, "Is it bad?"

"It isn't good." Hunt dialed Sam.

She picked up after three rings. "What can I do for you this time, Greg?"

"I need you to tell me everything you can about your friend, Noble."

"This is a really bad time for me," Sam said. "I'm not supposed to be talking to you, and I'm definitely not supposed to be talking about *him*."

"Sam, it's important."

She sighed. "You're asking me to put my head in the lion's mouth, Greg."

"I've just been ordered to retire him." Hunt gave that time to sink in. "If you know anything that might affect that decision, now is the time to tell me."

CHAPTER FORTY-SEVEN

Zona Rosa is a gay mecca located smack in the heart of Mexico City. The whole place feels like one big Mardi Gras parade. Rainbow flags are everywhere. Same-sex couples stroll arm in arm. Lap dogs are a common accessory. The stink of sweat and liquor permeates the air and the sonorous beat of dance music pulses from every door and window. The brutal heat wave and carnival atmosphere were the perfect excuse for locals to shed clothes and inhibitions.

Noble and Alejandra walked through an outdoor market. Vendors sold everything from pirated movies and knock-off sneakers to sex toys and produce. While a merchant haggled over the cost of a handbag with a gaggle of young girls, Noble swiped a bright purple scarf from a rack. He turned his collar up, draped the scarf around his neck and turned to Alejandra for approval.

She chuckled. "All of your gay culture comes from Hollywood."

"You're not wrong," Noble admitted.

She stopped him, untucked his shirt and then opened a few more buttons.

"Better," she said, and they resumed their course.

Noble attracted the attention of several men. A transvestite in a corset and fishnets gave him a wink. He fended off advances with polite rejections.

Alejandra led the way to an apartment built over a club called *Wild Stallions*. Blythe's pimp lived in number three. They entered a small foyer and mounted the stairs. Music from the club shook plaster from the walls. The deep rhythmic pounding would help mask the sound of a fight if it came to that. Noble reached behind him and put a hand on his pistol. He didn't know what to expect at the top of the stairs. "Has he got security?"

"Don't know." Alejandra shook her head and brought out one of the Sigs they had collected from Hunt's support crew. "I don't know how much good I'll be aiming with my left eye."

"I'll do most of the heavy lifting," he told her.

The staircase ended at a small landing with a stout door painted green. There was a peephole set in the door and a brass knocker shaped like a pair of nuts.

Noble said, "You do the honors."

Her lips pressed together. She rapped three times. The hollow booms echoed around the barren stairwell. There was movement on the other side of the door and then the tiny light at the center of the peephole winked out. Noble blew a kiss.

The door opened to the end of the security chain. A graying man with a neatly trimmed goatee appeared in the gap. His shirt was unbuttoned to reveal a thick mat of black curls. "The club is downstairs," he said in a foppish lisp. "This is a private residence."

Noble stepped back and crashed his foot into the door. The chain popped loose with a shriek of splintering wood. The door smacked the pimp in the face. His head snapped back. Blood burst from both nostrils and he went down on the floor in a heap.

Noble entered with his gun up. The apartment was garishly decorated in what passed for gay vogue. There was a leopard print rug on the floor and posters of Judy Garland from her Wizard of Oz days on the walls. In one corner was a chair in the shape of a giant, plastic hand.

Alejandra put her gun into the pimp's cheek while Noble checked the rest of the apartment. Both kitchen and bedroom were empty. A Twister mat had been framed and hung over a platform bed. Crossword puzzle books were piled on the night stand. The whole place was impeccably clean. Some stereotypes hold up, Noble decided.

The pimp cringed at the steel pressing into his cheek. Blood oozed from his busted nose and dripped on the leopard print rug. "Please, don't hurt me. I abhor violence. It makes me sick."

"How do you feel about pimping out little boys?" Noble asked.

"I have no idea what you're talking about," he said.

"I should let Alejandra dust you right now."

"No!" he shrieked. "Wait. What do you want? You want money? There is fifty-thousand dollars in the copy of *Alice in Wonderland*." He pointed a shaking finger at the bookshelf.

Noble pulled down the book and rifled the pages. He found fifty crisp one-thousand dollar bills in U.S. currency, which he folded and stuffed in his pocket. It would go to paying off his mother's medical bills. He tossed the book on the floor. It landed with a flat smack.

"You supply Henry Blythe with little boys," Noble said.

"I don't know any Blythe. I don't know what you're talking about. I'm an editor for an online zine."

"Yeah? What's your *zine* called?" Noble asked. "Pedo Monthly?"

"It's called the Queer Guide to Latin America."

"Selling boys is just your part-time gig?"

The pimp found his courage and said, "You know what you are? You're a cisgender homophobe and a bully."

"I'm a terrible dancer too," Noble said. "How does it work? Does Blythe reach out to you, or do you contact him?"

The pimp insisted he didn't know anything about prostitution. Alejandra pressed the gun deeper into his cheek, pinning him to the rug. Sweat collected on his brow. His eyes went from Noble to Alejandra and back again.

"Look at her face," Noble said. "She look like somebody you want to piss off?"

Alejandra pulled the hood back to reveal blood stained bandages and yellow bruises.

His chin trembled, but he needed more convincing.

Noble went to the kitchen and rummaged through drawers, making a lot of noise. Silverware jangled and dishes shattered on the floor. He found a wine bottle opener and carried it back to the living room.

The sight of the corkscrew had the desired effect.

"I'm just a middle man," the pimp said between sobs. "The seller sends me pictures of his newest boys. When he has one that matches a client's type, I arrange a meeting. Blythe wires the money and I contact the seller. I tell them where to take the merchandise."

"*Merchandise*," Noble said. "That's all they are to you?"

"Look, I never did it myself. I like men. I just make the connections. That's all. I forward the money into the seller's account and keep ten percent."

Noble waved the corkscrew under the pimp's nose. "You're going to contact Blythe and tell him you've got a boy for him."

"He might not want to meet right away."

"You better hope that's not the case," Noble said.

"If I arrange a meeting for tomorrow night, do you *promise* not to hurt me?"

"I promise to hurt you if you don't," Noble told him.

He swallowed hard, palmed blood away from his nose and nodded. "Okay, I'll do it."

Noble said, "What's your name?"

"Hector Sanchez."

"Time's wasting, Hector."

"I need my computer," Hector said.

Alejandra took the gun out of his cheek. Noble grabbed his arm and yanked him to his feet. Hector let out a frightened squeak. Noble shoved him at the computer desk. "Get to work."

Hector dropped into the chair and, after a sullen glance at Noble, opened a web browser. Noble watched every keystroke. He said, "If anyone shows up here to rescue you,

I'll kill them and then throw you out a window, understood?"

"You are so violent. You must be a meat eater," Hector muttered. He sent the email. They waited several minutes for a reply. The laptop chimed. Hector said, "It's done."

"When?" Noble asked.

"Tomorrow night, just like you asked. The Hotel Plaza Suites at six."

Noble patted him on the cheek. "Good boy."

Alejandra had gone into the bedroom. When she came back she was holding a pair of handcuffs and a ball gag.

Noble turned up an eyebrow. "Kinky."

"Like you never," Hector said.

"I'm a meat and potatoes kind of guy," Noble told him. He wheeled the desk chair—with Hector still in it—into the kitchen where he handcuffed Hector to a water pipe. The metal ratcheted together with a sharp clink.

Noble said, "Make trouble and you get the gag."

"What if I have to pee?"

Noble found a plastic cup in a cabinet over the sink. He handed it to Hector and then raided the refrigerator. The shelves were stocked with fruit, wheat germ, lox, pita bread and what smelled like hummus. Noble grabbed an apple, wiped it on his sleeve, and headed for the living room.

"Bully," Hector muttered at his back.

"What's the plan?" Alejandra asked. She had bolted and locked the front door as best she could. Together, they dragged the sofa in front of it.

Noble took a chomp out of the apple and spoke with his mouth full. "We should be safe here for the night. He hasn't got any food, but we can order in. Tomorrow, I'll get to the hotel ahead of Blythe and we'll have a chat."

"And if Blythe isn't chatty?"

"I can be very charming," Noble told her.

She looked at Hector, handcuffed to a pipe in the kitchen, and said, "Yeah, I see that."

CHAPTER FORTY-EIGHT

The hotel plaza suites is a towering glass and steel horseshoe on Paseo de la Reforma. The monument to Cristobal Colón commands an island of green in the middle of the busy street. One tarnished bronze finger points to the heavens while traffic hums past. At night, the hotel glitters like a jewel in the heart of the city.

Noble arrived just after four. Layers of smog turned the sun into a shimmering red disk overhead. Exhaust stung his eyes and sweat soaked through his shirt. He spent the next hour watching foot traffic on the surrounding blocks. If Blythe had security, they were staying out of sight. Noble was betting the Brit kept his illicit liaisons hush-hush. Some sins earn the disapproval of even hardened criminals.

He entered the lobby at 5:15 and headed for a bank of elevators. Blythe had reserved 1402, his regular suite, according to Hector. The Englishman had a routine which he followed to the letter. He would arrive at five-thirty and the boy would be delivered at six. A "cleaner" would come by around midnight to dispose of the mess and sanitize the room.

Noble rode the elevator up to twelve and walked the floor. Modern hotels secure their rooms with cardkey readers, programed with a corresponding binary code embedded in the magnetic strip. Each card opens a single door. Keycards add to a guest's feeling of safety. However, cleaning crews can access any room in the hotel with a universal card. And because hotel management is notoriously severe when it comes to the cleaning staff, most room maids clip their keycard to their trolley for fear of accidentally locking it in a room.

Noble walked the twelfth floor, returned to the elevator and rode to thirteen where he found what he was looking for; a maid's trolley parked in front of a door near the end of the hall. A vacuum cleaner droned inside the room. The door was propped open with a rubber wedge. Noble glanced inside. The maid had her back to him, her attention was on the rug. She had a pair of headphones in, mouthing lyrics while she worked.

Her keycard was attached to the rolling cart by a retractable wire. While she ran the vacuum over the rug, Noble pried loose the plastic spindle. It had been glued down and came off with a small ripping noise. He glanced inside the room. The maid was still focused on the rug. He pocketed the card and returned to the elevator. For hotel staff, the only thing more terrifying than losing a universal card is having to report the loss to management. Noble was banking on that fact to give him the time he needed.

Down the hall, the vacuum cut off. The maid wrestled the big Black and Decker onto her cart, still unaware that her card was missing. She would figure it out when she got to the next room.

The elevator dinged. The doors rolled open. Noble stepped inside and thumbed the button for fourteen.

He stopped outside room 1402 and knocked, making sure Blythe hadn't gotten there first. When no one answered, Noble let himself in. The room had a deep piled rug and modern art hanging on the wall. The bed was big enough to have its own zip code. Cars looked like toys from this high up.

Noble settled into a plush armchair in the corner and waited. It's a skill most people never learn. They get antsy. They get impatient. They fidget. They need something to occupy their mind so they start tapping, or check their phone. Maybe they decide to watch TV. Noble sat in the dark without moving a muscle. The hands on his TAG Heuer revolved slowly on their axis.

It was 5:28 p.m. when he heard the sound of a plastic card pushed into the electronic reader. There was an audible click and the door swung open. Blythe didn't look like an ex-con. He looked like a history professor, with a paunch and thinning hair. He was dressed in slacks and a button-down. Reading glasses rode low on his nose.

Noble had Hunt's Kimber resting on his thigh. Blythe moved deeper into the room and flicked a light switch. The overheads stabbed Noble's eyes, forcing him to squint.

Blythe, his hand still on the switch, froze like a wild animal that had just blundered across the path of a larger predator. His mouth opened. His eyes got big behind the gold-rimmed spectacles. "Who are you?"

"What's the matter, Blythe? Too big for you?" Noble aimed the gun at Blythe's belly.

"What's this about then?" Blythe stammered. "Who are you?"

"You ought to know. Your boss has been looking all over town for me."

The last of the color drained from Blythe's pale face. "Jacob Noble."

Noble waved the gun at the bed. "Sit."

Blythe reached for the corner and lowered himself gently onto the mattress. "Do you mind if I smoke?"

"Actually, I do," Noble said. "Who's the traitor?"

"I don't follow," Blythe said.

"Machado bought or blackmailed someone in the CIA," Noble said. "You're his money man. Who is it?"

Blythe shook his head. "It's not at all what you think."

Noble thumbed back the hammer.

Blythe held up a hand. "Wait. What I mean is, it's not someone in the CIA."

"Keep talking, Blythe."

"I'm not sure you'll believe me."

"You better hope I do."

"Her name is Helen Rhodes," Blythe said.

"The Secretary of State?" Noble said. "You're telling me a presidential candidate is passing secrets to the cartel?"

Blythe nodded.

"You're right," Noble said. "I don't believe you."

"It's the truth," Blythe insisted. "Machado has been funding her political campaigns for decades. He keeps her war chest well-stocked and she makes sure he has nothing to fear from American law enforcement. It is a rather tidy arrangement, you'll admit."

Noble sat in stunned silence.

"Funny old world we live in, isn't it?" Blythe said like a man commenting on the weather. "Your man was sold out by the very people he worked for."

"Hilarious," Noble said in perfect deadpan. "Tell me about the security around Machado."

Blythe tittered and shook his head. "He has his own private army. You'll never even get close. Besides, there's a hit squad hunting you as we speak. The leader is an ex-cop. He's got connections inside the department. I'm surprised you survived this long."

"You're talking about Santiago?"

"Machado's top lieutenant," Blythe said. He pronounced lieutenant *leftenant*. "He's the one that killed your mate."

"Where do I find him?"

"That would be like telling the pigeon where to find the cat."

"Let me worry about that."

Blythe shrugged. "He and his bully boys hang out at a bar called Paquita's. Machado runs the whole neighborhood. They'll know you're coming the moment you show your face in that part of town."

"I'm counting on it," Noble told him.

Blythe said, "What happens now, Mr. Noble?"

"Smoke your last cigarette, Mr. Blythe."

"It's like that, is it?"

"It's like that," Noble told him.

Blythe shook one out of a pack. It took him three tries to

get a flame. He took a drag, blew smoke at the ceiling and said, "It didn't start out this way, you know?"

"It never does."

Blythe talked while he smoked. He told Noble about his failed marriage and his first hesitant foray into homosexuality. It was like he needed to tell someone and Noble was the only person there. So Blythe talked and Noble listened. He explained his descent into pedophilia, his arrest, how he moved to Mexico and fell in with the likes of Machado. When he had smoked the cigarette down to the filter, he dropped the butt on the floor and ground it under his heel, leaving a small mess of black ash. "Are you going to shoot me?"

Noble shook his head. "Nice of you to choose a hotel with windows that open."

Blythe got up and took a deep breath. He seemed strangely resigned, as if he had been waiting for this day to come. He must have known when he took up with drug dealers that it would end badly. Blythe went to the window and turned the latch. Air rushed in. It was like someone turned the volume up on the traffic. He stared down at the pavement fourteen stories below. "They'll think I'm a suicide."

"Time's wasting, Blythe."

Blythe squeezed his eyes shut and stuck one leg out. It was a narrow window—probably to prevent people from jumping. Blythe had to grip the frame and force himself through. He got stuck halfway. "I—I really don't think I can—"

Noble stood and gave him a kick.

Blythe popped out the window like a cork. He fell face

first, his arms and legs pin-wheeling like he could run on air. A shriek ripped from his throat. Far below, there was a wet smack and the scream abruptly stopped.

Noble stepped away from the window, filled with a savage sense of justice. Blythe had been a monster. There was no telling how many lives he had ruined. He deserved to die. Forcing him to take a fourteen-story swan dive felt fitting. There was one less child-molesting creep in the world.

Noble let himself out and rode the elevator to the ground floor. A crowd had gathered. One limp hand could be seen through a forest of legs. Two hotel security guards rushed across the lobby. Noble strolled past humming *Sympathy for the Devil.*

CHAPTER FORTY-NINE

HUNT TROLLED THE SLUMS UNTIL HE FOUND SOMEONE willing to sell him a black-market piece. A ponderously fat man occupying a barstool in one of Mexico City's many dives asked for double the price of a new weapon in the States. He knew Hunt had money and he was desperate. With no other options, Hunt forked over seven hundred dollars American.

"This going to blow up in my hand the first time I use it?" Hunt asked.

"It would make you prettier," the fat man said. That got a good laugh from the other patrons.

Hunt tucked the weapon into his waistband and stepped outside into heat so intense it almost buckled his knees. He flagged down a taxi. Sliding into the back seat felt like climbing into a frying pan. Fake leather burned the backs of his bare arms. As the driver nosed out into traffic, Hunt rapped on the partition. "Driver, can you turn on the air?"

The driver waved a hand. "Air broke."

"Perfect." Hunt leaned forward, doing his best not to let his bare skin contact the seat.

They passed a high-rise hotel with a pair of ambulances out front, lights flashing. A police car screamed past, headed to the hotel. Hunt craned around in the seat, wondering what had happened.

At the embassy, Hunt tossed money over the seats and launched himself out of the sweatbox.

His phone vibrated as he hauled open the heavy glass door. A wave of cold air washed over him, drying the sweat on his face and leaving his shirt clammy. He waited until he was on the elevator to check his messages. It was a street address, sent from an unknown number. Hunt frowned. The elevator dinged. He went down the hall to the cramped office.

"How did it go?" Ezra wanted to know.

"Fine. No problems." Hunt said. "Gwen, I need you to run a check on an address."

He read off the street number and she plugged it into the computer.

"It's an apartment in a section of the city described as 'artsy.' No red flags. No connection to any past or ongoing operations. What's up?"

"I'm not sure," Hunt admitted.

He found the location on a map, circled it, and added a question mark.

The text hadn't come from Foster; the DDI wouldn't bother hiding behind an unlisted number. And it hadn't come from Burke, who didn't want Hunt taking down his prized pupil. It might be from Sam. Maybe she dug up something sensitive and needed to pass it along without exposing herself?

"Any hits on Noble or his whereabouts?" Hunt asked.

Ezra and Gwen shook their heads in unison.

Hunt checked the action on the secondhand pistol. The text could just as easily have come from Noble. The crazy bastard might be flipping the script, trying to lure Hunt into an ambush. He said, "I've got to check something out."

"Alone?" Gwen asked.

"You two weren't much help on the last one."

Zona Rosa made Hunt's skin crawl. The district looked like a live performance of Rocky Horror Picture Show. He found the address. The front door had been broken down and then propped up against the jamb. Hunt pulled the 9mm Makarov and threw the door aside. Someone had scrawled a note and stuck it to a computer in the corner. It read; CHILD PROSTITUTION RING. In the kitchen, Hunt found a man handcuffed to the radiator with a ball gag in his mouth. Another note had been taped to the man's forehead. This one read; MIDDLEMAN.

The pimp pulled at the handcuffs and moaned through the ball gag. He stank of sour sweat and urine. His eyes rolled in their sockets.

Hunt checked the rest of the apartment, then pulled out the gag and wiped his fingers on his slacks. "Just when I was starting to think I had seen everything."

Hector couldn't get it out fast enough. Sweat rolled

down his face in little torrents while he babbled. He told Hunt about the break-in and the meeting with Blythe.

Hunt leaned against the stove, crossed his arms over his chest, and tucked the Soviet Makarov under his arm. "So Noble went after Machado's accountant?" he said, mostly to himself.

Hector pulled on the cuffs. "The key is in my dresser drawer, next to my wallet."

"Why would he do that?" Hunt wondered aloud.

"How should I know?" He tugged at the cuffs, rattling the chain against the radiator pipe. "I told you everything. *Please* un-cuff me."

Hunt stuffed the ball-gag back in Hector's mouth, took out his cell and dialed Gwen.

She answered on the first ring.

He said, "Find out who's in charge of Mexico branch. I busted the middle man in a child prostitution ring. I've got his computer here. If we move fast, we can take down the whole network and maybe get the two of you back in Foster's good graces."

CHAPTER FIFTY

Paquita's WAS A RUNDOWN BAR IN A RUNDOWN section of the city. The buildings were layered in Graffiti and bars covered the windows. The government had recently tried to revitalize the neighborhood with a series of projects designed to lure businesses to the area. There was a half-finished strip mall where abandoned construction equipment was turning slowly to rust. Looters had carried off anything of value. Despite the attempt at urbanization, the neighborhood remained a sad jumble of brick and asphalt that decent people avoided.

Noble, behind the wheel of the stolen sedan, circled the block. A knot of girls hung out on the corner near *Paquita's*, plying their trade. All of them were hustling except one. A curvy girl in a purple tank top and a miniskirt was watching cars go by.

Noble did one more lap around the block and told Alejandra, "Climb into the backseat and get down."

"Why?" she asked.

"You stand out," he said.

She scrambled over the seats, into the floorboard.

Noble held Hunt's Kimber next to his thigh. He pulled over at the curb, buzzed the window down, and waved the watcher over.

Her eyes narrowed. Her face was just short of beautiful but her body made up for it.

Noble gave her a big, toothy American grin. "*Hola, señorita.*"

She sauntered over and stuck her head in the passenger side window, giving him a generous view of her cleavage. "Want some company, handsome?"

Noble showed her the gun. "Get in."

If she was a pro, the sight of the gun would have sent her screaming. Instead she pressed her lips together, opened the door, and climbed in.

Noble pulled away from the curb. "Let's have it."

She spread her legs. The leather skirt rode up to reveal a nickel-plated .38 revolver strapped to the inside of one thigh.

Noble said, "Get that for me, would you, Alejandra?"

Alejandra sat up and the prostitute gave a start. She let Alejandra reach between her thighs and remove the revolver. The snub nose barrel had been drilled to dampen the sound. The chambers were loaded with sub-sonic ammunition—a poor man's silencer.

"Is Santiago and his crew at the bar?" Noble asked.

The prostitute crossed her arms over her breasts and looked out the window.

Noble said, "Shoot her in the knee."

Alejandra ratcheted back the hammer and pressed the barrel against the prostitute's kneecap.

"Yes," she said.

"How many?" Noble asked.

"Five, including Santiago."

"How were you going to make contact when you spotted me?"

She reached a hand into her tank top.

"Slowly," Noble said.

She gave him a baleful look and brought out a cellphone.

Noble thrust his chin at the open window.

She tossed it.

He parked on a deserted side street away from the spill of the street lamps. "Get out."

"What are you going to do with me?" she asked.

"Less than you had planned for me." Noble popped the trunk and followed her around to the back of the car. "Inside."

She threw one leg over the lip of the trunk. "Machado is going to cut your heart out, *bastardo*!"

"I haven't got one." Noble tore off the emergency release tab, tossed it over his shoulder and slammed the trunk on the cartel assassin.

"Are you sure she can't get out?" Alejandra asked as they climbed back in the car.

"No," Noble admitted.

"Where are we going now?"

"Shopping."

He used his phone to bring up a list of hardware stores

and found one open until nine p.m. That gave him an hour. He told Alejandra, "This could get ugly."

She pointed to her face. "I'm already ugly."

"Fair enough."

CHAPTER FIFTY-ONE

Santiago held the phone two inches from his ear. Machado's screams distorted the speaker. The only thing coming out was static. Santiago didn't need the particulars. Blythe was splattered all over the sidewalk in front of a hotel and Machado was on the warpath. Santiago grunted occasionally to let Machado know he was still listening. The ceiling fans rocked on their mounts, stirring up the heat, making his blood sluggish and his thoughts slow. The line went dead and Santiago dropped the phone on the tabletop. He looked around at his crew and said, "Blythe is dead."

Esteban stopped peeling the label off an empty beer bottle and whistled.

Jorge asked, "How?"

"Someone threw him out a window," Santiago said.

"The gringo?" Esteban wanted to know.

"Who else," Santiago said.

"What are we going to do?" Lorenzo wanted to know.

Santiago rubbed the back of his neck. "If we don't put

that gringo in a body bag soon, our heads are going to be on the chopping block."

They exchanged tense looks.

The door opened and El Lobo entered. A bib of sweat had soaked through his gray shirt. He saw their expressions and asked, "What happened?"

Santiago shook a cigarette from a pack, stuck it between his lips and flicked his lighter. "The *Americano* killed the accountant."

El Lobo cursed. "Does Machado know?"

Santiago exhaled. "How do you think we found out?"

Jorge thrust his chin at El Lobo. "What are you doing to find him?"

The rest of the crew turned to the Wolf.

El Lobo spread his hands. "He's a ghost. Santiago, I'm telling you, no one has seen this gringo anywhere."

"Blythe saw him," Santiago said.

El Lobo went behind the bar and poured himself a drink. "Every cop and crook in Mexico is looking for this guy. What can I do?"

"You never failed before," Santiago pointed out.

El Lobo drank the head of foam off his beer. "You know what I think? I think Machado is losing his hold. First he let a *Norteamericano* spy into the organization and now his accountant is dead. Maybe it's time for new leadership?"

Santiago pulled his Glock from his waistband.

"You going to shoot me?" El Lobo asked. "Go ahead. But you know it's true, *amigo*. Machado has lost a step."

The door opened and Lucita limped in looking like she had just crawled out of bed. Her hair was a mess and her clothes were rumpled. One shoe had lost a heel.

Esteban laughed. "He must have been one horny customer. You need an ice pack?"

She flipped him the bird and said, "The crazy *gringo* kidnapped me and stuffed me in a trunk."

Santiago took his feet off the table. "What? When was this?"

"An hour ago," she told him. "Right out front. He drove up and waved me over to his car, then forced me into the trunk at gun point."

The rest of the crew was already checking their weapons.

"How did you get away?" Santiago asked.

"He drove somewhere, stopped for forty minutes, and then he let me out six blocks away. He wants you to know he's at the construction site half a mile north, across from the abandoned shopping mall. The Domingo woman is with him."

Jorge said, "It's a trap."

"Of course it's a trap," Santiago said.

"What are we going to do?" said Lorenzo.

"What we failed to do the first time." Santiago scraped his chair back and stood up. "Break out the hardware."

Esteban reached under the bar top, brought out an AK-47, and tossed it to Santiago.

CHAPTER FIFTY-TWO

FIFTEEN MINUTES LATER, SANTIAGO AND HIS CREW stood on the street in front of the abandoned construction site, peering through chain link at a darkened warzone of half-finished storefronts, discarded building materials and hard-packed earth crisscrossed by bulldozer tracks. Cones of yellow light from street lamps made the shadows deeper and distance hard to judge. Santiago scanned the dark landscape for movement. At his back was an apartment building. The residents, sensing trouble, had drawn the curtains and turned out the lights.

Jorge shifted his weight from foot to foot. Sweat gathered on the tip of his long nose and fell in heavy drops. "I don't like it," he said. "We should call Machado. Get a dozen more guys out here."

"We aren't calling anybody." Santiago turned his head and spit. "The gringo killed Ramone and made us look like fools."

"He's right," said Esteban. "Let's go get this guy."

Lorenzo nodded in agreement. "There are five of us and two of them."

"Don't forget the girl is blind in one eye," Santiago pointed out. "She can barely walk."

He hauled open the gate with a rattle of chain link. The noise underscored the pressing silence. Without speaking, Jorge and Lorenzo took the east side. Santiago, along with Esteban and El Lobo, took the west. The plan was to squeeze the *Americano* in the middle, catch him in a cross fire.

Santiago and his team moved in a crouch toward a block of low concrete structures. Jorge and Lorenzo sprinted for a stack of abandoned lumber next to a rusting concrete mixer. They had covered half the distance when a loud pop shattered the silence. Jorge lay sprawled in the dirt, writhing in pain. Lorenzo clutched a bloody arm, but was still on his feet.

The rest of the crew opened fire on the empty storefronts. They sprayed full auto bursts through open doorways and dark window cavities. Bullets chewed through cinder block walls, kicking up tiny dust storms. Santiago waved his hand and yelled. "Hold your fire!"

It took several attempts, but he finally got the message across. Silence crowded in around them as the last echo of gunfire drifted across the rooftops. Brass shell casings winked in the dirt. Esteban swapped mags. Smoke drifted from the barrel of his rifle.

Santiago, his nerves on high alert, waited and watched. No one was shooting at them. The explosion had been a simple IED designed to thin their ranks. It worked. Jorge pressed both hands over a chest wound oozing blood. His eyes bulged from their sockets. He wasn't getting up.

Santiago looked at Lorenzo. "You okay?"

Dark red blood had soaked his forearm from the elbow down. He switched his rifle to his left hand and nodded. "I can fight."

El Lobo grabbed Santiago's shoulder. "The American had an hour head start. He could've rigged dozens of booby traps."

Esteban said, "He's right. We don't even know if he is really here. He might be leading us on a wild chase. Let's get out of here, Santiago."

There was no point in wading through a minefield. The gringo had killed one and wounded another without firing a single shot. Santiago cursed and motioned for a retreat.

Gunfire erupted from the row of apartment houses behind them. Bullets burned through the air, kicking up divots in the turf. A slug hammered Esteban's shoulder. He fired blindly at the apartment houses. Windows blew out of their frames. People screamed.

Santiago sprinted through the construction site for the safety of the half-finished storefronts, where at least he could find cover. The others followed. They hadn't gone twenty feet when another loud pop assaulted Santiago's eardrums. Shrapnel buzzed overhead. He didn't stop. He forced his legs to move faster. Air burst from his lungs in panicked gasps.

A third explosion lifted Esteban off his feet. He went down flat on his back.

Santiago sprinted through two more explosions with bullets chasing him the whole way.

There was an open doorway directly ahead and Santiago knew it would be rigged. He slowed down, letting Lorenzo overtake him. They had been friends a long time, him and Lorenzo, but now it was every man for himself. Lorenzo dashed through the open door. An earsplitting bang flung him aside like a rag doll. He landed in a jumble, like a broken marionette.

Only Santiago and El Lobo remained. They leapt through the opening into the dark interior of the half-finished building. The shooting stopped. El Lobo was cursing and dancing a jig, holding onto his butt. Blood stained the seat of his pants. His face pinched. He limped around in a circle until the pain subsided. When he had mastered himself, he pointed at Santiago's forearm. "You got clipped."

Santiago looked down. He had a bloody hole no bigger than a BB in his forearm and seeing it made the pain set in. "*Bastardo*!"

El Lobo put his back to the wall. His face was pale. "We have to get out of here, amigo."

Santiago spoke through clenched teeth. "I'm not leaving until I kill the American."

"There's only two of us," El Lobo said. "We're both wounded, and the police will be here any minute."

Santiago shrieked in rage and frustration. El Lobo was right. The American had dismantled his entire crew with a few fireworks. This fight was over. He nodded. "Okay, let's get out of here before the police show up. See if you can find a back exit. I'll cover you."

El Lobo moved deeper into the darkened retail space. He was limping from the shrapnel in his butt. Santiago stayed several meters back on the pretense of guarding their rear flank. They passed a frightened hobo, cowering in a corner, surrounded by the detritus of homeless life. El Lobo located a back door and threw it open. A bright flash slammed him into the doorframe with bone crushing force.

"Sorry, old friend," Santiago muttered and stepped over El Lobo's broken body. He sprinted across seven meters of open ground, then scaled the chain link and disappeared into the neighborhood.

CHAPTER FIFTY-THREE

Noble had purchased ¾ inch plumber's pipe, caps, ball bearings, fishing wire and household chemicals from the hardware store. Building a pipe bomb is relatively easy; rigging trip wires in the dark took more time.

When they finished, Alejandra had located an empty apartment in the building across the street. Noble bought a filthy overcoat and a moth-eaten cap from a homeless man living in the derelict construction site before advising him to clear out. Then he laid down under a moldy tarpaulin and watched as Alejandra herded the cartel enforcers through the deadly hail of shrapnel. Only two of the assassins had survived, Santiago and the long-haired guy in snakeskin boots that Alejandra called the Wolf.

They walked right past him in their hurry to escape. It took all his willpower not to gun them down, but he waited, betting his last little surprise would cripple both. No such luck. Santiago let the Wolf go first.

Noble heard the earsplitting pop of the pipe bomb and threw off the musty overcoat. By the time he reached the back door, Santiago was gone. The Wolf lay writhing in pain, clutching a pair of bloody legs.

Noble had used an old cinderblock to direct the blast at knee height. The Wolf's lower legs were mangled, but he would live. He held up one blood-soaked hand as Noble approached. "Wait! I didn't off Diaz."

Noble hunkered next to him. "Who did?"

"He offed himself," he said through clenched teeth. "We had him cornered in a hangar and he shot himself. I swear on my mother's grave."

Noble took the key out of his pocket. "What's this go to?"

The wolf looked at it with genuine confusion, shook his head. "Don't know."

"Let's talk about Machado," Noble said. "How do I get close to him?"

"You don't," he said. "His house is a fortress."

"He has to leave sometime," Noble said.

"He'll kill me if I talk."

Noble stood up and stomped the Wolf's injured knees.

His eyes bulged and his mouth stretched wide in a scream. It took a second for the sound to catch up. When he finished, he took a deep breath and managed to say, "He scheduled a meeting."

"Now we're getting somewhere," Noble said and motioned for the Wolf to continue.

He rattled off an address. "Tomorrow night. Top floor. Penthouse. All the cartel heads will be there."

"What's the security situation like?"

"The rank and file will be in the parking garage," he

said. “Only the cartel heads and their bodyguards are allowed in the penthouse.”

Noble pressed his gun to the Wolf’s forehead. “You sure that’s everything you know?”

“I’m just a foot soldier,” he said. “They tell me when and where.”

Sirens screamed in the distance. Noble took the gun out of the Wolf’s face and stood.

“Wait,” the Wolf gasped. “Don’t leave me here.”

“Police are on their way,” he said. “They’ll get you to a hospital.”

“Exactly,” He said. “Machado finds out I talked, I’m as good as dead. Please, don’t leave me here.”

CHAPTER FIFTY-FOUR

Sam capped off an extra long workout by pummeling a heavy bag until she split the knuckles on both hands. Blood soaked through her wraps. A meathead on the squat rack had been trying to catch her eye for an hour. She ignored him. Even a polite smile would bring him over and then she'd never be rid of him. She tucked a loose strand of hair behind her ear, went to the locker room for her gym bag and left without bothering to shower. She could do that at home.

The sun had gone down, but hadn't taken with it any of the heat gripping the Foggy Bottom. Sam tossed her gym bag into the passenger seat of a gray Volkswagen. Her hands shook so badly it took two tries to slot the key in the ignition. She finally managed and the engine hummed to life. She cranked the air up and aimed the vents at her chest.

There was a knock on the window.

Sam jerked and closed her mouth on a scream. One hand darted into her gym bag, for her Smith & Wesson

M&P. She recognized the meathead from the squat rack. He gave her a smug grin.

She buzzed the window down a crack and said, "Not interested."

He laughed at that, like she had told a joke. "I saw you checking me out back there."

"You got that backwards, champ."

"Some friends of mine are throwing a party. You like to party, don't cha?"

"I said I'm not interested."

"Don't be like that." He frowned. "You don't even know me."

"I know your type," Sam said and buzzed the window up.

"Damned tease."

Sam took her phone out of her gym bag. She wanted to pull the gun, but that might get the cops involved and she didn't need any more trouble. The sight of the phone was enough to send him packing. He called her a slut and stalked back the gym on legs the size of tree trunks.

She watched him go and then noticed she had a text. It read, *Wizard would like a word.*

Her stomach did a nauseating summersault.

Getting summoned to a late night meeting with the DDO was not good. Sam put the Volkswagen in gear and backed out. Her shower would have to wait. She tried Burke's cell and got no answer. By the time she slotted the VW into a spot in the parking garage beneath Langley, her knees had turned to Silly Putty. Sam walked to the elevators in yoga pants and a sweaty tank top, blood caked on her knuckles.

After Hong Kong, joining the Company had seemed like the next logical step. She had always been a fan of thrillers. She devoured mysteries by the armload, reading as many as fifty books a year. Meeting Jake and helping him rescue Bati had given her a taste of the real thing. Suddenly, working a 9 to 5 job was impossible. She had spent her time in the hospital, recovering from a gunshot wound, wondering how she would ever return to a normal life. She had looked into the police, the military, even the FBI. It wasn't exactly what Jake did, but it was close and she would get to solve crime. She was all set to submit her application to Quantico when Burke had paid her a visit. Now, less than a year later, she was getting called onto the Deputy Director's carpet.

Foster was waiting in front of the elevators, checking his watch. His bald pate gleamed under the fluorescents. He spoke in clipped nasal tones. "Good of you to finally join us, Ms. Gunn."

"I was at the gym, sir. I got here as quick as I could."

He made a small disapproving note, like chalk on a blackboard, and said, "This way, Ms. Gunn."

Sam followed him through the clandestine operations wing. It felt like someone else was in control of her body. Her legs moved on their own. She chanced a peek inside Burke's office on her way past, but the lights were out.

Foster stopped in front of Conference Room C, opened the door, and motioned her inside. A nasty grin turned up one corner of his mouth. It was a vindictive little smile that turned Sam's blood to ice.

C was one of the nondescript interior offices without windows. It was swept for listening devices twice a day.

Cigarette smoke had turned the walls a sickly yellow and coffee rings stained the tabletop. Burke was slumped in one of the chairs. He looked tired. Dark circles ringed his eyes and Sam thought, or maybe just imagined, the streaks of gray at his temples were more pronounced.

The Director of Operations sat at the far end of the room. He looked like an anemic vulture hunched over the table. A cigarette dangled from a mouth that was a hard gash in his weathered face. It was impossible to tell how old he was; decades of smoking had turned his skin into a roadmap of deep-set wrinkles, but he had been working for the Company since the Cold War. He was dressed in a somber gray pinstripe and a skinny black tie that had gone out of style when Elvis was at the top of the charts. His thinning hair was combed straight back and a pair of sharp blue eyes peered out from beneath a pair of bushy eyebrows.

"I'm sorry I'm late, sir," Sam started.

He waved away her apology. His voice sounded like a knife on a sharpening stone. "Have a seat, Ms. Gunn."

Sam took the chair across from Burke and caught his eye, hoping for support. All she got was a simple nod of recognition, nothing more.

Foster seated himself to the right of the Deputy Director Intelligence, still wearing his peevish little grin. Two others were present; the Deputy Director's secretary and a middle-aged man with dark hair and a twitchy eye, named Coughlin. He was a long-time Company man whose unfortunate facial tick excluded him from field work. Sam had seen him around but never been officially introduced.

Wizard brought out a bottle of pills and shook a pair into his palm. "I take these twice a day for my blood pressure," he rasped. "The sawbones says my ticker is running on borrowed time."

His secretary poured a glass of water from a pitcher.

Wizard tossed the pills in his mouth, swallowed, ignored the water, and chased the medication with a drag from his cigarette. Smoke shot from his nostrils. "Did we interrupt a workout, Ms. Gunn?"

"Yes, sir," Sam said. "I mean... no, sir. I was just finishing up, sir."

Wizard chuckled and went into a coughing fit. His secretary tried to make him drink water. He shook his head and wiped a tear from one eye. A file lay open on the table in front of him. He paged through the contents. "You went to Yale."

Sam wasn't sure if it was a question or a statement. "That's correct, sir."

"I was a Yale man" he said. "Did you pledge?"

"Kappa Kappa Gamma, sir."

Foster frowned, unhappy with the direction the conversation had taken. The vein in his forehead was in danger of bursting.

"I was Alpha Phi Alpha," Wizard said. "That was long before you got there. Before schools turned into indoctrination centers. Used to be, universities encouraged kids to think for themselves. Now they're socialist echo chambers."

"If it's any consolation, sir, I left with my faith in the free market system firmly intact."

Every eye in the room turned to Sam. She wanted to shrink down into her seat and disappear. Foster actually snickered.

Wizard fixed her with those piercing blue eyes. The

trace of a smile tugged at the corner of his mouth. He nodded. "Good to know, Ms. Gunn."

Foster's nostrils flared. He looked like he had just swallowed a nasty bug.

Burke tried and failed to hide a grin.

Wizard continued flipping through her file. His bushy brows twitched as he read. "You graduated the Farm three months ago?"

"Yes, sir."

He closed the file, leaned back, and said, "Tell me about your current operation, Ms. Gunn."

From the corner of her eye, Burke gave a barely perceptible nod. She desperately wished she had showered, or at least taken a comb to her hair. She felt ridiculous and out of place in her workout clothes. She took a breath and let it out. "Sir, I've been posing as a Secret Service Agent assigned to Secretary of State Helen Rhodes."

CHAPTER FIFTY-FIVE

Cafebrería El Pendulo is a two-story bookstore and café with the kind of lighting you would expect in a museum. Ivy crawled along the second floor banisters and a tree grew up right in the middle of the space. The strong aroma of rich coffee filled the air. Noble preferred dimly lit bookshops full of musty old tomes, but this one had a certain charm to it. They had scoped it out ahead of time. It was less than a mile from the construction site. He could still hear the wail of sirens. Alejandra was on a sofa in the History section. Noble collapsed next to her. The adrenaline was wearing off and his hands were starting to shake.

"You did good," he said.

"Did we get them all?" she asked.

"Santiago got away." He saw the disappointment in her eyes. "We just dealt a serious blow to Machado's operation. We took out his top hitters and got away clean. He lost his money man and his best soldiers all in one day. He's going to be feeling the pressure."

A waitress appeared. Noble ordered two cups of coffee.

"Is it safe to be seen in public?" Alejandra asked. She had her hood up to hide her face.

"I doubt Machado has anyone watching the local bookshop," he said.

The waitress returned with two artsy mugs of steaming coffee. Noble drained half of his in one long swallow. Hot liquid burned down his throat into his belly. He slouched deeper into the seat, sighed, and ran a hand over his eyes.

Alejandra took up her coffee in both hands and blew off the steam. She looked small and pathetic, swaddled in clothing three sizes too big with yellowing bandages on her face. A few patrons threw curious glances in their direction. She said, "What's our next move?"

He told her about his brief conversation with the Wolf.

She nodded as he spoke. "The cartels own the hotel. The penthouse is neutral ground, a place where they meet to discuss business."

"You've been there?"

"Once, during one of their meetings," she told him. "It's heavily guarded but less difficult to infiltrate than Machado's compound."

"Have you got the general layout?" he asked.

She inclined her head. "I could sketch a map. What are you thinking?"

A swarthy man with beady eyes watched them from the Philosophy section. When he took out a cellphone, Noble said, "I think we need to find some place else to be."

CHAPTER FIFTY-SIX

Wizard leaned back in his chair, took a drag, and blew smoke at the ceiling. His eyes bore into Sam. She held his gaze.

"I wasn't aware of any such operation," he said.

Foster cleared his throat. "That's because it was completely off the books. It was laid in and orchestrated by Burke to further his own personal political agenda. He used a recent graduate of the Farm in an unsanctioned operation designed to sabotage a presidential election. If that wasn't bad enough, now he's got his protégé, Jake Noble, running around Mexico waging a vigilante war against the cartels."

"I have nothing to do with Jake Noble's presence in Mexico," Burke said.

"You met with him in Saint Petersburg." Foster leaned forward like he was about to climb over the table at Burke.

"I went to see him." Burke shrugged. "So what? He's a friend. It doesn't mean I divulged Company intel."

Foster drummed the table top with a boney finger. "Lie

all you want about Noble, you shanghaied a rookie officer into an unauthorized operation."

Coughlin spoke up. "It's true, sir. I checked with the head of the Secret Service. They have Ms. Gunn listed as Vanessa Klein. She's been assigned to the Secretary of State's detail for the last several weeks. The whole thing was arranged by an agent named Thomson, a confederate of Mr. Burke's inside the Secret Service. They served together in the Army."

Sam cut in, "I was not *shanghaied*, Director."

Foster held up a hand. "Please, Ms. Gunn. You aren't to blame. Burke has a long history of rule breaking. He used you for his own ends. Answer our questions honestly and you might make it out of this with your job intact."

Sam turned her attention to the Director of Operations. "Sir, Helen Rhodes passed top secret information to enemies of the United States and used the Secret Service to plant false evidence against FBI Director Standish."

Foster's eyes bulged in their sockets. "Ms. Gunn, I am ordering you to stop talking!"

Burke raised his voice. "What's the matter, Foster? Afraid she'll kick over a rock and a few of your secrets will slither out?"

"You're the only one trying to bury secrets," Foster fired back. "Is that why you sent Noble to Mexico? Trying to keep your skeletons in the closet?"

Coughlin joined the fray. "We aren't here to discuss Jacob Noble's presence in Mexico City. There's no evidence that Burke fed him intel on Company operations in Central America."

"We are here to discuss a CIA officer laying in operations without authorization," Foster said.

Wizard raised a hand and the room fell silent. It was like hitting mute on the television remote. He stabbed out his cigarette and said, "Clark, step into the hall and give yourself a few minutes to calm down."

Foster sat there a moment, stunned, like the DDO had just slapped him across the face. He came back to himself, stood up, and walked out.

When the door had shut behind him, Wizard turned to Burke. "Want to tell me what's going on?"

Burke's eyes danced between the Wizard's secretary and Coughlin.

"Playing this a little close to the vest, aren't you?" The Director asked.

Burke inclined his head.

"Okay," Wizard said. "I'll play along. Everyone clear out."

Sam rose along with the rest.

"Not you, Ms. Gunn," Wizard said. He pointed at her chair.

She sat back down while the others filed out of the conference room. The door clomped shut with a heavy sound, like the lid closing on a casket. Sam was alone with Burke and the DDO.

Wizard looked at Burke. "What's this all about, Matt?"

"A mole hunt." Burke propped his elbows on the table and laced his fingers together. He told the Director of Operations everything he had told Sam. He finished by saying, "Rhodes has been trading top secret information to foreign powers in order to fill her own personal piggy bank."

Wizard lit another cigarette. "Can you prove any of this?"

"I don't have physical evidence."

Wizard shook his head. "We don't deal in politics, Matt. You know that. Our job is to collect intelligence, not dictate policy."

"If I'm right," Burke said, "and she becomes the president, our enemies will be the ones *dictating* policy. This country's intelligence apparatus will be crippled. Every agent we have in the field will be at risk. You want to work for a president who owes favors to drug traffickers and terrorist regimes?"

"If you are wrong, you'll go to jail," Wizard said. "You trot this out into the light and Rhodes will muddy the waters until the voting public can't tell the truth from all the *boolsheet*. She'll dig up your past and turn this whole thing on its head. You'll be the one on trial."

Burke spread his hands. "I have to do something, Al. She's guilty as hell and people died because of it. I can't sit back and watch her sell out America to the highest bidder." After a minute, he added, "Neither can you."

Wizard leaned back and watched smoke rise in lazy curlicues. "You're a good officer, Matt, and I trust your instincts. I've covered for you a lot over the years. Even put myself out on a limb a few times. But I'm not sure I can protect you this time. If this goes sideways, your career is over. You really want to risk your pension?"

Burke's large black hands clenched. He took a deep breath, held it, let it out slow. "She willfully exposed a CIA officer to the head of a Mexican drug cartel. I have to draw the line somewhere."

Wizard crushed out his cigarette. "Let me hear you say it."

Burke said, "I stand by my actions, sir, and I'm prepared to face the consequences."

Wizard turned his eyes on Sam. "Ms. Gunn, you made high marks all the way through training and you have the makings of a first-rate intelligence officer, so I'm going to give you a choice."

Her stomach did a flip.

He jerked his head at the door. "You can stand up right now and walk out of here. I'll personally clear you of any wrongdoing in this matter. You were a rookie following orders from a senior officer. No harm, no foul. Or, you can stay and face the fallout as a willing participant."

Burke said, "Get outta here, Sam. No need for you to go down with me."

Here was a chance to make a clean break of this mess. Everything in her said *get up and run—don't walk—to the door*. It was the smart thing to do. But she'd never have a single night of guilt-free sleep for the rest of her life. The Secretary of State was selling out spies to further her own agenda. Sam couldn't let that slide. She swallowed a knot in her throat. "Thank you, sir, but I'll stay."

He managed to look surprised without moving a single muscle in his face. His eyes just sort of twinkled. "Then you had better debrief me on your actions inside the Rhodes campaign."

Sam gave a full account, telling him everything, including how she had planted evidence against Standish.

He stopped her several times to ask for clarification on a certain point, and had her repeat parts. When she finished, he said, "That was quick thinking, putting the files on his wife's computer instead. I'll bet the investigators never even bothered to check her laptop."

"Thank you, sir," Sam said.

"One question," he said.

"Did Rhodes order you to plant evidence against Standish?"

"Sir?"

"Did Helen Rhodes personally tell you to plant the evidence on Standish's laptop, or did Guy Taggart?"

It was several seconds before Sam could muster words. "It was Taggart."

He smoothed one bushy white eyebrow with a nicotine-yellow fingertip. "See the problem that creates for us?"

Burke said, "Rhodes will claim Taggart was working on his own."

Wizard nodded.

Sam raked a hand through her hair. "What about my recordings?"

Burke shook his head. "Everything points to Taggart. We need ironclad evidence that Rhodes can't explain away. Torres had a paper trail, but he's missing."

"What about your man in Mexico?" Wizard asked. "Is he close to obtaining the missing files?"

"I'm not in contact with him," Burke said. "Foster sent Hunt to run interference."

Wizard leaned back in his seat. "I don't want to see a traitor sitting in the oval office any more than you, but without those files, we're dead in the water. If Noble manages to lay hands on actionable intel, something we could *accidentally* leak to the press, then we might be able to steer public opinion and avoid any direct involvement. At the very least, we can throw a public spotlight on Helen Rhodes' criminal activities. That should turn public opinion against her and strong-arm Standish into filing charges, making her ineligible for president."

"A lot could go wrong with that plan," Sam said.

The Wizard took his time lighting up another cigarette. "Until we have something concrete, there is nothing more to discuss. Ms. Gunn, please ask the others to rejoin us."

She went to the door, stuck her head out, and told them to come back. After they had taken their places, Wizard said, "The particulars of my discussion with Mr. Burke and Ms. Gunn will remain private for the time being. Before I can decide if there was any wrong doing on their part, I'll need to collect more information. As of right now, I'm placing both on unpaid administrative leave."

Ten minutes later, Sam was in the parking garage with Burke. Everything she had spent the last six months working toward was crashing down. Her mind was racing and getting nowhere fast. Sam bent over, put her hands on her knees and shook her head. "What are we going to do?"

Burke patted his pockets, found his keys and said, "I could use a drink."

A hysterical laugh jerked out of her throat. "A drink would be good."

CHAPTER FIFTY-SEVEN

NOBLE RAPPED AN OPEN PALM AGAINST THE BACK DOOR of the Santa Ana Mission.

"This is your plan?" Alejandra asked, looking around the trash-strewn alley. "We barely escaped the first time."

"They'll never expect us to come back." He pounded on the door some more and heard footsteps. The lock opened. Cordero peeked out. Both eyes were swollen purple slits and his nose was a fat red welt. He threw a quick glance over Noble's shoulder at the empty alleyway. When he spoke, it sounded like he had a mouth full of cotton. "I didn't expect to see either of you again."

"We're trying hard not to *be* seen," Noble told him.

Cordero opened the door wide and stepped back. "Then you'd better come in before someone sees you."

They gathered around a table in the kitchen, sipping a Spanish wine. Dinner was a loaf of stale bread and cheese. Cast iron skillets hung from a rack overhead. The air was hot and stuffy. The sharp stench of incense permeated everything, ruining Noble's appetite. He asked, "What happened to you?"

"Machado's men." Cordero prodded gently at his bruised cheek. "Paid me a visit two nights ago."

"Why didn't you ask for police protection?" Alejandra said. "They would have put a patrol car out front."

"Would it have made a difference?" Cordero asked. "Machado owns the police."

"Not all of them," Alejandra said.

"Did you tell them anything about me?" Noble said. "Or Diaz?"

Cordero shook his head. "Don't worry. I told them the girl came seeking aid and it was my Christian duty to help. They didn't believe me at first." He pointed to his swollen face. "But I stuck to my story."

"You're lucky they didn't kill you," Noble said around a mouthful of stale bread.

Cordero shrugged.

"I'm sorry about the sister," Noble said.

"Rosalita is with God now," Cordero said, as if that settled the matter.

"Sure," Noble said.

Cordero heard the doubt in his voice. "You don't believe?"

"I'm not sure what I believe," Noble admitted. He sipped his wine. "Someone—a friend—prayed for my mother once."

"And?" Cordero asked.

Noble hitched up a shoulder. "She had cancer. Now she's in remission. Hard to say if it was prayer or chemo. I guess I know where you come down on that issue."

"I will offer a prayer for her continued improvement." Cordero used a knife to cut a slice of bread. The act of chewing reopened cuts on his lips. He dabbed at the blood with a napkin.

"I was raised Catholic," Alejandra said. "But I haven't been to confession in years."

"It's not too late," Cordero told her.

One hand went to the bandages over her left eye in an unconscious gesture. "Tomorrow perhaps."

Cordero nodded. "Whenever you are ready."

She tore off a hunk of bread. She was getting her appetite back. After dinner she finished her wine and said, "I'm exhausted."

"Rest well," Cordero said.

She told them goodnight and went in search of a bed. Noble found himself thinking of Sam. The idea of her and Hunt together made him want to kick a hole in a wall. He should have told her how he felt. He might not get another chance. That brought him back around to Machado. He said, "Do you think God is still in the miracle business, Padre?"

"I don't think he ever left."

"I suppose you have to believe that," Noble said. "Sort of an occupational requirement."

"It certainly helps." Cordero cut off another slice of bread. "Are you going after Machado?"

"He killed my friend," Noble said by way of explanation.

"And you will make him pay for what he did?"

Noble nodded.

"Unless he kills you first."

"That's a possibility," Noble admitted.

"A very good possibility from where I sit."

"Thanks for being honest."

"Another occupational requirement."

Noble laughed. "I didn't know priests came with a sense of humor."

"I bought it on Amazon."

"Money well spent," Noble said. They sat in silence and the minutes ticked slowly past. His thoughts turned to death and the afterlife. Every soldier thinks about it sooner or later, even if they won't admit it. Finally, Noble said, "Want to hear my confession?"

Cordero motioned for him to continue.

"Don't we have to lock ourselves in those little cubbies?"

Cordero grinned. "Confessionals are a formality. God hears you just fine."

Noble nodded. "Machado had a British accountant on his payroll named Blythe. He was a pedophile that got his jollies rolling little boys. I encouraged him to step out a fourteen-story window."

"How did that make you feel?"

"You a priest or a psychiatrist?" Noble asked.

"Sometimes there is not much difference."

"I didn't feel the least bit bad about it," Noble said. "In fact, I felt pretty damned good about it, at first."

"And now?"

"Now I don't know," Noble admitted. "Tomorrow I'm going to kill Machado. Or he's going to kill me. The Bible says 'thou shalt not kill', but how can killing a monster like Machado, like Blythe, be a sin?"

Cordero put down his slice of bread and brushed

crumbs from his fingertips. "You bring up an interesting point. The Bible does not say 'thou shalt not kill.' A closer translation would be 'thou shalt not murder.'"

Noble questioned him with a glance.

"There are several different words in the ancient Hebrew which mean to take a life. To 'kill' is a broad term that covers everything from slaughtering a chicken for supper to soldiers on a battlefield. That word in Hebrew is *harag*. However, that is *not* the word used in the Ten Commandments. *Ratsakh* is the word used in the Old Testament. It means to murder someone in an act of criminal violence or out of selfish ambition. It doesn't apply to soldiers on a battlefield."

"I'm not exactly a soldier on a battlefield," Noble pointed out.

Cordero's brow pinched. "This *is* a war, *señor*. Ten thousand people die every year at the hands of the cartel. They are animals. Sometimes I think all the killing has driven them mad. Your friend, Diaz, he understood this."

Noble drained the rest of his wine. "Sounds like you want me to kill Machado."

Cordero clasped his hands together. His knuckles turned white. "If I was a man of your... skills..."

Noble grinned. "Go on."

"I would be tempted to take the law into my own hands." Cordero let out a shaking breath, like admitting it had required a physical effort and, now that it was out, a weight had been lifted.

"Glad to hear it," Noble said. "Because I'm going to need you to do some shopping for me tomorrow."

"Please don't ask me to purchase anything illegal," Cordero said.

"Just a few household supplies," Noble assured him.

CHAPTER FIFTY-EIGHT

The Smoke & Barrel was packed for a week night. Helen Rhodes was giving an interview to George Stephanopoulos on the television and college kids had crowded the bar to watch. They gulped over priced whiskey and assured each other Rhodes would fix the sexist, homophobic, bigoted cesspool that was America. To hear them talk, there was no way the insurgent could win. Wizard was right; the education system had brainwashed an entire generation.

Sam directed Burke's attention to an empty high-top. They beat a pair of hipsters to the table. "That could have gone worse," Burke said.

Sam pinched the bridge of her nose between thumb and forefinger. "I don't see how."

"Wizard didn't have to kick Foster out of the room." Burke sipped a slushy pink concoction from a curly straw. "He could have put us on the spot with a room full of witnesses, forced us to incriminate ourselves. Foster would have insisted on enhanced interrogations. Right now, you would be at a black site, strapped naked to a chair, spilling your guts."

"He could do that?" Sam asked.

Burke nodded. "As the Deputy Director of Intelligence, he has that jurisdiction."

An image flashed through Sam's mind of herself in a dark room, handcuffed to a hard-backed chair under the harsh glow of a hooded bulb while her interrogator, a shadowy figure, stalked restlessly back and forth like a jungle cat. A shiver tip-toed up her spine.

"All in all," Burke said. "We got lucky."

"Forgive me if I don't do backflips," Sam said.

"Don't look so glum," Burke said. "I've been on administrative leave before."

"I haven't even been with the Company a year, Matt. Do you know what my parents are going to say when they find out?" She stuck out her thumb and pinkie and spoke into an imaginary phone. "Hi Mom, hi Dad, remember when I told you I went to work for an international design firm in D.C.? I lied. I actually took a job with the CIA, got fired, and now I might be facing criminal charges."

Burke cringed and glanced around, but no one in the noisy bar was paying them any attention. "Relax, you won't get fired. Wizard likes you."

"Really? How could you tell?" she asked. "That guy is like a chain smoking vulture. I'm pretty sure the last time he cracked a smile, Calvin Coolidge was in office."

"Don't be too hard on him," Burke said. "He's been running counterintelligence operations since the Tet Offensive. He gave three marriages and a kidney to the job."

"A kidney?"

Burke nodded.

"And he still smokes?"

Burke shrugged. "If there is a no smoking sign on the pearly gates, Albert Dulles won't go in."

They finished their drinks and ordered more. Sam said, "Think Torres is still alive?"

Burke shook his head.

"And if Jake doesn't find the missing files?"

Burke drew a finger across his throat.

Sam groaned.

"Relax. If anyone can find those files, it's Jake."

"How can you be so sure?"

"That kid is like a dog with a bone."

"Does he even know what he's looking for?" Sam asked.

"He's got a key that Torres mailed shortly before he disappeared. I'm assuming it will lead Jake to the missing documents."

"How do you know all this?"

Burke grinned around his curly straw. "Been doing this a long time, babe."

On the television, Rhodes ended her speech by promising to "Move America Forward." The college kids cheered at the campaign slogan. Sam thrust her chin at the screen. "Can you believe this? She's the first female nominee in American history and the only one under investigation by the FBI."

Burke frowned. "If she wins, Wizard will be forced into retirement and she'll appoint Foster head of the CIA. You and I won't be able to get a job walking dogs."

"Great." Sam massaged her temples. She felt a

headache coming on. "Well, I'm going back to the Philippines. What's your plan?"

"I'll be exploring a career in alcoholism," Burke said and lifted his glass.

"Maybe this was a huge mistake," Sam said, more to herself than to Burke.

"Don't say that. You have the makings of a good agent. Maybe even a great one. I saw it right away. Wizard sees it too.

"Really?"

"Don't let it go to your head." He smiled, showing the gap between his teeth. "You're not as good as Jake."

"He's the reason I joined."

"He's the reason I recruited you."

She questioned him with a look.

Burke shrugged. "He had me check up on you during the unpleasantness in Manila. Spoke *very* highly of you."

Sam didn't know whether to be offended that Jake had vetted her or proud that he gave his stamp of approval. The two emotions battled for supremacy. Then she remembered that her career with the Company was over almost before it began.

"I had this whole fantasy worked out in my head," Sam told him. The wine helped loosen her tongue. "We would see each other in the office. He would be so surprised to learn that I had joined and made it through training. Then we would get teamed up on an operation..."

"Except Jake refused to come back to the reservation," Burke said.

"That messed up my plans a little."

"And then you met Hunt."

"Yeaaaah." Sam stretched the word out. She thought they had kept their romantic escapades quiet. They had been extra careful but it was surprisingly difficult to keep secrets in a job where keeping secrets *was* the job.

"Jake's a better fit," Burke said.

"You don't like Hunt?" It was more a statement than a question.

"Hunt is slippery as an eel. Jake is a straight shooter. What you see is what you get. If he gives you his word, he'll come through or die trying."

"Jake is..." Sam searched for the right words.

"Silent? Brooding? Hard to read?" Burke suggested.

"All of those things." Sam nodded. "But he is also Jake. If that makes sense. There is something about him that is incredibly primal."

"That's what makes him so good," Burke said.

"Hunt, on the other hand..."

"Will break your heart," Burke finished for her.

Sam admitted that with a nod. She had always known it; Burke just put it into words. She shook her head and shifted the focus of the conversation. "What about you? You going to be happy with Dana?"

"It was stupid. I never should have let it happen. But I'll probably end up at her place again tonight."

"We're quite a pair," Sam said.

Burke lifted his glass. "To the losers."

"The losers," Sam echoed.

They touched glasses and drank. One toast turned into three and soon Sam was feeling lightheaded. Burke tried to order another round. Sam begged off. She had to drive and she didn't want to add drunk driving charges to her troubles.

CHAPTER FIFTY-NINE

Noble spent the next morning mixing potassium chloride, petroleum and wax together in a Tupperware container the size of a ham sandwich. It was slow, nerve-wracking work and it didn't help that Alejandra hovered over his shoulder the whole time.

Father Cordero had found most of the ingredients on the shopping list at a farm supply store. The rest he picked up from a hardware store. He didn't ask what it was for, saving Noble the trouble of lying. While Cordero was out shopping for potassium chloride and petroleum, Noble had risked a trip to a nearby electronics store for pre-paid cell-phones. He took a circuitous route back to the mission, wasting two hours to be sure no one had picked up his trail.

Then came the arduous task of heating and mixing in careful measurements, so the concoction didn't blow up in his face. The kitchen was a sauna. Alejandra had sweated through a white tank top and the dark points of her nipples peeked through. The worst of her bruises were healing and some of her natural beauty had come back. The scars would be with her for life, like graffiti on a priceless work of art.

Noble, stripped to the waist, sweat glistening on his bare chest, kept his eyes off Alejandra's breasts while he stirred the explosive compound.

Cordero came in as Noble was finishing up. His eyes went to Alejandra and then away. He hooked a finger in his collar and tugged. "The weatherman says a storm is rolling in from the Pacific. Hopefully it will give us a break in this heat. What's for lunch?"

"A thermite charge," Noble told him.

Alejandra watched him spoon boiling potassium chloride from a large aluminum mixing bowl into the Tupperware container. She said, "You're going to blow up the penthouse? What about the other residents?"

"Don't worry," Noble said. "I'm not going to fire bomb the building. This is just a little insurance policy."

"What are you going to do with it?" Cordero wanted to know.

"I'm going to attach it to the underside of Machado's limo. The armor plating meant to keep bullets out will contain the blast, redirecting the force of the explosion inward."

"Won't it need some kind of shrapnel?" Alejandra asked.

"A conventional explosive would," Noble told her. "This is a thermite charge. It burns white hot, like napalm, but it doesn't explode."

"So anyone inside the car will cook?" Alejandra said.

"That's the idea."

He finished mixing the lethal cocktail and took one of

the burner cells, stripped off the back, and attached a copper wire to the receiver. He carefully inserted the other end into the thermite jelly, placed the lid on the Tupperware and duct taped the whole thing tight. "All it needs is a text message to set it off."

"I hope you don't get a telemarketer," Cordero said.

Noble grinned and stuffed the Tupperware into a black satchel like the kind carried by bicycle messengers. "With any luck, I won't even need it."

CHAPTER SIXTY

THE GLASS AND STEEL HIGH-RISE STOOD AT THE HEART of downtown Mexico City, a few blocks from the American embassy. Despite the weatherman's prediction of rain, the mercury continued to climb. Heat mirages shimmered in the distance.

Noble and Alejandra sat in a stolen Explorer with the engine running and the air conditioner on full. It was 5:27 p.m. Traffic crawled past on the boulevard. Two of the party guests had already arrived. They watched as the motorcades turned down the ramp to the underground garage.

Tension inside the Explorer mounted. Noble chewed the inside of one cheek. He had the bones of a plan, but no idea how to pull it off.

Alejandra glanced in the rearview and sat up. A three-car convoy had just turned onto the boulevard—a pair of black Range Rovers flanked a spotless white limousine with mirrored windows.

"That's him," Alejandra said.

"You have to be absolutely sure that's Machado's car," Noble told her.

"I'm sure."

The convoy pulled even with the stolen SUV.

Noble said, "Get down."

Alejandra ducked between the seats as the motorcade rolled past. The lead vehicle turned into the parking garage followed by the limo and the rear security vehicle. Dark window tint made it impossible to get an accurate head count. Noble counted five in the lead car and another four, at least, in the rear car.

"One more to go," Noble said.

Alejandra gave a jerky little nod. The corners of her mouth turned down. She gripped a pistol with white knuckles. Noble was worried she would accidentally pop off a shot but didn't say anything. He put that fear aside and focused on the task ahead.

The last of the cartel leaders showed up just after 5:40. Two Jeeps, a black limo and a Lexus SUV glided down the ramp into the underground parking garage.

"Showtime," Noble said.

He took the black satchel from between the seats. "Slide into the driver's seat and be ready. We'll need to make a quick getaway when I come out. Think you can handle it?"

"I'm going in with you," Alejandra said, like it was a forgone conclusion.

Noble shook his head. "You're too keyed up. You want Machado dead and you're ready to die for the chance to kill him. No way."

"He took everything from me," she said through clenched teeth.

"And he's going to pay for it," Noble said. "But I can't trust you to stay cool in there. You'll be thinking with your heart instead of your head. You're just as likely to get *me* killed. So you stay."

Her nostrils flared.

"You stay," Noble said. "Understand?"

She glared at him with her one good eye, but nodded.

"Be ready to drive when I come out," Noble told her.

He climbed out and dodged traffic. Beads of sweat gathered on his forehead. His shirt clung to his back. The satchel bounced against his hip with every step, reminding him that he had two and a half pounds of thermite jelly strapped to his side. If it went off, he would do an impression of the human torch. He hauled open the heavy glass door and stepped into air so cold it made him shiver.

A pretty Mexican girl in a navy blue suit smiled at him from behind the concierge desk. A security guard in an ill-fitting blazer was posted next to a potted plant in one corner of the lobby. Noble slumped his shoulders and pretended to smack gum. If anyone asked, he was an express courier.

He rode the elevator up to seven, waited to be sure no one got on, and then pressed the button for the underground. When the car started moving again, he climbed onto the handrails and pushed up the access panel. A breath of warm air hit him in the face. The temperature in the shaft was well over one hundred degrees Fahrenheit. Small red emergency bulbs in wire housings gave enough light to see by. Thick metal cables twanged and popped. The sound filled the narrow shaft. Noble stepped carefully around the large pulley system to the edge of the car. Far below he saw the spill of light from an air vent.

It was a short ride to the bottom. The bell chimed and the doors opened. A blade of light appeared along the top edge of the car. He had assumed the cartels would have people checking everyone who stepped off the elevator for the next couple hours and he wasn't disappointed. A hired thug stuck his head in the car and said, "It's empty."

Another voice said, "Maybe someone pushed the button by mistake."

A minute later the doors rolled shut.

Noble slid over the side of the elevator and hung by his fingertips in the narrow space between the box and the wall. He dropped to the bottom of the shaft, right into a puddle of standing water.

A voice said, "Did you hear something?"

CHAPTER SIXTY-ONE

The top floor penthouse was calculated decadence. Maintained jointly by the drug cartels, it was accorded neutral ground in the never-ending turf wars, someplace they could meet and talk shop. There was a private wait staff made up of exotic young women in short dresses, with plunging necklines and easy smiles. Original oil paintings by Spanish and Italian renaissance masters graced the walls. Chinese vases stood on rich mahogany accent tables. The floors were covered in Oriental rugs.

Santiago followed Machado into the billiard room. The sweet odor of Cuban cigars hung in the air. A fat man in a white suit with gray hair, known to the police as el Cazador, lined up a shot. He tapped the cue ball. It kissed the three, which sank in a corner pocket. El Cazador grinned. The other players each counted out enough money to buy a new car lot. Some of the hired muscle in the room clapped while the rest eyed each other with open hostility.

Santiago rolled his shoulders. Every nerve ending in his body was on high alert. Being an ex-cop in a room full of hired goons with automatic weapons made him jumpy. This was neutral ground, but these were stone-cold killers. The slightest provocation could start a fight and Santiago already knew how that would go down. He had played the scenario out in his head a dozen times. It didn't end well for anybody.

While Machado greeted his rivals, Santiago accepted a glass of champagne from a serving girl. As a lieutenant, he was afforded that privilege. The rest of the security detail was expected to be sober and silent. Santiago had replaced his dead team with three up-and-comers. They weren't as good as the guys he had lost, but they would do.

"Sorry to hear about your accountant," El Cazador was saying as he chalked his stick. "He had been with you several years, no?"

"Eleven," Machado said.

"I hear he threw himself out of a window."

Escobedo, a tall man with a thin face, said, "I heard he was pushed."

"Embarrassing," said el Cazador.

The muscles in Machado's jaw bunched. "He had outlived his usefulness."

"Then his death did not come as a surprise to you?" Escobedo commented.

"Not at all," Machado assured them.

"I see." El Cazador lined up his next shot. "Perhaps it was for the best then."

Escobedo said, "I hear rumors of an American vigilante."

"The *Americano* is being dealt with," Machado said. "And the two events are unrelated."

El Cazador sunk the four. "Well, by all means, let us know if you need assistance dealing with this lone vigilante."

Machado showed his teeth in what was supposed to be a polite smile. It looked more like a shark's grin. "Shall we get down to business?"

"Of course," *El Cazador* said. "We can finish our little game later." They left their sticks on the table and filed out of the billiard room, down a short hall toward the drawing room.

Machado caught Santiago by the arm. His powerful fingers sunk deep into Santiago's bicep. They fell behind the rest of the group. When the others were out of earshot, Machado said, "The gringo must not be allowed to disturb the meeting."

"You think he would attack us here?" Santiago asked. "With all this security?"

"If he does," Machado said, "I'll hang you upside down and slit your throat."

Santiago's nostrils flared. He bit back a sharp rely. Machado was as good as his word. If the gringo interfered Santiago's life would be worth spit.

Machado let go of his arm and joined the meeting in the drawing room.

Santiago drained his wine, put the empty glass on an occasional table and went to the private elevator.

CHAPTER SIXTY-TWO

Every muscle in Noble's body tensed. He was at the bottom of the elevator shaft with nowhere to go. If the cartel thugs found him, they would cut him down like a cornered rat. He pulled Hunt's Kimber and listened.

"I thought I heard something."

"It was my stomach growling."

"Shut up and listen."

Noble stood still, careful not to disturb the water pooling around his feet, and tried to control his breathing.

"It's nothing. Come on."

Noble exhaled slowly. He holstered the weapon and crept across the floor of the shaft to an exhaust vent which faced away from the elevator doors. Through the slats, he could see oil-stained concrete and the tires of an SUV. Using the ambient light, he found the latches securing the vent and turned them, one by one, with painstaking care. They made small scraping noises, like a mouse in search of cheese. Noble winced. He went slow, twisting the knobs a fraction of an inch at a time until they released. That done, he lifted the grate and hoisted himself up.

The elevator bank was a square of concrete in the center of the underground garage. Fluorescent lights glowed on the roofs of the cars, creating an artificial brilliance and deep pockets of shadow. Gasoline fumes filled Noble's lungs. Around the corner on his right, a pair of hard cases with submachine guns guarded the elevator doors. Another pair hovered near the exit ramp. Bright sunlight turned them to silhouettes.

There were footsteps on his left. Noble eased the vent shut, took two long strides and rolled under the nearest vehicle—an SUV—as a cartel soldier with an MP5 rounded the corner. Noble lay in the shadows and waited for the soldier to pass. He rounded the corner to the elevator doors and paused to bum a cigarette from a buddy.

The drug lords had parked their motorcades in the aisles. Locating Machado's white limousine was easy enough. The driver of the rear vehicle had gotten out to stretch his legs and smoke. The limo driver had the window down and a magazine open. The lead vehicle was empty. The driver must be roaming around someplace. Maybe he was on elevator duty.

Noble crept along the lanes, pausing twice for patrols, until he reached Machado's motorcade. He waited behind the bumper of a Hyundai. The driver of the rear Range Rover smoked his cigarette down to the filter, tossed it, and climbed back inside. He switched on the radio. Mexican rock blasted from the speakers.

Noble used the opportunity to dart across the aisle.

The driver dialed in a pop station. In back of the Range Rover, Noble dropped to the ground and belly crawled. The engine was still hot and had warmed the concrete. *This must be what a waffle feels* like, Noble thought. He paused at the front bumper. Less than half a meter separated the Range Rover from the limousine. He took a deep breath, flipped onto his back and shimmied forward until his head and shoulders were under the limo. His hips were exposed to anyone who might happen by. The limo's gas tank was directly overhead. He wedged the satchel between the tank and the tire well, made sure it was snug, then flipped onto his belly and did an awkward backwards crawl.

A two-man patrol chose that moment to wander past. Noble waited until they were gone, let out a shaking breath, and palmed sweat from his face. The first part of the plan was done. Now all he had to do was cause enough chaos to get Machado back in the limo. He shimmied backwards until he was out from under the Range Rover and rose to a crouch. His knees popped and his back ached. Thirty-four was too young for bad joints, but Noble had put a lot of mileage on his body. He was getting ready to retrace his steps when he saw Santiago crossing the parking garage towards the convoy.

Noble darted behind a gray Lincoln Navigator. The Los Zetas *sicario* stalked between lanes to the lead Range Rover and rapped on the driver's window.

The glass buzzed down.

"Keep your eyes open. Call me on the radio if you see anything suspicious." Santiago went to the limo, repeated the message, and then to the rear SUV.

He was less than ten feet away. The ghost of Torres

screamed at Noble to take the shot. From this distance, he could lean around the bumper and drill a bullet through Santiago without aiming, but he stayed put. *Stick to the plan,* he told himself, *stick to the plan, or this whole thing falls to pieces.*

CHAPTER SIXTY-THREE

Santiago stalked away, his heels echoing on the garage floor. Noble waited until he was out of sight, then retraced his steps to the elevators. The grate squeaked gently. Noble slid back into the stifling heat and darkness of the shaft. The elevator car was still on the underground level but getting on top of it was going to be difficult. He put his back against the car, planted his feet against the wall and shimmied up. It took ten minutes, but he was able to scramble onto the roof.

With gun in hand, he lifted the access hatch, made sure the elevator was empty and then swung his head and shoulders down through the opening. He had to strain and almost lost his grip, but was able to use the barrel of his pistol to press the button for seventeen.

The car hurtled up through darkness. Noble knelt on one knee, one hand pressed against the top of the elevator, listening to the cables hum. Red maintenance bulbs flashed past. On his left was a long drop, getting longer by the second. Noble tried not think about that.

The cables slowed and the car stopped one floor below the penthouse. A soft red glow lit a pair of double doors overhead. On the other side of those doors was a small army of killers with enough firepower to fight a war.

Long odds, Noble told himself.

He rolled his shoulders, loosening up. *Slow is smooth and smooth is fast,* he repeated inside his head. *Make enough noise to get Machado back in the car and let the thermite finish the job.*

Standing on tip-toes, he managed to trip the door activation arm with the barrel of the Kimber.

Time slowed down. The doors rolled open like the curtain parting on a deadly ballet. Light filled the elevator shaft—a spotlight drawing the crowd's attention to the main performer. But this show was unscripted. Who lived and who died was entirely up to chance.

A trio of cartel soldiers stood in front of the doors. They were bunched together under a crystal chandelier in the middle of the entry hall. All three had automatic rifles slung around their necks. They turned in unison as the doors opened.

Six months ago, Sam Gunn had prayed before a firefight in a rock quarry north of Kowloon and they had won against overwhelming odds. Now, as the doors reached their bumpers, Noble offered up a quick prayer in the hopes that God—if he existed—would grant some divine protection. A little luck at the very least.

He sighted on the first man and rolled the trigger back until he felt the Kimber breathe fire. A deafening boom filled the elevator shaft. A hole the size of a quarter opened in the thug's forehead. The back of his skull disappeared in a grisly spray of blood and brains. His knees buckled.

At the same time, the second man thrust a submachine gun out in front of him and mashed the trigger. The little automatic sounded like an angry buzz saw. Empty shell casings jumped from the breech. Lead impacted the floor, digging trenches and skipping up to drill holes in the elevator shaft over Noble's head.

He crouched, making himself as small as possible and fired a pair of rounds. Both bullets punched through the cartel soldier's chest, driving him backwards.

The third man held down the trigger until the bolt locked back on an empty chamber. As his friends fell dead, he ejected the spent magazine and tried to reload, but in his haste, had the magazine backwards. He realized his mistake a second too late. Noble put a pair of rounds through his chest.

All three targets were down. A thick cloud of blue smoke hung in the air. The floor had deep gouge marks and the wall of the elevator shaft two feet above Noble's head was shot full of holes.

If that didn't qualify as a miracle, what did?

He hauled himself up, grabbed the dead man's AK-47 and snagged a radio off his belt. There were shouts from an open door on Noble's left. He shouldered the weapon and triggered a three-round burst in time to catch a cartel soldier coming to investigate. Slugs stitched the soldier's chest. His head and shoulders went backwards. His feet shot out from under him. He landed flat on his back. He was still breathing, but not for long.

Noble turned to his right, clearing the penthouse

counter-clockwise. His only chance for survival was to create chaos, keep the enemy off balance, and make them kill each other instead of killing him. He mashed the button on the radio and, in his best Spanish, yelled, "The Los Zetas are attacking!"

He didn't know if the radio he was holding belonged to the Los Zetas or one of the other gangs, but it was bound to cause confusion. He entered a well-lit hall with parquet floors and oil paintings hanging on the walls. A long table with high-back chairs suggested a dining hall. He was moving fast and nearly ran over a girl in a short dress with a tray of champagne glasses. The tray hit the floor. Glass shattered. Her eyes looked ready to pop right out of her skull. She opened her mouth to scream.

"Don't scream," Noble warned her. "Do *not* scream."

The sound died on her lips.

He clapped his left hand over her mouth and drove her against the wall. There were shouts coming from the other end of the penthouse.

He said, "How many other civilians working here?"

He lifted his hand so she could speak.

"Seven."

"Any other way out?"

She shook her head. "Just the elevator."

"Where is the fuse box?"

She pointed to a door at the other end of the room. "Through there. Two doors down, on your right."

"Lie down on the floor and put your hands over your head," Noble ordered.

She hurried to obey, pressing herself into the corner.

CHAPTER SIXTY-FOUR

Alonso, head of the Caballeros Templarios, was a middle-aged man with a pair of chins. He was telling the gathering that he had begun equipping his coyotes with night vision goggles. If the U.S. border patrol had them, he reasoned, why shouldn't they? It also allowed them to excavate new tunnels without worrying about installing electricity. The Templars were responsible for roughly two dozen tunnels stretching from Tijuana all the way to San Diego, many of which had light and ventilation.

The cartel heads had gathered around a low table in the conference room. They were surrounded by their security details. The wait staff kept their drinks filled. Cigar smoke hung in the air, stirred into slow-moving eddies by ceiling fans. Beyond the windows, dark storm clouds gathered in the west, blotting out the sun.

Escobedo shook his head. "We avoid the need for technology altogether if we simply buy off more of the U.S. border patrol."

"That is getting harder to do," Alonso argued. "Americans are tired of the killing on their southern border. The *Norteamericano* border patrol are vetting their people better. It's hurting business."

"That is why I called this meeting," Machado told them. The time had come. He had spent decades putting all the pieces in place. It required patience and no small investment of capital but the fruits of his labor had finally ripened. He took a long drag from his cigar and exhaled. "What if I told you, in a few short months the border patrol will no longer be of any concern?"

Alonso snorted.

"I'd say you have been using your own product," Escobedo muttered.

"I've been working on a deal to end America's war on drugs and allow us open access," Machado told them.

"Go on," El Cazador said.

"You talk of buying off the border patrol." Machado laughed and a cloud of smoke burst from his nostrils. "You think too small, my friends. Why buy the border agents when you can own the president?"

Alonso shook his head. "You'll never buy off the President of the United States. Even America isn't that corrupt." After a pause, he added, "Yet."

"What if I told you I already had?" Machado said and let the statement sink in. "What if I told you the current frontrunner for the DNC is in my pocket?"

El Cazador leaned forward. "This is incredible news."

All eyes were on him. He took his time, enjoying the moment. "For decades now, American politicians have been taking campaign contributions from foreign governments, like Iran and Saudi Arabia. I thought to myself, why should the ragheads be the only ones dictating American policy?

"Several years ago, I began financing political campaigns in the calculated gamble that sooner or later one of my investments would pay off. One thing you can always count on, my friends, is greed. Helen Rhodes was all too eager to accept my *campaign contributions.* It was my money which helped secure her run for Governor of New York and my money is funding her presidential campaign."

"I have seen her speeches," Alonso said. "She argues for open borders."

"Once she is in the White House, we can move product without fear of the border patrol."

"How can you be sure of this?" Alonso asked. "It's one thing to give her money. It's something else entirely to expect she will give us open access."

"I recorded our conversations and kept a detailed paper trail of the money I funneled into her Swiss account," Machado told them. "When she is president, I will *request* she open certain routes for us to move product. If she refuses, I release the recordings."

Alonso laughed and clapped his hands. "Bravo! No politician wants the voting public to see the skeletons in the closet."

Machado nodded.

Escobedo champed on the end of a cigar. "You alone will know which routes are safe to use. In fact, if you wished, you could use your connection with America's president to bring the law down on us."

Machado offered a friendly smile. "You worry too

much, my friend. I will happily provide you safe passage, for a modest fee. Say, twenty percent?"

Escobedo snarled. "You won't get a single peso out of me!"

Machado leaned back and slung one arm over the back of the sofa. "Then, I am afraid, you will find it very difficult to move product."

El Cazador spoke through clenched teeth. "You think you can strong-arm us, Machado?"

"You're looking at this all wrong, my friends. I am making it safer and easier to move product. No more fighting over tunnels in the desert. No more war. No more bloodshed. We provide *Norteamericanos* with the drugs they need to numb their pointless existence and we make more money than God."

"But you make more than all of us," Alonso pointed out.

"The price of doing business—"

A deafening peal of automatic fire cut off his words. The cartel leaders froze where they sat. The lieutenants pulled their weapons. The muscles in Machado's back tensed, ready for action. Blood pounded in his ears. His worst nightmare was coming true. He stood on the precipice of victory and his plan was being undone by a lone American with a grudge. He cursed the gringo CIA agent and that incompetent fool, Santiago.

The shooting stopped just as suddenly as it began.

"What the hell is going on out there?" Alonso wanted to know.

"The police?" Escobedo said.

All around the conference room, armed men eyed each

other. The air felt electrified. They sat on a powder keg. A single spark would set the whole thing off.

A radio crackled. Static broke up the transmission, but a garbled voice came through. "...Los Zetas...attacking..."

Machado felt all eyes on him. The other cartels swiveled their guns in his direction. His enforcers responded in kind. Panic flooded his limbs. He started to stammer out a denial but he was interrupted by more gunfire.

Escobedo jumped up so fast his chair toppled. Everyone in the room was on their feet, pointing guns at each other. The three Los Zetas soldiers with Machado were severely outnumbered. They shifted their focus between the other cartel leaders and rival enforcers.

"Wait!" Machado threw up his hands. "Just wait!"

"Tell your men to put their guns down!" Escobedo ordered.

"Order your men to hold their fire," Machado growled.

The lights went out, plunging the room into darkness. A pistol barked. The muzzle flash lit the faces of fourteen armed and angry men. Machado felt the bullet sizzle past his ear. He lunged for the door as a hailstorm of lead filled the air.

In his panic, he collided with someone in the dark and they both went to the floor. A fist slammed into the side of Machado's head. It glanced off his ear, leaving him more surprised than hurt. The man beneath him was a writhing mass of flailing arms and legs. Machado didn't know if he was wrestling a soldier or one of the other gang lords. He took a punch to the lips and the hot copper taste of blood filled his mouth.

Machado locked his hands around the man's head and gave a powerful twist. All the gunfire had shorted out his hearing, but he felt vertebra crack. The man's arms went limp, like someone had pulled the battery from a child's toy.

Men screamed. The sharp stench of gun powder filled the room. Lead, like a swarm of angry hornets, buzzed overhead. Machado groped for a weapon and latched onto a dead man's shoe instead. He gave up the search, pushed himself off the floor and ran for the exit. He hit the door with his shoulder. Wood shrieked. The door burst open, spilling him into the long corridor connected to the entryway. The red emergency exit light revealed the bodies of four dead enforcers in front of the elevators.

A bullet zipped past his head. Machado flinched and pulled his shoulders up around his ears. He heard Escobedo scream, "*Machado, you traitor*!"

Machado ran for the elevator

CHAPTER SIXTY-FIVE

Noble found the circuit breaker in a library full of books that had never been read; none of the spines were even cracked. A pair of leather armchairs flanked an electric fireplace. The room was an affectation of refinery, someplace the drug dealers could go to make believe they were civilized men instead of petty crooks. A tapestry hid the fuse box. Noble opened the door and tripped the main breakers.

The lights winked out.

From the opposite end of the penthouse, there came the hard rattle of machine guns. The deadly roar lasted a full minute then tapered to a single handgun clapping in the dark. A savage grin turned up one side of Noble's mouth. The paranoid cartels had just done his work for him. The upper floor was still crawling with enforcers, but it sounded like the bosses had dusted each other.

He left the library and worked his way through the penthouse—the AK-47 leading the way—clearing rooms one at a time. His pulse hammered in his ears and the darkness played tricks on him. In the distance, he heard deep thunder and, closer to hand, sporadic gunfire.

The billiard hall had been transformed into an Alamo by three of the hired thugs. They had tipped a pair of tables on edge and were using them for cover. Floor to ceiling windows looked out over Mexico City. A dark line of ominous storm clouds had gathered in the west and, below the cloud bank, the sun shimmered on the horizon. Four dead men, the grisly results of a failed attempt to storm the defenders, lay in the middle of the floor. Empty shell casings littered the rug.

Noble took two long strides and launched himself over the bar top.

The hard cases hosed the far end of the room with automatics. Lead splintered the polished bar, shattered bottles, and obliterated the back mirror. Noble landed on a rubber mat. Broken glass and booze rained down on him.

Bullets raked the bar like an angry beast trying to claw its way through. When it finally stopped, the silence was deafening.

A terrified bartender hunkered in the corner where the bar curved to meet the wall. He put both hands up and begged for his life in halting English.

"I'm not going to hurt you," Noble said in Spanish.

The bartender shrank back against the shelves, trying to make himself small. His eyes darted around and his chin trembled.

Noble chanced a peek and almost got his head blown off. More bottles shattered, showering him in bourbon and whiskey.

Noble thought the cartel soldiers were probably putting

too much faith in those pool tables. A 9mm round can punch through a wall and Noble's AK-47 fired a heavy 7.62mm.

He rose to a crouch and triggered three short bursts. The rifle kicked against his shoulder. Brass casings leapt from the breech. The bullets impacted the pool table with heavy splats, ripping holes in the green felt and the wood beneath, but got trapped in the complicated ball return system.

The manufacturer had crafted a quality piece of recreational equipment. *Damn it.*

The *sicarios* responded with a hail of lead, dousing Noble in more liquor. It gave him an idea. He grabbed a bottle of tequila, twisted off the cap and took a rag from a shelf. Bullets continued to hammer the bar. The cartel soldiers were taking turns, one shooting while the others reloaded, keeping Noble pinned. He soaked the rag, stuffed one end in the open bottle, then cast about for something to light it.

The barman produced an orange Bic from his breast pocket.

"*Gracias,*" Noble said.

"*De nada, Señor.*"

Ghostly blue flame raced up the rag toward the neck of the bottle. Noble tossed it overhand. The bottle turned end over end and shattered against one of the table legs with a hungry whoosh. An orange blaze enveloped the defenders. Their panicked shrieks filled the air. All three ran in a desperate attempt to escape the fire.

Noble popped up from behind the bar and caught the first with a burst from his AK-47. The second man collapsed and rolled around while fire blackened his skin. The third man danced a jig, slapping at his arms and legs. Noble hit him with a short burst. Bullets drove the cartel soldier backwards through the windows. He fell screaming.

There was a distant smack. Tires screeched.

The smell of charred flesh choked Noble's lungs and brought tears to his eyes. He coughed, waved a hand in front of his nose, and stepped around the bar to the shattered window. The cartel soldier had landed in the street. Traffic was backing up along the boulevard. Several drivers had gotten out of their cars for a better look.

CHAPTER SIXTY-SIX

Machado stabbed at the call button. Sweat glistened on his bald head, glowing red under the glare of the emergency exit lights. He watched, on the verge of panic, as the floor indicators blinked to life one by one. The elevator would never reach him in time. He went to a blank section of wall and groped for a hidden switch. The cartels had installed a private stairwell in case they were ever raided by the police. Machado had forgotten all about it, until now. He never expected to actually use it. Like a spare tire in the trunk of the car, it was an added layer of security that you didn't think about until you needed it. His fingers found the button and a cleverly disguised door swung in on silent hinges.

Santiago was in the parking garage, waiting on the elevator, when the radio squawked, "Los Zetas... Attacking..." Two Gulf Cartel members stood ten feet away. Both men turned to stare at him. Santiago's stomach did a somersault. He saw the accusation in their eyes. The elevator dinged and the doors rolled open.

Instead of trying to reason with them, Santiago drew his service issue Glock, emptied the magazine and retreated into the waiting elevator car. The nearest soldier doubled over. The other enforcer stitched the front of the elevator with rounds from an Uzi. Santiago pressed himself into the corner and jabbed the button for the penthouse.

Machado burst through the door into the parking garage. All hell had broken loose. The cartels were shooting at each other over the roofs of parked cars. Bullets blew out windows and skipped off concrete. A Gulf Cartel soldier lay on his back in front of the elevators. A short-barreled AR-15 lay near his outstretched hand.

Machado started for the rifle, but a swarm of bullets forced him back. Lead chewed through the wall, showering him in dust. He reversed directions and sprinted across the parking garage to his armored convoy.

The Los Zetas soldiers were out of their vehicles, spraying automatic weapons at the Caballeros Templarios. Machado reached the lead SUV and yelled, "Let's go!"

He shoved the driver out of his way. The man went down on his butt with surprise etched on his face. He opened his mouth, but the side of his head exploded before he could protest. Machado threw himself in the driver's seat of the SUV, slammed the door, and stamped the gas. Bullets impacted the windshield, scarring the glass. The armor held.

Noble, looking out the shattered window, spotted Machado's limousine shoot from the underground parking garage like a gleaming white missile launched from the deck of a ship. A pair of SUVs bookended the limo. The lead SUV rammed a Mazda. The driver zig-zagged through traffic, blaring his horn, using the bumper to push other vehicles out of his way. He mounted the sidewalk, swerved around a delivery truck and then back onto the street. The limo driver had a hard time keeping up.

Noble took the burner cell from his pocket and dialed. There was a flash. An orange fireball lifted the back end of the limo off the ground.

The lead SUV never stopped. So much for honor among thieves.

Noble watched long enough to make sure no one escaped the limo, then gave a thumbs-up to Alejandra. Mission accomplished.

She put the Suburban in gear and veered out into traffic, colliding with a sedan. She stamped the gas, ripping off most of the side paneling, then rammed another car out of her way, mounted the curb, and shot past the burning limo in pursuit of the lead SUV.

Noble cursed and ran for the elevator. Sirens wailed in the distance. He needed to escape before the police cordoned off the building. He jabbed the call button and waited. Every second brought the sirens closer. The first thing they would do was set up a perimeter to net anyone coming out.

"Come on," Noble urged. He heard the lift on the other side of the doors and discarded the AK-47. He couldn't carry it out of the building. It clattered across the floor. The bell dinged. The doors rolled open and Noble was face to face with Santiago.

CHAPTER SIXTY-SEVEN

THE CIA STATION CHIEF IN CHARGE OF MEXICO HAD put the right people onto the child prostitution ring. Local authorities managed to nab the leader and save a dozen kids. The pimp was sitting behind bars, spilling his guts, and Hunt came off looking like a hero. The only thing he couldn't figure out was why Noble had turned him onto the whole thing in the first place. Was he trying to help or hinder?

Hunt stared out the window of the embassy at a line of dark clouds massing in the west. The sun was a hot, red crescent on the horizon, dropping fast. He turned from the window and stretched. "Anything?"

"I'm working on it," Ezra assured him. He was at his computer, slumped so far down in his seat it looked like he might slide right out of the chair onto the floor.

"How long does it take?" Hunt asked.

Gwen was getting annoyed. She said, "It's called a burner cell for a reason. It's hard to trace."

Hunt rubbed at his eyes.

"Finally," Ezra said, sitting up.

"You got something?" Hunt asked.

"It was purchased seven blocks from the pimp's apartment."

Hunt crossed his arms and made a face. It only proved what he already suspected—Noble had sent the text—but it didn't explain why. "Where is it now?"

"It's not pinging any towers. He probably disabled it right after he sent the text."

Noble had surfaced and disappeared again, like those annoying whack-a-mole games. He popped up in one location and by the time Hunt got there, he was gone again, only to turn up someplace completely different. Hunt bared his teeth.

Gwen snapped her fingers. She had a headphone pressed against one ear, monitoring the police band. "There is shooting in a high-rise penthouse. Multiple shots fired. All available units are responding."

"Where?" Hunt leaned over her shoulder.

She read off the address.

Ezra went to the map. "That's less than two miles from here."

The whack-a-mole had popped up within easy reach this time. Hunt holstered the tarnished Soviet-era pistol and hurried down the hall to the elevators. Noble was going down. To hell with the benefit of the doubt. If Sam got pissed, well, she'd get over it.

CHAPTER SIXTY-EIGHT

Santiago brought his gun up and Noble had a split second to react. There was no time to draw his own weapon. He stepped inside the elevator car and slapped Santiago's hand with an open palm. The 9mm Glock breathed fire. Heat licked the left side of Noble's face. The bullet missed his ear by fractions of an inch. It felt like an icepick to his brain. He screamed, but managed to get both hands around Santiago's pistol.

They grappled for control of the weapon inside the elevator. Noble wrenched the gun up and Santiago pulled the trigger. One of the overhead fluorescents disintegrated in a shower of sparks. The empty shell casing bounced off the wall and rolled around the floor.

Noble kicked at Santiago's knee and the cartel enforcer elbowed Noble in the face. It felt like a ballpeen hammer to his cheek. He reeled backwards into the wall. Santiago forced the gun barrel down. Noble leveraged his weight on Santiago's wrist and turned the muzzle at the last possible second. Two slugs drilled holes in the wall.

Santiago was a street fighter. Unlike Hunt, he had honed his skills in countless life or death struggles. His attacks were less polished, more lethal. Noble had to end this fast or Santiago would beat him to a pulp.

Noble slammed him against the bank of buttons and half the floor numbers lit. The doors slid shut and the elevator started down. Noble slammed him again, forcing all the air out of Santiago's lungs. He lost his grip and the gun clattered across the floor. The car stopped and the doors slid open. Noble blocked a flurry of knees and elbows. The doors slid shut. Knuckles mashed Noble's bottom lip. The taste of copper filled his mouth. The elevator stopped on fourteen, thirteen, and again on ten. Santiago's knee threatened to re-break Noble's rib with a painful blow. Noble clapped both hands over Santiago's ears.

The attack was designed to burst the eardrums and disorient an attacker. It worked. The cartel lieutenant screamed and reeled backwards. A trickle of blood dribbled down his cheek.

Noble dived for the gun. Santiago wrapped him up in a headlock. It took all Noble's strength, but he managed to lunge forward and grab the weapon. He stuck the pistol around his side and fired blind. Santiago jerked, let go, and slumped against the wall.

Noble turned, lost his footing on an empty shell casing, and sat down hard.

Santiago sat across from him, one hand pressed against his stomach and blood soaking through his shirt. His eyes held Noble like he could continue the fight with the depth of his hatred alone. But he wasn't getting up. They both knew it.

He struggled for breath. "Your friend... he died... like a coward."

"When you get to hell, tell them Jake Noble sent you." He pulled the trigger. The gun clapped thunder. Blood painted the wall in a violent red shout.

The elevator stopped on two. Noble limped out and took a moment to collect himself. Pain marched up his body in ranks. He probed his aching ribs. They were intact, but they would be bruised. Before the elevator doors closed, Noble tossed Santiago's gun into his lap.

He took the stairs to the parking garage, eased down the latch on the heavy door, and opened it enough to peek. Three of the convoys were still parked. Police cruisers had barricaded the exit ramp. Officers ordered them to surrender, but the cartels were armed to the teeth and not going down without a fight.

"Mexican standoff," Noble muttered to himself.

No one was watching the stairwell. Noble opened the door, aimed over parked cars, and shot the nearest thug in the back. The Kimber roared. In the concrete cave of the underground garage, the report echoed, making it impossible to tell where it had come from. Everyone started shooting at the same time. The sound was deafening. Bullets skipped around inside the parking garage, obliterating windows, setting off car alarms, and blowing out tires. Men screamed in pain.

Noble swung the door shut before one of the bullets bounced into the stairwell. He raced up to the first floor. There were two doors on the landing. One led to the lobby. The other was a fire exit. He holstered his weapon and shouldered his way through the fire door into an alley.

"Hands up!"

A pair of police officers in tactical gear pointed AR-15s at him. Their car blocked the mouth of the alley. The other end was open, but too far to run. Noble would just die winded. He raised both hands.

They ordered him to lay down.

He played the hapless foreigner card. "*Er... perdón... no hablo español.*"

One of the officers came forward while his partner hung back near the car. Noble stared down the barrel of the AR-15 and reminded himself to breathe. The cop could end his existence with a twitch of his finger. Noble's heart drummed against the wall of his chest. He put his hands up.

The officer lowered the weapon. It was attached by a single point sling around his neck. He let the rifle dangle and grasped Noble's outstretched arm. Noble reversed the hold. Now he was gripping the officer's wrist. He pulled the officer in close and jammed his knee into the cop's groin. The officer doubled over in pain and Noble snatched the AR-15.

The second cop couldn't fire without hitting his partner. He started forward, shouting orders. Noble brought the rifle up, and pulled the trigger. The bullet hit the cop in the chest and he went down flat on his back.

Noble pressed the quick release on the rifle sling and struck the first officer with the butt of the weapon. His legs buckled and his eyes rolled up. He went over on his side.

The second cop coughed and clutched at his chest. Noble had been counting on the cop's vest to stop the bullet, but from this distance it was a gamble. He probably had broken ribs and tomorrow he'd have one hell of a bruise, but he'd live. He tried to lift his rifle with hands that flapped around like dying butterflies.

Noble centered the front sight on his forehead. "Toss it."

The cop released the buckle and pushed the weapon aside. It clattered on the asphalt. Fear flooded his eyes.

Noble collected two full magazines from the unconscious cop at his feet and then stepped over to the fallen partner. He kept the barrel aimed at the officer's head while he pulled two more magazines from the man's tactical harness. In Spanish, he asked, "Did it penetrate?"

The officer shook his head.

"Keys?"

"In the car," he croaked out.

"Count to one hundred, slowly," Noble told him. "Then call an ambulance."

The officer nodded.

Noble grabbed the second AR-15, climbed into the driver seat of the police cruiser, and tossed the rifles into the passenger seat.

The wounded officer rolled onto his hands and knees and crawled over to his unconscious partner. They were probably good cops. Noble felt bad about taking them down.

He reversed out of the alley. Traffic around the high rise was at a standstill. Cops poured bullets down the ramp into the parking garage. Motorists panicked and tried to back up, causing dozens of fender benders. Noble searched the dash, switched on the flashers and drove on the sidewalk until he had worked his way past the traffic jam. He headed east, past the American embassy, following Alejandra. He didn't see Hunt going the opposite direction.

CHAPTER SIXTY-NINE

Tonight marked the first presidential debate. Rhodes was squaring off against the loud-mouthed real estate tycoon from New York. The debate would be moderated by Shawn Hennessy from Fox. The cable news pundit would grill her with questions about the deaths of four Americans in Libya, her private email servers, and the recent allegations that she had planted false evidence against the head of the FBI.

There's nothing worse than a journalist who doesn't owe allegiance to the establishment. They ask tough questions instead of sticking to the narrative. After thirty years in politics, Rhodes knew what the plebeian masses really wanted; someone to keep the lights on so they can swill beer and watch football.

She was backstage in a private dressing room. A colored girl was doing her makeup. Rhodes believed in the work of Margaret Sanger and thought blacks should be sterilized. Crime and rising welfare costs were their only contribution to society, but they voted democrat. Herd them into slums and supply them with enough cash to toke up, they'd keep voting democrat. Much as she hated to admit it, she needed the black vote. The redneck, inbreeds in flyover country certainly wouldn't be voting for her.

While the colored girl applied concealer, Rhodes read over her talking points, mouthing silently to herself. Her staff was making too much noise: working social media, making telephone calls, and discussing contingency plans for any embarrassing questions that might come up. Under all the racket, Rhodes thought she heard the crowd chanting the insurgent's name. Her left eye started to twitch.

"Try not to do that," the colored girl said, "It messes up your mascara."

Her Chief of Staff, Mateen Malih, appeared over her shoulder holding a cellphone and whispered, "Call for you."

"What idiot would be stupid enough to call me fifteen minutes before a debate?"

Mateen dropped her voice another octave. "It's *him*."

"Be more specific."

"Our *biggest* donor." Mateen raised her eyebrows.

"Blythe?"

Mateen shook her head. "*Him*."

Her nostrils flared. "He knows better than to call me. That's not how it works."

Mateen put the phone to her ear and started to issue an excuse. She stopped mid-sentence. The color drained from her face. She listened for several seconds and then handed the phone to Rhodes. Her lips trembled. "He *threatened* me."

Rhodes snatched the phone. "I'm about to go on stage. What's so important?"

It sounded like he was in a car. Rhodes heard the engine revving. Machado yelled into the phone. "The CIA assassin sparked a war between the cartels and blew up my car!"

Rhodes flicked a hand at the colored girl, who politely stepped away. "And you decided to call me on a cellphone?"

"Worried somebody might be listening?"

Rhodes lowered her voice. "I understand how that might be upsetting, but there is no reason to be uncivil. I'll see what I can do to remedy your little problem. Right now I'm about to go on stage."

"It is not a *little* problem," Machado said. "Noble just destroyed everything I spent the last two decades working on. I want him dead."

She stood up and stamped a foot. "Who do you think you are? You don't give me orders!"

Everybody in the room was watching her.

"You ignorant cow!" Machado exploded. "How would you like the American public to find out about our little arrangement? How would that affect your poll numbers?"

"Are you threatening me?"

"I don't make threats," Machado said. "I make promises. I have recordings of every conversation and a paper trail of every dollar I ever donated to your campaigns over the years."

Rhodes gripped the edge of her stool and lowered herself onto the seat. Her eye twitched.

"Now, listen to me very carefully," Machado said. "I want Jake Noble dead or I'll have your daughter kidnapped and mailed back to you in pieces."

The threat against Kelsey was immaterial. The twenty-two-year-old ball and chain could drop dead for all Rhodes cared. But the threat of leaked recordings... that would destroy her. It was an effort to keep her voice in check. "Don't do anything rash..."

The line went dead.

The colored girl made a motion to ask if she should continue. Rhodes shook her head. She dialed and put the phone to her ear.

"This is Clark S. Foster."

"I said I wanted the rogue agent dealt with," Rhodes said. "Was I not clear?"

"My best officer is down there right now," Foster said. "But we've hit a few snags. The Wizard is running interference for Burke. Instead of hanging in the wind, he's on administrative leave. Once you're president and I'm in charge, I'll clear out the riffraff. Cowboys like Burke will no longer be a problem."

"It's too late for that," Rhodes said.

"What are you talking about?"

She retreated to a corner of the room. "I'm talking about Machado. He's become a problem. He needs to go away."

"I'm not sure I understand you," Foster said.

Her voice was a dangerous whisper. "Eliminate him."

"I would need to clear an operation like that with the Director first," Foster said.

Rhodes gripped the cellphone so hard her bony knuckles cracked. "You don't work for the Director. You work for me. I'm going to be the next president and I'm giving you a direct order. Kill Machado or pray I lose this election."

She hung up before Foster could protest. She missed the days when you could slam a phone to make your point. Everybody was watching her. She barked, “Show’s over, people.”

CHAPTER SEVENTY

Three blocks up, police waged war against cartel. The hard crack of automatic rifles echoed along the boulevard. Pedestrians ran for cover. Drivers fought clear of the traffic jam and then stepped on the gas. Hunt watched as a squad of Mexican cops in riot gear advance on the parking garage, pouring round after round from AR-15s down the ramp. One of the officers took a bullet in the leg, staggered, fell.

Hunt sheltered in a recessed door and watched the battle unfold. He felt his cell vibrating in his pocket, dug it out and recognized Foster's number. He put the phone to his ear. "Now's not really a good time, sir."

"Do I hear gunshots?"

"Yes, sir."

"Jake Noble's not dead, is he?"

Hunt frowned. "Er... no, sir. Not yet."

"Good," Foster said. "The situation has changed. Machado needs to be eliminated."

Hunt turned away from the action and plugged an ear. "Say again."

"I'm switching the op. Make contact with Noble and support him in any way you can." Foster said.

"You want me to *help* Noble?"

"It's complicated." Foster sounded like a school teacher lecturing a dimwitted student. "I don't have time to educate you on the intricacies of foreign policy. All you need to know is, Machado's continued existence threatens America's best interests. He needs to be dealt with. Can you handle it?"

"Yes, sir," Hunt said. "What about Noble?"

"If he lives, fine. If he dies, all the better. But make sure Machado is taken care of."

"Consider it done."

Hunt stood there fuming. His plans for Noble would have to wait. He pocketed the phone and watched the battle, eager to see how things shook out. He was in no hurry to square off against a drug cartel. That kind of thing was better left to the military. Then, Hunt recalled, Noble was a former Green Beret. Still, even with Noble on his side, Hunt didn't like their chances against a narco army. With any luck, the Mexican police would make a clean sweep of it.

His hopes were dashed when a police cruiser shot backwards out of an alley. Tires screeched. The rear bumper stopped just short of a paneled van. Noble was behind the wheel. He jammed the car into gear and stamped the gas. The engine roared. He used the sidewalk to get past the line of stalled cars.

Hunt turned his face away as Noble rocketed past.

Where is he going?

Hunt walked out into traffic where a motorcyclist was walking his bike backwards. The biker cleared the worst of the jam and got turned around. Hunt drew his gun and let the biker see it. The guy passed the handle bars over without further prompting.

Hunt threw a leg over the seat, popped the clutch and the front tire jumped into the air. He threw his weight over the handlebars, forced the wheel back onto the pavement and swerved around a tractor trailer. The police cruiser was less than half a kilometer ahead. Hunt eased off the throttle. He kept low over the handlebars, making himself harder to spot in a rearview mirror. Noble wasn't checking for tails. Wherever he was going, he was in a hurry. He used the sidewalk again and ran a red, forcing Hunt to keep up or be left behind.

CHAPTER SEVENTY-ONE

NOBLE'S HEADLAMPS REFLECTED OFF THE BACK OF THE Suburban parked on the shoulder. The driver side door was open. Rocky, hardscrabble terrain and stunted trees flanked both sides of the road. Dark storm clouds boiled overhead. Noble slowed down as he passed. No blood. No bullet holes.

He pulled over, parked, cranked open his door, and waited. A lone cicada buzzed. Electric light limned a ridgeline on Noble's right. He didn't need satellite to tell him Machado's compound lay just over the hill of broken teeth. Alejandra was probably already on the other side.

He took both rifles and started up the rocky incline. Loose rock shifted underfoot. Thorny brambles raked his thighs. He was forced to go slow or risk turning an ankle. A collar of sweat formed around his neck. Near the top, the grade turned sharply upward. Noble used one hand to pull himself along. It took ten minutes to reach the summit.

On the other side of the hill lay a sprawling complex of stucco buildings surrounded by a high wall, complete with an Olympic-sized swimming pool, tennis courts, and a garden maze full of Greek statuary. Arc sodium security lamps banished the darkness. The armored SUV that had escaped the hotel was parked in front the main building.

From atop the ridge, Noble counted twelve guards. There would be more inside. A jagged fork of lightning blazed across the sky, leaving its afterimage printed on his retinas. A low rumble followed. The first promise of a breeze lifted his hair.

He scanned the dark crags and boulders, spotted movement near bottom. Alejandra crept along the rocks twenty meters below. She was planning a single handed assault on the compound. Hate was eating her up. She had been living with it so long now it overruled her common sense. Hurt *anyone* deep enough and they'll storm the very gates of hell for revenge.

A little voice at the back of Noble's head asked; *And what are you doing in the middle of the desert with a pair of automatic rifles?*

Looking for justice, Noble thought.

Justice? Or vengeance?

Tomato, to-mah-to.

He heard an engine and turned. There was a tiny spark of light, like a lightning bug in the dark. It grew to a single headlight. A motorcycle pulled up and stopped in back of the parked cars. Even from this distance, he recognized the rider.

"Damn, that guy is persistent."

Hunt swung his leg off the motorcycle, looked around, started up the incline.

While Hunt was working his way up, Noble started

down the other side. Going down was faster, if no less dangerous, and he caught up to Alejandra as she hunkered behind a large outcropping of rock.

"Machado was in the lead car," she said without preamble.

"I figured as much," Noble said. "What's your plan? Go in guns blazing, like Butch and Sundance?"

"Who's Butch Sundance?" she asked.

"Butch *and* Sundance," he corrected.

"Who's that?"

"Never mind," Noble said.

"I'm not asking you to come with me," she said.

Noble caught her arm. She turned to face him. He said, "I wouldn't be here if I wasn't planning on going over that wall."

"No more tricks," she said. "No more traps, no more bombs underneath cars. This ends tonight."

"Fine." Noble handed her a rifle and two full magazines. "But if we are going to do this, let's at least do it right."

She checked the action on the weapon. "I'm listening."

"Hang on a second," Noble told her.

Atop the ridgeline, a dark shadow moved against the deeper black of the night sky. Noble used the flashlight mounted on the AR15 and flashed twice. Several minutes passed. Nothing happened. Noble signaled again. Finally, Hunt started down the embankment, staying low and skirting the larger rock formations.

Another loud rumble announced the storm. Lightening flashed across the sky. Noble felt a heavy drop on his shoulder. A moment later the sky opened up and rain came down in thick sheets, cutting visibility to a few yards.

Hunt swam out of the darkness a few minutes later.

"Him again?" Alejandra said. She had to raise her voice over the driving rain. "Should have killed him."

"Nice to see you too," Hunt sneered. His GQ model hair was plastered to his skull. Water ran off his chin. All his swaggering confidence was gone, replaced by a sullen, hangdog look.

"What the hell is he doing here?" Alejandra asked.

"Looking for answers."

Noble made a surprised face. "I was starting to wonder if the CIA was still in the fact-finding business."

"Think what you like, Noble. I've got my orders."

"And those are?"

Hunt looked like he had just swallowed a slug. "To help you take out Machado."

"Curiouser and curiouser," Noble remarked. "Why the sudden change of heart?"

"I didn't ask."

Noble grinned. "You didn't ask, or Foster wouldn't say?"

"I follow orders. You should try it some time." Hunt drew a Soviet-era 9mm Makarov from his waistband.

Noble cocked a brow. "That thing will probably blow up in your hand."

"Someone *stole* mine," Hunt said.

Alejandra said, "We're wasting time."

Noble passed Hunt the other AR15.

"What's the plan?" Hunt thrust his chin at the compound wall. "There are a dozen guys in there and a lot of AK-47s."

"Alejandra and I are going over the wall," Noble told

him. "You're going to cover us from that ridgeline. Think you can handle it?"

"That's your plan?" Hunt said. "Not exactly Winston Churchill, are you?"

"You aren't exactly Eugene Sledge," said Noble. "Work your way back up the slope until you've got a good view of the layout. Signal with your flashlight when the coast is clear."

Hunt nodded. "Alright, but if this goes sideways, I'm back over that hill and you're on your own."

CHAPTER SEVENTY-TWO

MACHADO DOUBLED THE MEN ON THE FRONT GATE before retreating to his private study. He poured a finger of scotch from the side bar, knocked it back, and refilled the glass. Liquor calmed his nerves. He wanted to kill: to break and rip and destroy. Jake Noble had pulled the rug out from under his feet. Instead of negotiating with the other cartel leaders for a cut of their revenue, he was running for his life. The damn Yankee would die badly, but first Machado needed to get out of Mexico. The other cartels would be out for blood.

He dialed Santiago and got no answer. Next he dialed his new pilot and waited.

The man came on the line after a dozen rings. "*Si, el Jefe?*"

"What the hell took you so long?"

The pilot started to stammer out an excuse.

"Never mind," Machado barked. "I want to be in the air in thirty minutes."

"*Perdón, señor*, but there is a storm."

"I don't care if fire is raining from the sky," Machado screamed into the phone. "Be on the runway and ready to fly by the time I get there!"

He hung up and sipped his scotch. *Maintain control,* Machado told himself. Have every man at the compound escort him to the airfield and once he was safely in the air, he would have Noble's family—if he had any—assassinated. After that, he would call a meeting with Helen Rhodes. He had lived up to his end of the deal. It was time for her to flex the might of the American border patrol. With her help, he could still bring the other cartels in line. He nodded to himself. Perhaps it was not a complete loss.

There was a two-way radio in a charger on a side table. Machado picked it up and turned it over in his hands, trying to figure out how the thing worked. Usually Santiago handled communications. Machado found the power switch and then toggled the transmit. His head of his security answered. Machado said, "Prepare the convoy. Take every man you can spare. We are going to the airfield. Let me know as soon as you are ready to move."

"*Sí, señor.*"

Thunder shook the house. The first drops of rain pattered on the window panes, then the clouds opened up, lashing the house with all the fury of mother nature. A small knuckle of fear twisted in his belly. Would they be able to take off in this mess?

Machado sloshed more scotch into his glass. Minutes passed. *What the hell was taking so long*?

The sporadic burp of small arms fire climbed above the

pouring rain. So much for making a clean getaway. He would have to fight his way to the airfield. He put down his drink and drew a pump action shotgun from under the desk.

CHAPTER SEVENTY-THREE

NOBLE AND ALEJANDRA CREPT ACROSS TEN METERS OF open ground to the wall. Alejandra used the flashlight mounted under her rifle to signal Hunt, then they waited. Noble checked the action on the Kimber and let out a nervous breath.

Alejandra said, "You don't have to do this, you know. It's not your fight."

Noble thought of Torres. If the roles were reversed, if he had been killed by Machado's butchers, Torres would chase the kingpin to the ends of the earth. That's why Torres stayed while Noble was pinned beneath a dead horse with mortar shells raining down on them.

Noble said, "Yeah, it is."

"We're going to die," Alejandra said.

"Probably," Noble admitted. "Nervous?"

She shook her head, throwing droplets of water. "I'm not afraid to die."

"Once we get inside, keep moving," Noble told her. "That's key. A moving target is hard to hit."

She gave another jerky nod.

"It's going to be chaotic," he said, then added, "Don't get jumpy and shoot me in the back."

Minutes felt like hours. Noble's legs started to cramp. Finally, Hunt returned the "all clear" with two quick beats from his flashlight.

"Can we trust him?" Alejandra asked.

"We're about to find out," Noble said.

Before they could move, the sound of a machine gun ripped through the gusting wind and rain. Alejandra had her rifle up looking for targets but the shots came from the front gate. Several automatics answered. One of the other cartels had decided to pay Machado back for the dust-up at the penthouse.

"Now's our chance," Noble said. "Go."

Alejandra slung her weapon and laced her fingers together. Noble put his foot in the stirrup. She hoisted him up. He grasped the top of the wall and hauled himself onto the ledge. A dozen pickup trucks and SUVs pulled up to the compound. Muzzle flashes winked like fireflies through the downpour. Bullets hissed and snapped overhead.

Alejandra jumped and Noble latched onto her wrists. His bruised ribs gave a tortured cry but he managed to pull her up. They dropped down on the other side with a splash. No need to worry about the noise. The battle would disguise their movements. The arrival of the enemy cartel had improved the odds of getting inside. Getting out was another matter. Noble took the lead. He hurried across the lawn, past the tennis courts, through the pouring rain to the main house.

Hunt counted two dozen attackers and seventeen defenders. The attackers had rolled up to the gate in pickups with belt-fed machine guns mounted in the beds. The home team had the advantage, though; they had good cover behind the wall and plenty of firepower. It was a full-scale war and Hunt had bleacher seats. This must have been what the Romans felt like sitting in the Colosseum. Hunt was halfway up the slope, a few short meters from the top. He wanted to be close enough to scramble over the ridgeline, back down the other side and be on the motorcycle if things went south.

He settled the barrel of his rifle in a wedge formed between two rocks and steadied his breathing. His pulse raced. He could feel his heartbeat in his ears. This was the first time he had ever been in a pitched firefight. And it was an ideal situation. For him at least.

He checked on Noble and the girl. They were moving south towards the main building, past a swimming pool big enough to float a yacht in. At the front gate, Machado's men were decimating the attackers. Hunt cursed. He needed the Los Zetas to lose. If the rival cartel overran the compound and killed Machado, Hunt could call it a day and go home.

He aimed at one of the defenders, let out his breath and his fingertip tightened on the trigger. The rifle kicked. The Los Zetas soldier tumbled from the wall.

Hunt, his heart tap dancing inside his chest, ducked down behind the rock, anticipating a hail storm of lead. He had just killed a man, shot him in the back. It was like a video game. Aim. Squeeze. *Bang*. One minute the guy was standing there, the next he folded up and hit the ground.

This was the second time Hunt had fired his weapon in the line of duty. The first time, he had been sprinting across a snowy parking lot in Pushkin. The whole thing happened so fast, Hunt never knew if he had hit the Russian agent and never found out what happened.

This was different. His bullet had found the mark. No doubt about it.

He chanced a peek over the rock. No one was shooting at him. The narco armies were caught in the fog of war and didn't realize someone was shooting at their backs. *Why would they?* A single rifle didn't attract any attention in the deadly barrage.

Hunt steadied his weapon, fired and watched another Los Zetas soldier collapse.

"I could get used to this," he told the rain. He felt invincible, like a god dispatching his enemies with cool detachment. He lined up another shot, missed, frowned, and then remembered to check on Noble and Alejandra.

Noble was at the side of the main building, moving in a half crouch, toward the backyard. One of Machado's men was going the opposite direction. They would both reach the corner at the same time.

Hunt held his breath. If Noble got himself killed and the rival faction took out Machado, all of Hunt's problems would be tied up in a neat little bow. He thought about breaking the news to Sam. *Sorry for your loss. Awful shame. If only he hadn't insisted on going in alone.*

CHAPTER SEVENTY-FOUR

Noble heard boots in the gravel and pressed himself against the stucco wall. Alejandra fell in beside him. He put a finger to his lips. It was too early to start shooting. He didn't want the Los Zetas to know the compound was breached. If he could take out Machado quietly and slip back over the wall, he might make it out alive.

An underfed Mexican in a faded T-shirt and combat boots hurried around the corner with an AK-47. Noble stepped up behind him, snatched a fistful of hair in one hand and clapped the other hand over his chin. Breaking a man's neck is no easy task. Neck muscles are some of the strongest in the human body—they carry an object the same approximate size and weight of a bowling ball all day long—and vertebra have more flexion than most people realize.

Noble wrenched the thug's chin over his shoulder and felt the muscles reach their limit. The guy tried unsuccessfully to elbow Noble. The tendons in his neck stood out like cords stretched to the breaking point. Noble smelled sweat and unwashed hair as he fought to control the struggling man.

He forced the guy down to one knee, getting the leverage he needed and gave a heroic twist. He felt the vertebra pop. The cartel soldier went limp. A dark stain spread over his pants. The harsh stench of urine filled the air. Noble dragged the dead man around the corner, dumped him in the gravel, and took his AK-47.

Hunt took his finger off the trigger. Noble had broken the guy's neck. It was like something out of a movie. Hunt watched, a little jealous, as Noble dragged the body out of sight. It was one of the coolest things Hunt had ever seen.

Noble took the dead man's weapon, checked the corner and then moved in a crouch—AK-47 leading the way—around the main building toward the back doors.

Hunt shifted his attention to the front gate. The battle had reached a stalemate. The Los Zetas had the advantage of position, but the attackers were entrenched behind their vehicles. They seemed content to wage a prolonged assault on the compound: popping up, squeezing off a few rounds, and then ducking back down. It was like they were waiting, but for what?

As if in answer to Hunt's unspoken question, a belt-fed machine gun opened up atop the ridgeline. A group of attackers had mounted the far side of the hill and come up directly in back of Hunt. They raked the compound wall with an M60. Bright green tracer rounds zipped through the rain, leaving a glowing afterimage. Three Los Zetas soldiers died before the others turned and sprayed the hillside. Lead hissed and snapped overhead, digging up puffs of sodden earth. A bullet whined off a rock, inches from Hunt's ear. He cowered behind the boulder, caught between the two opposing forces.

Machado opened the MacBook Pro on his desk and brought up the feed from state-of-the-art video surveillance. He zoomed in on the front gate. Cartel soldiers didn't wear uniforms, so it was hard to be sure, but it looked like Escobedo's men.

The whip crack of high powered rifles was punctuated by a blast of thunder so close it shook the house. The lights blinked. Machado unlocked a tall cabinet and took out a pair of night vision goggles in case the storm knocked out the power.

He tried to get his head of security on the two-way but got no answer. That left Machado on his own. If he could make it downstairs to the garage he could escape in one of his armored vehicles. Several of his hotrods had been outfitted with Kevlar plates and bullet-resistant glass.

He checked the surveillance feeds and spotted two figures creeping up to the back doors. Machado zoomed in. He recognized Alejandra at once. The man would be Jake Noble, the bothersome fly who had killed his accountant, and brought Escobedo's men to his doorstep. While Machado watched, Noble tried the back door, found it locked and put his elbow through the glass.

A vein stood out like an engorged python in Machado's

forehead. His muscular frame shook with rage. The gringo had ruined everything. Now he had the nerve to break into Machado's house? *Does he think he can walk in here and assassinate me in my own home?* Machado fumed at the arrogance of the American.

CHAPTER SEVENTY-FIVE

They reached the back doors. Noble knocked out a pane of glass while Alejandra covered him. He reached through, felt around for the deadbolt, and let himself in. Evidence of Machado's hubris was everywhere. The house was a palace. There was a painstaking recreation of the Sistine Chapel painted on the ceiling. Only in this version, Adam looked suspiciously like Machado. The floor was pink marble. A crystal chandelier hung overhead. Intricately carved pillars held up the roof. A sweeping staircase led to the second floor.

Alejandra shuddered. "He keeps it freezing here."

Noble grunted. He was too keyed up to pay any attention to the temperature. His senses were on high alert. His stomach muscles clenched in nervous excitement. So far, the operation had gone off without a hitch. The thunderstorm and the rival cartel had been an unexpected bit of luck, but that sort of luck never lasts.

"Where's the kitchen?" Noble asked.

Alejandra pointed.

"Lead the way," he said.

She took him through an expansive dining room, past a table long enough to host a UN summit, to a kitchen with a range big enough to feed the delegates.

Alejandra shut the door and put her back to it. "You hungry?"

"Starving," Noble told her. He hadn't eaten since lunch, but he wasn't thinking of food. He slung his rifle, grasped the stove and scooted it out from the wall until he could reach behind and jerk the gas line loose.

The smell filled the kitchen. Alejandra covered her nose.

Noble rifled the cabinets and said, "There aren't any power lines running to the compound and it's too far for underground cable, so Machado must have his own power source. You've been here before. Do you know where the generator is stored?"

"It's in another building," she said. "Why?"

Noble found a cloth napkin, stuffed it in a stainless steel toaster and plunged the lever. Then he grabbed Alejandra's elbow. She didn't need convincing. They jogged the length of the dining room, back to the marbled hall.

Three cartel soldiers were coming down the steps as Noble and Alejandra slammed through the dining room door.

Noble and Alejandra dodged behind the nearest pillar. Bullets blasted chunks from the stonework and skipped off the marble floor. Noble pulled his arms and legs in. Alejandra crowded in next to him, but she wasn't fast enough. A lead bee stung her forearm. Her face pinched in pain. She made a noise somewhere between a bark and a scream.

"Bad?" Noble shouted over the roar of gunfire.

She pressed a hand over wound. Her mouth was a strict line. "I'll be alright."

From the kitchen, there was a hungry *whoosh.* Noble closed his eyes and opened his mouth to equalize the pressure in his ears. A second later, a blast shook the house. Lights flickered. Plaster rained from the ceiling. The explosion had taken out the kitchen and a good portion of the dining room. But that was just the opening act. The fire would race back down the gas pipe to the generator.

Noble held his breath.

Seconds after the first explosion, a second blast rent the air. The lights winked out, plunging them into darkness. Beyond the French doors, Noble saw an orange fireball through the pouring rain.

The twin detonations had stunned the cartel soldiers. Noble used the distraction to break cover. He leaned around the pillar and sighted on a dark silhouette, triggering three short bursts. His bullets stitched two of the soldiers and they went down. The third man fired and tried to retreat up the steps at the same time. He caught his heel and sat down hard.

Alejandra's left hand wasn't working so she propped the rifle in the crook of her elbow, leaned out, and drilled four rounds through his chest. He slumped over and a line of dark blood ran from his mouth.

A bullet whined off the rock that Hunt crouched behind —*more like cowering,* he had to admit, at least to himself. Sooner or later one of those bullets would bounce the wrong way. He needed to move. But no one had seen him yet and he was sure the moment he broke cover the machine gunner would spot him. The deadly firestorm would sweep across his position and that would be the end of Gregory Alastair Hunt Jr. He let out a small, terrified breath that sounded a lot like a whimper, though he would never describe it that way to anyone else. Another ricochet buzzed past his ear.

Got to move, he told himself. *Got to move before I catch a bullet.*

But where?

He couldn't go up. The machine gunner was at the top of the hill, blazing away. Down didn't feel any safer. The rocks and vegetation petered out toward the bottom of the hillside. Then there was the compound wall, a ten-foot-high concrete barrier slick with rain. Noble and Alejandra had helped each other over. Hunt would be on his own, trying to mount the wall in the middle of a firefight where anyone might see. He had an image of himself reaching the top and getting shot in the back, just like in the old movies he had watched as a kid. The convict makes the top of the prison wall, a search light finds him, there's a bang. The actor throws his hands in the air and tumbles out of sight. Credits roll.

Hunt pressed himself against the boulder, soaking wet and deaf from the constant buzz saw of the M60, too terrified to move.

In the courtyard, Los Zetas soldiers produced a rocket propelled grenade launcher. The RPG is a favorite among

Islamic extremists, third world despots and Mexican drug lords because they're cheap and easy to use. They're also notoriously inaccurate.

The rocket sizzled over the compound wall but instead of obliterating the M60 gunner, it exploded halfway up the hillside, a few meters to Hunt's left. The sharp thunderclap shorted out the last of his hearing. Shrapnel blistered the side of the boulder. He felt a pinch on his left thigh, like an ant bite. Hunt hissed and touched his leg. His fingers came away wet with blood.

That sealed it. He rolled around the boulder and belly crawled down the incline. As soon as he moved, the pain started in earnest. It felt like an iron spike in his hamstring.

Another rocket went sizzling up the slope. This one got closer, but still missed. Dirt and debris rained down on Hunt's back. The machine gunner zeroed in on the rocket launcher. A hailstorm of bullets felled the Los Zetas soldier holding the rocket tube.

Hunt scrambled between rocks and through thickets. He was half way to the bottom of the hill when the side of Machado's mansion disappeared in flash of light and sound. The explosion shook the ground and lit the night sky. Hunt buried his face in the dirt. A moment later, one of the annex buildings disintegrated.

CHAPTER SEVENTY-SIX

Alejandra tried to stand. Her legs gave out. She sagged against the pillar, slid to the ground and pressed a hand to her side. Blood had soaked through her shirt. She let out a trembling breath.

Noble knelt next to her. "Let me see."

He eased up her shirt. A bullet had burrowed a hole, no bigger than a nickel, through her side and out her back.

She managed to smile through the pain. "That stings."

Noble's brow drew down. If they had been in the city with emergency medical crews close by, she might live. Sam Gunn had survived a very similar wound six months ago. But they were miles from the nearest hospital and Noble would have to get her out of the compound and past Machado's men. He stood a better chance of becoming the next pope.

She read the expression on his face and nodded. "It's okay."

"We have to stop the bleeding," Noble said.

She grabbed onto his arm and wouldn't let go.

"Kill Machado," she said. "For me."

Noble hesitated.

"For Diaz," she said.

He nodded.

She let go.

He put the AR-15 rifle into her hands, laid his AK-47 across her lap and pointed at the French doors. "You kill anybody that comes through these doors, understand? Two in the chest, one in the head."

She nodded.

Leaving her was a death sentence. Noble knew it and he felt bad about it, but she was going to die and there was nothing he could do to stop it. Maybe she would kill a few Los Zetas soldiers before she stepped out. He patted her uninjured cheek. She kissed his open palm.

Noble's heart clenched. He felt like there was a rebar spike jammed through his chest. A white-hot fire had been building in his belly since he learned Torres was dead. Now it spilled over into blind, unthinking rage.

Hunt was still face down in the mud when someone nearly stepped on him. Several cartel soldiers were creeping up the incline, whispering to each other in the dark. One passed within inches of Hunt. He counted three men, then spotted two more, on their way to ambush the machine gunner. Hunt stuck his face in the mud and tried to look like part of the scenery. Noble's little plan had gone to hell.

Hunt's escape was cut off. He couldn't go back over the hill without being seen and he didn't like the idea of going down any better. It crossed his mind to lay there all night, sinking into the mud. Let the cartels kill each other and when they were dead, then maybe he could make his escape.

The Los Zetas soldiers reached the summit and opened fire on the machine gun crew. There was a short, fierce firefight, then silence. Hunt, his leg still smarting, raised up for a peek. It was hard to see through the driving rain, but it looked like both sides had killed each other. He waited. A wave of dizziness hit. Probably from blood loss. Several minutes ticked by. He didn't see any muzzle flashes. He pushed to his feet, intent on scaling back up the incline, but his leg gave out. He went down on his face in the mud and came up spluttering.

"I hate you, Noble," he muttered. "I hate your guts."

Using his rifle as a cane, Hunt hobbled up the embankment. He stopped five meters short and waited some more to make sure no one was alive and faking. Below him, the cartels had battled each other to a standstill. The frantic din of automatic weapons had given way to sporadic bursts. Dying men with broken bodies littered the ground. Their screams made Hunt's heart tremble inside his chest.

Closer at hand, one of the cartel soldiers gave a weak moan. Hunt shouldered his rifle and fired. The man coughed and his eyes rolled up. Hunt had the hilltop, again. And an M60. He limped over the uneven terrain and found three full belts of ammo among a litter of spent brass.

"Alright, Noble," Hunt said. "Maybe we can pull this off."

He took the machine gun from the dead thug and limped to a large, flat-topped rock. He carried over the ammo belts and then checked the action on the weapon. Ready to rock and roll.

Hunt turned the sights on the attackers and, using one hand to keep the belt up so it would feed, eased back on the trigger. The big gun burped out a steady *chunk—chunk—chunk* of 7.62mm NATO rounds. Smoking brass leapt from the breech. Green tracer rounds arced through the pouring rain. Hunt walked his line of fire across the attacking cartel. Three fell and the rest tried to scramble around the other side of their vehicles only to be cut down by the defenders.

Hunt held the trigger for a seven count and let go, allowing the barrel cool. As soon as he stopped, bullets drilled the hillside with heavy, sharp *thwacks*. He responded with short bursts, chewing through the belt of ammo until the weapon locked back on an empty breech.

The few remaining attackers decided they'd had enough. They piled into their vehicles and tore off down the dirt road. The men inside the compound gave a victory shout.

"That's right *amigos*," Hunt said, loading a fresh belt of ammo. "Keep cheering."

He hauled back on the charging handle and loosed another long burst of deadly automatic fire. The Los Zetas soldiers broke and ran. This time Hunt held down the trigger and the M60 barrel started to glow.

Noble worked his way through the first floor, going slow, clearing each room before moving to the next. He hadn't met anyone in the dark and was starting to feel like he had the place to himself. Machado could have slipped out in all the confusion. There might be a secret tunnel in case of emergencies. Plenty of drug lords used them. Machado could be miles away by now.

Outside, the battle was winding down. The gun fire tapered off. *Wonder who's winning,* Noble thought. It wouldn't matter much. With his skin tone, either cartel would shoot him on sight. And people say there's no such thing as reverse racism. But survival was the farthest thing from his mind.

He opened the door to a garage with a automobile collection that rivaled Jay Leno's and Clive Cussler's. Three rows of classic muscle cars lined the showroom floor. Chrome bumpers winked in the starlight streaming through floor to ceiling windows. Machado had all the hallmarks of a good collection: the Mustangs, Camaros, Chevelles, Pontiacs and Challengers. He also had more eclectic finds: a Renault, a Rolls Royce Phantom, a Ford Edsel. A fully restored Model T sat next to an Aston Martin DB9. On Noble's left, was a '67 Ford Fastback painted light gray with dark stripes. He let out a low whistle. There was enough wealth in this room alone to solve all of his financial problems. Too bad he couldn't take it with him.

Noble moved through the garage to a door on the far side. He was halfway when he heard movement and turned. Machado entered the garage with a shotgun and night vision goggles. Noble suddenly knew how David must have felt facing Goliath. Machado was built like a bulldozer. His massive shoulders threatened to burst his suit coat. The weapon looked tiny in his steam-shovel hands.

CHAPTER SEVENTY-SEVEN

Noble threw himself behind a '67 Pontiac GTO and the shotgun roared. The windshield exploded in a shower of broken glass. Night vision goggles let you see the bad guys before they see you, but they make aiming difficult. It takes practice. *Lots of practice.* Soldiers in the Special Forces log countless hours learning to use their weapons with night vision. Machado had not and it saved Noble's life.

He thrust the Kimber around the front bumper and fired blind. He wasn't aiming, just trying to rattle Machado. It didn't work. The drug tsar racked the slide and fired again, blowing out the driver's side headlamp and blasting holes in the grill. The sound was like a railroad spike in Noble's ears. His lips peeled back from clenched teeth. His heart ping-ponged around inside his chest.

"You think you can kill me in my own house?" Machado yelled.

Noble heard him stuffing shells into the breech. He needed to put more distance between him and the shotgun.

He took two long strides and launched himself behind the Model T. It was a step down in terms of cover. The shotgun coughed fire and the old automobile pissed coolant from a busted radiator. Noble circled the back bumper of an Aston Martin, looking for a better vantage point. Machado fired. Buckshot skipped off the hood of the car, spider-webbing one of the floor to ceiling windows that looked out across the garden. It gave Noble an idea.

Machado yelled, "Keep running little man. Soon you run out of cars to hide behind. Then what?"

The smell of spent gun powder hung in the air. Noble heard the *click-clack* of the shotgun over the ringing in his ears. He aimed over the hood, squeezed off two rounds and then sprinted across the garage. The shotgun boomed. Buckshot snapped overhead. The small hairs on the back of his neck stood up. Noble covered his face with both arms and threw himself through the window. It felt like jumping into a pile of loosely stacked bricks. He impacted with his shoulder, the window shattered, and Noble burst through. But his arm wanted to know who had hit him with a baseball bat. He landed on the rain soaked lawn.

Buckshot blew out another window, showering Noble in glass. He returned fire. He couldn't see through the pouring rain and didn't wait to find out if he hit anything. He pushed himself off the ground and stumbled into the maze of tall hedges and topiaries, shaking chips of broken glass from his hair.

Hunt held down the trigger on the M60. Bright green tracer

rounds flashed through the rain. Los Zetas soldiers fell like wheat before a sickle. He fired until the barrel melted and the weapon jammed with a loud *clank*. His ears rang like someone was holding down the E chord on an electric piano. Rain obscured his vision and his hands shook from the heavy recoil. He wiped his eyes and picked up the AR-15 to continue the fight but the Los Zetas army was in tatters.

Machado had probably died in the explosion, and if he hadn't, Noble had probably killed him. It was time to go, before the cops showed up. *Get back on the motorcycle and lay down rubber*, Hunt told himself. *That was the smart thing*. But there was a remote possibility Machado was still alive and it would be the final disgrace to tell Foster that he was dead only to have his name pop up on an intelligence brief in a month or two.

Alejandra's eyelids drooped. Her toes were little blocks of ice. She couldn't feel her legs. The pain in her stomach had dulled. She forced her eyes open but they closed again almost immediately. Everything had gotten very quiet. The guns had stopped. This must be dying, she told herself.

Her chin sank to her chest. Diaz was smiling at her. They were in bed. She felt his hands on her skin. She reached for him. The *pop—pop—pop* of small arms fire shattered the dream. The gunshots sounded far away, like they were coming from the Gulf of Mexico. Alejandra realized her eyes were closed and forced them open. Four cartel soldiers ran past, headed in the direction Noble had gone.

How long ago was that?

She couldn't remember. They either hadn't seen her or thought she was dead. With a concentration of effort, she planted the butt stock on the floor, gripped the barrel in both hands and levered herself up. Her head swam. Blood stained her pants. There was a crimson puddle on the marble floor. She wavered and clung to the rifle for support. When the dizziness subsided, she followed the soldiers along the corridor toward the back of the house. She had to stop several times. It took forever just to go the length of the hall. She rounded a corner and saw the gunmen go into the garage. She leaned against a wall, marshalled her strength, and shouldered the rifle. Another wave of dizziness hit and she fought to stay on her feet until it passed.

Through the garage door, she heard Machado growling orders. Her eye focused. She forgot about dying and remembered what she had come for. Her mouth formed a grim line. She pushed off from the wall and stumbled forward on trembling legs.

Noble sprinted through the garden, putting as much distance between himself and Machado's shotgun as possible. The shock of throwing himself through a window had worn off and he got his legs moving again. He ran along the hedge maze, taking turns at random, past a row of Greek statues, then ducked behind a gazebo of white stone.

The rain was letting up. It fell straight down, in heavy drops, the way it does when the storm has spent all of its fury and is wringing the last of the moisture from the clouds. Noble crouched next to one of the stone pillars and pressed the magazine eject on his pistol. He had two rounds left in the mag. One in the chamber. His lips pulled back from clenched teeth.

His ears pricked up at the sound of footsteps squelching in the soggy grass. His heart leapt. He aimed at a gap in the hedge and fired two rounds as a dark silhouette stepped through the opening. The man went down flat on his back, his arms flung out to either side, an AK-47 lying next to him.

The garden came alive with the deadly riot of automatic rifles. Bullets buzzed around like angry bees. Noble hunkered next the gazebo, trying to make himself as small as possible. A round blew a chunk from the handrail, inches from his head. He broke cover and hustled across the lawn to the fallen soldier.

CHAPTER SEVENTY-EIGHT

ALEJANDRA ENTERED THE GARAGE IN TIME TO SEE Machado and four of his enforcers step onto the lawn through a shattered window. They fanned out in search of Noble. Machado, in his business suit, armed with a shotgun and night vision goggles, disappeared behind a hedge.

Alejandra staggered between cars, leaving a trail of blood, to the windows. Broken glass crunched beneath her feet. Rain fell in heavy drops. Outside, a cartel soldier stalked alongside a decorative pool carpeted with large lily pads. He was so focused on the garden he never bothered to look behind him.

Shots rang out from a dark corner of the maze. The soldier turned his rifle in the direction of the sound and held the trigger down. He whipped his rifle back and forth like a fireman turning a hose on a burning house.

Using the noise as cover, Alejandra raised her weapon, sighted on his back and squeezed. The rifle kicked, sending a lance of pain from her wounded belly, up her spine, to her brain. Her bullets punched through the soldier's back. He splashed face-first into the pond. The shooting stopped. Silence descended on the garden. The only sound was the steady patter of rain falling on leaves.

Noble snatched up the AK-47 and checked the mag. It was hard to say how many bullets were left without taking them out and counting. Instead he pressed down with his thumb and felt a mostly empty spring. His situation had improved only slightly. He rammed it back in the weapon and patted the dead thug's pockets. No luck.

His only chance was to keep moving and pick off the bad guys one at a time. He retreated further into the garden, looking for another likely spot to use for an ambush, but hit a dead end. The garden butted up against the compound wall. Noble jogged along it in search of a hiding place.

A cartel soldier pushed through a hedge, saw Noble and yelled, "He's here!"

The shout was like a shot of adrenaline. Noble side stepped, aimed, and mashed the trigger. The hired goon fired at the same time. Bullets whip-cracked over Noble's shoulder, impacting the wall. Noble's bullets found their mark, knocking the man backwards through the hedge.

His first thought was to take the dead man's weapon. He started in that direction, but the ear-splitting thunder-clap of a shotgun rent the air. Buckshot obliterated a hedge less than a foot from Noble's elbow. He ducked and pulled his shoulders up around his ears like a turtle trying to crawl inside its shell.

Machado stepped around a large topiary. The green dot

on his night vision goggles glowed like the hateful eye of Homer's mythical Cyclops.

Noble was already moving, making himself a hard target. He leveled the AK-47 and loosed three short volleys before the hammer fell on an empty chamber.

Machado racked the shotgun. Another sharp clap assaulted Noble's ears. Buckshot whistled through the air. He dodged a pair of benches and a stone cherub pissing into a fountain. Machado squeezed off three more rounds in quick succession. *Boom—click-clack—boom—click-clack—boom.* The cherub lost a wing and most of one chubby arm. Machado racked the weapon again. This time there was a hollow *click.*

Noble stopped and wheeled around.

Machado threw aside the shotgun and came at Noble like an enraged bull. His muscular legs ate up half the distance in the time it took Noble to drag the Kimber from his waistband. Machado slammed into him like a beer delivery truck without brakes. All the air went out of Noble's lungs in a loud *Oof!* He lost his hold on the gun. It landed in the fountain with a *ker-plunk.* Machado carried Noble to the ground. Two-hundred and twenty pounds of muscle came down on his bruised ribcage. He let out a grunt. Meaty fists impacted the side of his head. Small fairy lights danced in his vision.

Noble's brain felt like a scrambled egg. Desperate to stop the punishment, he jackhammered a fist into Machado's cheek. His knuckles connected with enough force to check a charging mastiff. Machado barely registered the hit. Noble struck three more times. It did no more good than a wad of newspaper blowing against a brick wall.

Machado wrapped both hands around Noble's neck and squeezed, cutting off his air supply. The vertebra in his neck creaked under the crushing force. His eyes bulged. He tried to pry Machado's fingers off. It was like digging at tree roots. His brain screamed for oxygen. His face turned an ugly shade of purple. His vision narrowed to a pin prick.

"I'm going to kill you," Machado snarled. "Just like your friend."

CHAPTER SEVENTY-NINE

Alejandra was losing blood fast. Her whole body shook from cold. Her left leg was a club, forcing her to drag it behind. It was everything she could do to stay on her feet. The urge to lay down and close her eyes was overpowering. She turned a corner near the gazebo and spotted a furtive figure creeping along a row of statues. She recognized him at once. She didn't know his name. He was one of the men that had raped her, after Machado finished and before she was too far gone to remember faces. He had taken a lot of pleasure in hurting her. Alejandra shouldered her rifle and whistled.

The color drained from his face.

She shot him twice in the belly.

He dropped his weapon and sat down in the grass, held his stomach and moaned. Alejandra stepped around him, pushing deeper into the garden. Shots rang out. It was a short, rapid exchange, and then silence. She wanted to run, but only managed a stumbling shuffle.

Noble's eyes rolled back in his head. He clung to consciousness through sheer force of will. His lungs screamed for air. One hand landed on his cellphone in his pocket. With the last of his fading strength, he pulled out the phone and snapped a picture. The flash triggered.

Machado shrieked, reeled backwards and clawed the goggles off his face. The sudden flash, magnified through the night vision goggles, must have felt like knitting needles in his retinas.

Noble gasped. Oxygen flooded his aching lungs. His eyelids fluttered open. His fingers and toes tingled as blood started to circulate again.

Machado was on his knees, blinking and rubbing at his eyes.

Noble lifted his foot and drove his heel into Machado's face. He felt the impact. A nice solid hit. Machado pitched over backwards with a noise like a wounded buffalo. His lips split open and two of his front teeth landed in the grass. Blood spilled down the front of his suit.

Noble kicked again, pressing his advantage, trying to put the big man out of commission. The force of the blow put Machado flat on his back. He rolled onto his hands and knees and tried to crawl. He looked like a drunk, flailing across the grass.

Noble struggled to his feet, almost fell, caught himself and kicked Machado in the ribs. The force of the blow lifted the big man a few inches off the ground.

Machado gasped for breath.

Noble kicked him in the face, rolling Machado over onto his back. Blood bubbled from both nostrils.

"You scared?" Noble croaked through a throat that felt like someone had scrubbed it with steel wool.

Machado coughed up blood. "Go to hell, *Americano*!"

Noble swung a kick at his face, meant to break his jaw, but Machado's hands moved like twin cobras. He caught Noble's foot and twisted. It felt like his leg would rip right out of socket. He went down in the grass with a piercing scream.

A fist the size of a bowling ball hammered his kidney. Noble grunted through clenched teeth. The giant fist impacted his temple. Fireworks exploded behind his eyelids. He managed to ward off another blow with his forearm. Machado swatted his arm aside, gripped Noble's head in both hands and twisted. Noble fought against it with the muscles in his neck but his head turned slowly, inexorably to the right, until his spine was at the breaking point.

"Let him go!" Alejandra shouted.

She pressed the muzzle of her rifle against the back of Machado's head.

The pressure on Noble's neck disappeared. He scrambled away, trying to get out of reach of those murderous hands, scooting over the grass until he bumped into the stone fountain.

Machado crouched in the wet turf, a bib of blood on his chest. His shoulders tensed, ready for action. He looked over his shoulder at Alejandra. "Go ahead. Pull the trigger, you whore."

Alejandra did. The rifle clicked on an empty chamber.

A small noise—one part surprise, one part disappointment—escaped her lips.

Machado ripped the rifle out of her hands and swung it like a club. Her head rocked to the side. She fell to the earth like a broken puppet.

While Machado was busy with Alejandra, Noble had pulled himself up on the fountain in search of the fallen Kimber. He spotted the gleam of polished steel under the water and lunged for it. His fingers closed around the pistol grip.

Machado dropped the empty rifle and turned to find himself staring down the barrel. He crouched slightly, a jungle cat ready to pounce. His hands twitched. His eyes narrowed.

Noble said, "Try it."

Machado leapt.

Noble pulled the trigger. The Kimber clapped thunder. A brass shell leapt from the breech, trailing smoke. The bullet punched a hole the size of a nickel in Machado's forehead and blew off the back of his skull. His legs went out from under him. He landed flat on his back, staring up at the sky with blank, lifeless eyes.

Noble, every muscle in his body aching, crawled across the grass to Alejandra and scooped her up in his arms. Her eyelid peeled open. Her lips moved. No sound came out. She tried again. "Machado?"

"Dead," Noble told her.

She nodded. Her face pinched in pain. A cough wracked her frame. Blood spilled from one corner of her mouth. She raised her left hand and Noble took it in his right. She urged him closer. He bent down. A long, rattling noise escaped her throat. In a small voice she managed, "Train station."

Noble touched the key in his pocket. She nodded. One last breath escaped her lips. A spasm gripped her body. Her pupil dilated. Noble felt for a pulse but she was dead. He laid her down in the grass, feeling exhausted and empty. A lump formed in his throat. The rain had stopped. It was time to get out of here. Before he could convince his legs to stand, someone pressed a gun to the back of his head.

CHAPTER EIGHTY

Every nerve ending in Noble's body hummed like a high-tension wire. His heart tried to crawl out through his throat. The muscles in his back tensed. He was just about to make a desperate attempt at disarming whoever was behind him when he heard Hunt say, "I want my gun."

Noble passed the Kimber over his shoulder.

"What did she tell you?" Hunt asked

"She thanked me," Noble said, "for avenging her parents' murder."

Hunt looked at the scattered bodies. "Your missions always end like this?"

"Pretty much." Noble climbed to his feet. His knees popped, letting him know he was getting old. "Anybody left?"

"A few. They took off in trucks. We're the last men standing."

Noble pointed to Hunt's thigh. "You got clipped."

"Shrapnel from an RPG."

"Hurt much?"

"Stings."

"So what happens now?" Noble wanted to know.

Hunt gave it some thought. "I still don't like you, Noble. The Company should have tossed you in a deep dark hole somewhere."

"But," Noble prompted.

"But Sam asked me to give you the benefit of the doubt," Hunt said.

Noble nodded.

Hunt said, "The next time we meet, I'm taking you down."

"Let's hope we don't meet," Noble said.

Hunt turned and limped away. Noble legged it back to the mansion. The explosion had destroyed a good portion of the house but the storm had put out the fire before it got out of hand. There was evidence of looting. Several of the more expensive artworks and a lot of electronics had been liberated by the last remaining Los Zetas soldiers before they fled. Ten minutes later, Noble roared out of the compound gate behind the wheel of the '67 Ford Fastback.

CHAPTER EIGHTY-ONE

THREE DAYS LATER, NOBLE WALKED INTO THE Buenavista Railway Station in downtown Mexico City with a laptop bag slung over one shoulder. A loudspeaker announced a train to Juarez departing in ten minutes. The electronic voice echoed around the cavernous terminal. Noble sat down at a lunch counter with a back mirror, ordered a cup of coffee and watched the crowd. No one stood out.

He nursed his coffee for five minutes then tossed a few pesos on the counter, crossed the busy terminal, located locker 314. The key fit. Noble opened it and peered inside. There were no files, no papers, no disks. *Nothing*. He stared into an empty metal cube. Noble chewed the inside of one cheek. Torres wouldn't have sent him the key to an empty box. He examined the inside of the locker for a message. He even studied the graffiti for hidden meaning. No dice.

Noble raked a hand through his shaggy locks. He closed the door and was about to turn the key when he got an idea. He opened the door and reached inside. There was a narrow metal lip where the door met the frame. A thumb drive was balanced on the ledge. A thrill of satisfaction went through him. He pocketed the USB, closed the locker, and turned toward the busy terminal. A hand came down on his shoulder. He felt the sharp point of a knife in his ribcage.

Hunt said, "I'll take that."

The last boarding call for the Juarez-bound train echoed over the loudspeakers. Busy travelers hustled past. Noble said "You're not going to stab me, Hunt."

"Yeah? Why not?"

"You want to know what's on this thumb drive as much as I do. If you give it to Foster, it'll get buried."

"That's what makes us different, Noble. I follow orders." He dug the knife a little deeper. "Now give me the thumb drive."

Noble spoke through clenched teeth. "I had a feeling you'd be that way about it."

"What's that supposed to mean?"

Noble had stopped through the local library on his way to the train station and filled the laptop bag with hardbacks. He used it to deflect the knife blade, then turned and threw an open hand strike to Hunt's throat. The knife bounced across dingy linoleum. Hunt's head snapped back. He lost his balance and sat down hard. His face scarlet.

Noble hustled through the terminal toward the gates.

Hunt scrambled to his feet and pressed a hand to his ear. It took him a minute to get words out. "Converge!" he said into a radio. "Converge on target. Cut him off. Don't let him on the train."

Noble saw the support team closing in from either side.

Ezra was closest. His eyes were full of fear. He took short, jerky steps, like Frankenstein's monster. He looked like a man stepping into the Colosseum with a hungry lion.

Noble gave him an icy stare and reached into the laptop bag.

"Oh my God." Ezra stopped in his tracks. "He's got a gun. He's got a gun."

Gwen fell back a step, looking for help that wasn't there. Hunt was too far away to provide any support, and she wasn't going up against Noble by herself.

"Get him!" Hunt croaked. "Don't let him on the train."

Noble reached the gate. He handed a ticket to a dour-faced Mexican who stamped it and wished him safe travels. Noble passed through the metal detector without setting off the alarm and down the steps to the platform. He had to hustle but he made it onto the train. He watched as Hunt reached the gate. The attendant held up a hand and asked to see his boarding pass. Noble grinned and waved his ticket as the pneumatic doors hissed shut.

CHAPTER EIGHTY-TWO

NOBLE PARKED THE '67 FASTBACK IN FRONT OF THE Hangar in downtown Saint Petersburg. He took the same booth overlooking the runway and ordered a plate of eggs with bacon and coffee. Steam rose from the mug in quiet little curlicues. Aretha Franklin was on the juke box, singing *Chain of Fools*. There was a high definition flat screen mounted in one corner showing the latest scandal surrounding presidential candidate Helen Rhodes. Shawn Hennessey had received a thumb drive from an anonymous source containing proof that Rhodes had been taking large sums of cash from a Mexican Cartel in exchange for classified intelligence in America's war on drugs. The report had been airing daily for more than a week. All the other major networks had picked up the story—except CNN, who was doing their best to discredit Hennessey.

Noble, gazing out the window at a Cessna taxiing onto the runway, picked up his coffee and sipped. He had almost finished breakfast when Burke squeezed his bulk into the booth. The cheap vinyl creaked under his weight.

Noble asked, "Were you followed?"

Burke shook his head. "The Company's too busy dealing with the fallout to bother keeping tabs on me. Everything Foster touched is radioactive. A lot of good operations had to be shut down." After a moment he added, "I guess that's better than the alternative."

"What's going to happen to Foster?"

"Undergoing enhanced interrogation right now." Burke flagged down a waitress, ordered a sweet tea and a turkey club.

"Those enhanced interrogations tend to break people," Noble commented over the rim of his mug.

Burke agreed with a nod. "He claims he had no idea Rhodes was passing intelligence. She promised him the director's chair in exchange for keeping her in the loop on Company operations. Hard to say how much he knew. One thing is certain. He's finished as Deputy Director of Intelligence. They're looking for his replacement as we speak."

"What about Sam?" Noble asked.

"She's been reinstated," Burke said. "But she's got a permanent black mark. One more and she's finished."

"And Hunt?"

"He's young. His reputation might recover." Burke hitched up a shoulder. "Might not. He blames you, by the way."

Noble dismissed that with a shrug.

Burke's food arrived. He ate in silence.

Noble watched planes come and go. "Think Helen Rhodes will go to jail?"

Burke spoke around a mouthful of food. "A good politician can wade through hip-deep horseshit and come out smelling like roses, but her shot at the White House is finished."

"You should have told Torres what you were up to," Noble said.

Burke put down his sandwich. "I never suspected Foster. I included the mission in Mexico to cover my bases, but I was surprised as hell when it went off the rails. Hand to God, Jake, it wasn't supposed to happen like that. I *ordered* Torres to walk away. I had no idea he was in love with the girl."

Noble leaned back in his seat and closed his eyes. He let the grief and anger burrow down inside where it would turn to bitterness. He could handle bitterness.

Burke dusted crumbs from his fingertips onto his plate. "This is a dangerous job. We make decisions and sometimes those decisions go bad. Good men die. You, of all people, know that."

"I guess it doesn't matter now," Noble said. "Torres figured it out in the end. That's why he sent me the key."

"Torres didn't send the key to you," Burke said. "He sent it to me."

Noble sat for several seconds trying to process that information.

Burke said, "I'm sorry like hell about what happened. I really am. But he knew the score and he traded his life for hers."

Noble chewed the inside of one cheek. A good man was dead and nothing Noble had done would bring him back.

Like he was reading Noble's thoughts, Burke said, "You got his killer and stopped one of the most corrupt politicians in American history from taking the White House. That's a win."

Noble drained the last of his coffee without comment.

Burke finished his sandwich and took a few bills out of his wallet. "We good?"

"We're good," Noble told him.

"Keep your nose clean," Burke said as he levered himself out of the booth. "Things are changing at the Company. You might be hearing from me soon."

Noble watched him go, then turned his attention to the television. FBI Director Standish had just called a press conference to announce the formation of a joint bi-partisan committee to investigate Helen Rhodes.

The End.

CAN'T WAIT FOR MORE JAKE NOBLE?

Sign up for the Jake Noble Fan Club and get, SIDE JOBS: Volume 1, The Heist for FREE! This story is available exclusively to my mailing list.

https://williammillerauthor.com/fan-club/

DID YOU ENJOY THE BOOK?

Please take a moment to leave a review on Amazon. Readers depend on reviews when choosing what to read next and authors depend on them to sell books. An honest review is like leaving your waiter a hundred dollar tip. And the best part is, it doesn't cost you a dime!

ABOUT THE AUTHOR

I was born and raised in sunny Saint Petersburg, FL on a steady diet of action movies and fantasy novels. After 9/11, I left a career in photography to join the United States Army. Since then, I have travelled the world and done everything from teaching English in China to driving a fork-lift. I studied creative writing at Eckerd College and wrote four hard-boiled mysteries for Delight Games before releasing the first Jake Noble book. When not writing, I can be found indoor rock climbing, playing the guitar, and haunting smoke-filled jazz clubs in downtown Saint Pete. I'm currently at work on another Jake Noble thriller. You can follow me on my website WilliamMillerAuthor.com

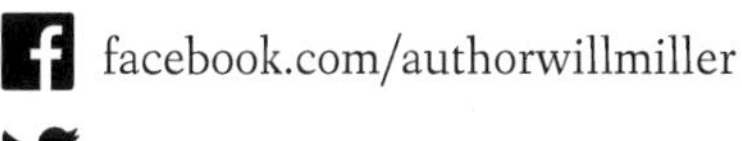

instagram.com/wmiller314

NOBLE INTENT

by

WILLIAM MILLER

CHAPTER ONE

A small craft nosed up to a stone jetty in the harbor town of Honfleur. Nestled on the south bank estuary of the Seine River, Honfleur is a picturesque port town of narrow lanes and closely packed buildings. It is home to medieval fortresses and the Sainte-Catherine church, built entirely of wood in the 15th century. The cafés and cobblestone streets have inspired Claude Monet and countless painters since. Rain was still falling, but now it was coming straight down. Sailboats bobbed on the water, sheltered from the worst of the storm by seawalls to the north and south. The fiberglass hull of the SeaVee bumped rotting wood pylons.

Duval tried to convince the pilot to take him down the Seine, all the way to Paris, but the old seaman only shook his head and cut the engines. The mercenaries leapt out and went to work securing the mooring lines.

The pilot said, "Good luck to you, Mr. Duval."

"Thank you." Duval paused to shake his hand.

While Jacques finished tying off the lines, Mateen went a little way down the jetty and checked their surroundings.

The harbor faced a quaint little row of seaside shops, all closed at the moment. Street lamps glowed like fairy lights through the steady drizzle. A few boathouses lined the seawall and a row of cars were parked on the boulevard, but the town itself was asleep. Mateen nodded, satisfied, and returned to the ship. "All clear. Get your luggage."

Duval grabbed the oversized suitcase and heaved it over the gunwale onto the dock. He grunted with the effort. Butterflies were zipping around inside his belly. He felt totally exposed. He didn't like being on the boat in the middle of the ocean, but he didn't like being out in the open either. He wanted to ditch his luggage and run to the waiting Renault. He would feel safer once they were in the car, headed south. He clambered over the gunwale, slipped on the clammy stone and went down on top of his suitcase.

Mateen said, "We need to hurry."

Duval pushed himself up. "You could help."

Mateen glanced around the empty harbor, sighed, and reached for Duval's overstuffed suitcase. The moment he did, a sharp *thwip-thwip-thwip* split the air. Jacques made a sound like a seal giving birth, bent over at the waist and staggered. One foot slipped between the pier and the boat. He hit the side of the vessel and went into the water with a splash.

Duval's heart climbed up into his throat. He hunkered down, looking for the source of the noise. A black-clad phantom appeared through the rain, wearing a ski mask and pointing a small automatic machinegun capped with a sound suppressor. Duval didn't know much about guns, but he knew enough to recognize professional hardware.

Mateen dropped the suitcase and shoved a hand into his

jacket. He didn't even get his gun out before another short burst of muffled claps ripped through the pouring rain. *Pthut-pthut-pthut.* Duval was close enough to hear the impacts and see wet droplets explode off Mateen's rain slicker.

The mercenary danced a jig. His hand came out of his coat with his gun. The assassin fired again. *Thwap-thwap.* Mateen's head snapped back. He let go of the weapon and pitched over onto the dock. The gun bounced over the stones and came to rest a few inches from Duval's feet.

His first instinct was to dive back into the boat, but his legs refused to obey. He felt rooted to the spot. His bladder surrendered the fight right then and there. He was standing up straight, leaning back away from the assassin. The weight of his duffel bag almost toppled him over.

The assassin moved along the dock, kicked Mateen's handgun into the water and then turned the stubby automatic on the pilot. The Englishman's hands went into the air and all the color drained from his face. He started to stammer out words. It might have been "Don't shoot," but it sounded like, "*Donchuma!*"

A woman's voice, muffled by the rain-soaked ski mask, said, "Do you want to live?"

The pilot nodded. "I've got two little girls at home."

"Get on the deck. Put your face down and count to one hundred, slowly."

He threw one terrified glance at Duval, muttered an apology, and then sank to the deck of the ship.

Fear turned Duval's arms and legs to rubber. A tortured sob escaped his throat. He screwed his eyes shut and waited to hear the *pthut-pthut-pthut* and feel the bullets punch through his chest.

Instead, the assassin grabbed his collar and hauled him along the deck. His toes caught on uneven paving stones and his knees threatened to give out. Air exploded from his lungs in panicked little gasps. He tried to beg for his life, but fear so powerful it was a physical force shorted out the circuits between his brain and mouth.

At the end of the jetty, the assassin steered him along the sidewalk toward an unmarked van with tinted windows. *This is it,* Duval told himself. He would be forced into the back of the van, duct taped, and driven to a black site where they would torture him. When they had wrung out every last bit of useful information, they would put a bullet in the back of his head. No one would ever find his body.

That thought finally tripped something in his brain. Survival instinct overruled his fear. In desperation, he drove an elbow over his shoulder, catching the assassin off guard. Her head snapped back. She made a noise that was more surprise than pain, but it was enough to throw her off balance. She lost her grip on Duval's collar and he ran for his life. He didn't know where he was going, only that he needed to put as much distance between him and the assassin as possible. Fear coursed through his veins, turning to blind panic, urging his legs to move faster.

CHAPTER TWO

Duval darted between parked cars and took off running along the line of shops fronting Quai de la Quarantaine. The duffel bag humped against his back as he ran. He was surprisingly quick for a paunchy, middle-aged man. Fear and adrenaline, mixed into a potent cocktail to give him a burst of speed. He turned down Rue des Logettes and then mounted the steps to Église Sainte-Catherine. He raced along the narrow corridor behind the old church that let out onto Rue du Puits. Fear carried him two more blocks before poor cardiovascular fitness took its toll. His tired legs started to slow and his feet grew heavier with every step. The muscles in his thighs burned with the effort.

He shot a glance over his shoulder, saw his pursuer and let out a terrified squeak. The assassin, built like a runner, was quickly closing the gap. Duval pumped his arms for speed. His head was on a swivel, like a rat looking for a bolt-hole to slip through. His eyes locked onto the glowing blue and white sign for the tram. A train car was pulling into the station. The long white shuttle slowed to a stop. Air brakes hissed and wires rattled. There were only two people waiting on the platform at this time of night. Fluorescent lights bathed them in a sickly artificial glow. Pneumatic doors sighed open. Duval was almost at the platform. If he could just make it onto the train...

The assassin stopped, shouldered the MP5, aimed low and triggered a three-round burst. The bolt carriage sounded out a rapid *clack-clack-clack.*

Pain, like he had never felt before, lanced Duval's right butt cheek. He clapped both hands over his bottom, gave a shout and went face down on the paving stones. The initial sting turned to a crushing throb that threatened to send him tumbling down a dark abyss. He fought the urge to pass out. He had to stay awake, had to escape. But all he managed to do was roll around on the ground, holding his bottom and moaning. Fear wrote itself on his face in large capital letters.

The train doors hissed shut and the gleaming white shuttle moved away from the station, slowly at first, then picking up speed. Duval made one feeble attempt to gain his feet but the exquisite hurt in his bottom convinced him running was, for the moment, out of the question. "Please, for the love of God, don't kill me."

The assassin closed the last few yards, knelt, and pulled off the ski mask. A long curtain of jet black hair fell around her shoulders. She was Asian, with high cheek bones and eyes that gave away mixed parentage. "I'm not going to kill you," she said. "My name is Samantha Gunn. I'm trying to save your life."

He spluttered. Rain flew from his lips. He heard the words coming out of her mouth, but they didn't make any sense. He took one hand away from his butt, inspected his palm and was surprised when he didn't see any blood. His face wrinkled in confusion.

"It was a rubber bullet," Samantha explained. "It'll sting, but it doesn't penetrate."

"Rubber bullet?" Duval muttered. His hand went back to his butt. The pain made him want to vomit. He had to fight down a wave of bile trying to climb his esophagus.

Samantha Gunn mopped rain water from her face. "Listen to me. We don't have much time. Those mobsters weren't your friends. They were going to sell you out."

Duval's brain was starting to catch up with events. He said, "Mateen? Jacques? They were going to turn me over?"

"I don't have time to explain it all," she said. "You're going to have to trust me. There's a CIA wetwork team on their way right now. We need to get you out of here. Can you stand?"

She gripped his elbow and helped him up. He put weight on his right leg and gasped. His eyes opened wide. "I can't." He shook his head, trying to lower himself back down. "You shot me. It hurts."

She hauled him back up. "They're going to do a lot worse if they catch you."

A pitiful whimper escaped his throat, but the threat had the desired effect. His legs started to move. His bottom still hurt. Putting weight on his right leg was utter agony, but once the shock wore off, he managed an ungainly trot. His rescuer urged him to go faster. Duval could hear his own pulse pounding in his ears. Every beat came with a stabbing pain.

PICK UP A COPY OF NOBLE INTENT TODAY!

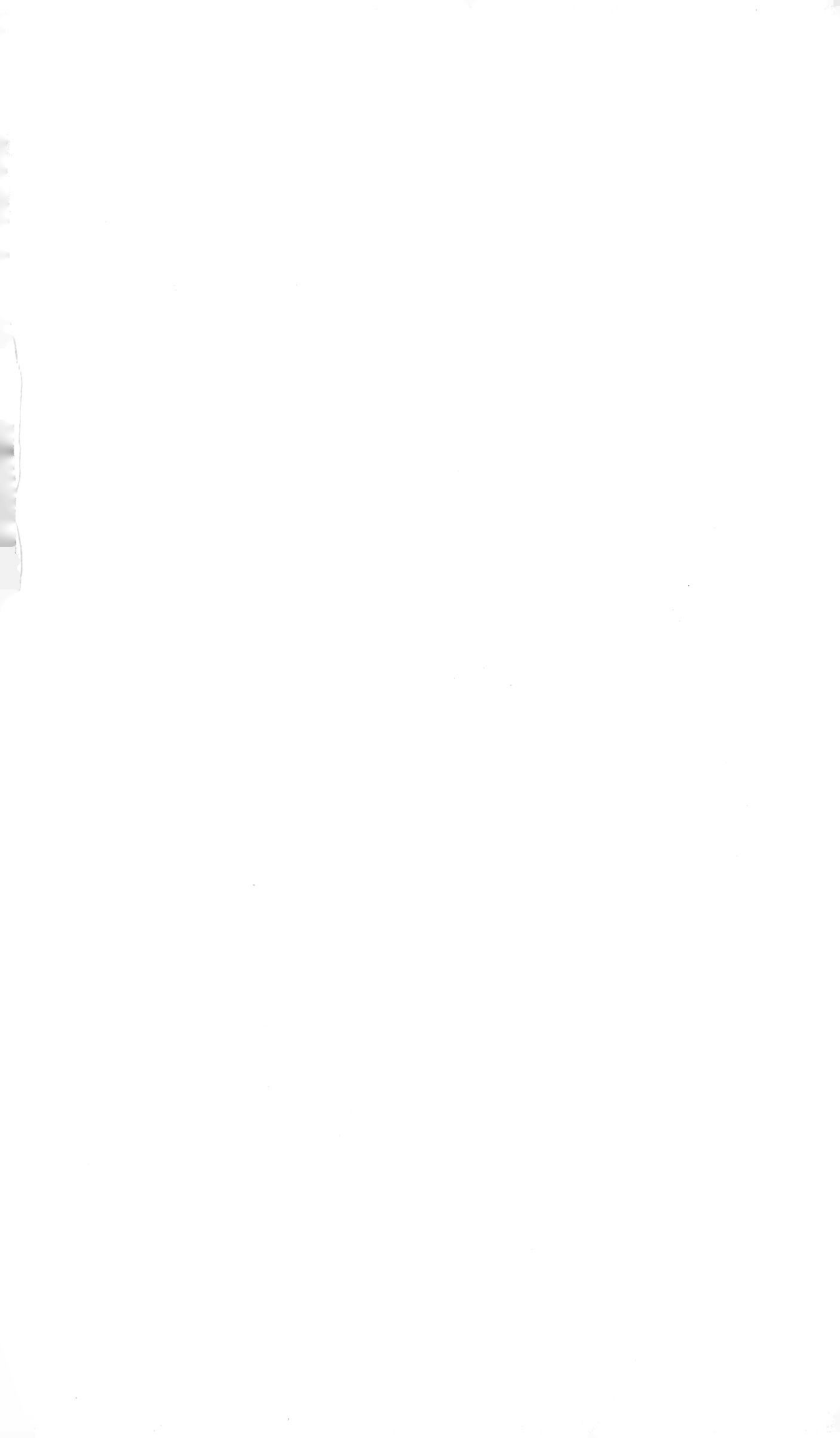

Made in the USA
Middletown, DE
10 March 2025